Praise for *The Parliament of Blood*:

'A rollicking ghoulish horror story written with great pace and historical detail. Children will love it.' *Daily Mail*

'Impressive . . . a rollicking historical yarn about street-wise boys foiling a dastardly conspiracy.' *Daily Telegraph*

'You can always trust Justin Richards to provide a rip-roaring story that will keep you on the edge of your seat from start to finish, and this follow-up to *The Death Collector* is no exception . . . This is the kind of book for reading late at night under the covers. A perfect Halloween read for anyone who prefers an adventure over gore.' *Waterstone's Books Quarterly*

Praise for *The Death Collector*:

'This is a real page turner. The book starts with a dead man walking back into his kitchen and then dragging his terrified dog out for a walk! . . . Once you've finished it, you'll want to find another book just as exciting.' *CBBC Newsround*

'A very exciting novel, reminiscent in some ways of Philip Pullman's Victorian novels . . . a real page-turner – and the ending is quite spectacular.' *Books for Keeps*

THE PARLIAMENT OF BLOOD

Justin Richards has written over twenty novels as well as non-fiction books. He has also written audio scripts, a television and stage play, edited anthologies of short stories, been a technical writer, and founded and edited a media journal. Justin is the author of *The Death Collector*, *The Chaos Code* and *The Invisible Detective* series. He is also Creative Director of the BBC's bestselling range of *Doctor Who* books. He lives in Warwick with his wife and two children, and a lovely view of the castle.

www.justinrichards.co.uk

by the same author

The Death Collector
The Chaos Code

THE PARLIAMENT OF BLOOD

JUSTIN RICHARDS

To Imogen

Best wishes

Justin Rich

faber and faber

First published in 2008
by Faber and Faber Limited
Bloomsbury House, 74–77 Great Russell Street
London WC1B 3DA
This paperback edition published in 2009

Typeset by Faber and Faber Limited
Printed in England by CPI Bookmarque, Croydon

A CIP record for this book
is available from the British Library

ISBN 978–0–571—23691–6

2 4 6 8 10 9 7 5 3 1

To Julian – blood relative

PROLOGUE

The carriage had been booked for over four thousand years, and the driver did not want to be late.

The photographer had no such worries. His name was Bernard Denning, and his breath smelled strongly of the cheap ale he'd been drinking. After his afternoon appointment, there was not enough time to get home to Ealing, so instead he spent the time in the Red Lion a few streets away. A pint and a meat pie was just the ticket.

He was supposed to be there ahead of the guests, but Denning didn't care that he was a little late. Let the guests and the academics mingle and chatter without him. Bernard Denning, Photographer, would be ready and waiting when it mattered.

That was one of the advantages of these new dry-plate methods – a smaller camera he could easily carry. Much faster exposure times, so you could just hold the camera and press the lever. Job done. And with a magazine camera already loaded with a dozen plates, he didn't even have to prepare for the next session.

The evening sounds of London were muffled by the cold, clammy fog. Denning pulled up the collar of his coat with his free hand, the other cradling his precious camera. He could feel the February chill seeping into his feet from the cobbled roadway. There was a carriage waiting at the side of the street, barely visible in the gloom – a pencil-sketch shape. Almost like an old, fuzzy photograph itself, the horses were so still and quiet. He could make out the dark profile of the Coachman – heavy, hooded cloak, poised whip. The shadows across the Coachman's face made his eyes seem deep and empty. Like a skull.

Denning shivered, and walked on.

Ahead of him, another shape coalesced out of the fog. A woman. She was standing at the corner of the street. She too wore a large cloak, and the deep red of the material bled into the misty air so it seemed to glow around her. Her face was almost white against the charcoal black of her hair. She turned as Denning approached, hearing the clip of his nailed boots on the cobbles.

The woman stretched out her arms, as if in greeting, and her cloak fell open. Beneath it she was wearing an evening dress that was as red as her cloak. It was cut low, and her neck was pale and slender. Denning's breath quickened as he saw how very beautiful the lady was. The mist from his breath joined the swirling fog around them. Had he been less distracted, he might have noticed that there was no breath from the woman's scarlet lips.

'You must be the photographer,' the woman said. She smiled, her dark eyes widening. 'The late photographer.'

'Denning,' he said, assuming she had seen the camera under his arm. 'Bernard Denning. At your service.'

'Really? How kind.' She took a step towards him, reaching out a hand to touch his cheek.

It was cold. Even through the long, white glove, her touch was cold as death.

'Are you going to the Unwrapping?' Denning asked, his voice a nervous whisper. He stared into her deep, dark eyes, unable to move as the woman reached out her other hand, holding his head between her chill palms.

'Indeed I am.' She was tall – almost as tall as Denning himself. Leaning forward, smiling, lips parting. Her cold eyes seemed to burn into his.

A sharp intake of breath. Denning leaned away, his feet frozen in position. As he felt the cold of her lips on his neck, he experienced a sudden rush of fear and struggled to pull away. But he was unable to move.

Then there was a crack of sound, like a gunshot, and

the spell was broken. Gasping, Denning took a step backwards. The woman was staring at him, her face twisted into a snarl of angry disappointment. All beauty gone.

The coach drew up slowly out of the fog, and Denning realised that the sound had been the Coachman's whip. The photographer looked up, trying to stammer a thank you. Shadowed by the hood of his cloak, the man's face still looked like a skull.

The woman stepped towards Denning again, teeth bared, hissing at him like an angry snake.

'No,' the Coachman said. He pointed the whip at the woman, and she stopped.

Denning felt another rush of relief. But it was short-lived.

'It must look like an accident, Clarissa.' The Coachman's voice was deep and dark and dry and brittle all at once. 'A tragic accident.'

There was a sudden clatter of carriage wheels across the cobbles. The sound of hoofs. Denning turned in time to see the horses bearing down on him. Nostrils flaring as they snorted – but no mist. The skull-faced Coachman cracked the whip. And the faces of the horses were like skulls too – pale and angular. Denning could see the ribs poking out of their sides. He could see the symbol painted on the door of the carriage as it turned slightly to head straight for him. He could hear the woman laughing.

Clarissa.

Denning's last thought was that Clarissa was such a lovely name. The last things he heard were her laughter, and the crack of the whip, and the unholy snarl of the horses. And the click of the shutter as he clutched the camera tight.

Clarissa stared longingly at the dark pool growing from under the carriage. She licked her lips, sighed, and turned to go.

The carriage moved slowly away again, back to where the Coachman had been waiting. He had been waiting a very long time, but now the waiting was nearly over . . .

Chapter I

Professor Andrew Brinson

**AT THE BRITISH MUSEUM,
EGYPTIAN ROOMS**

**THURSDAY, 11 FEBRUARY
1886**

**A MUMMY FROM SAQQARA TO
BE UNWRAPPED AT
HALF-PAST EIGHT**

TO: George Archer Esq.

George Archer had forgotten about the invitation. He felt the stiff card in his inside pocket as he put his jacket on. He took out the invitation and read it again. Tapping it against his fingertips, he considered his options. It was the end of a long day and he had been looking forward to getting home. But now his priorities had altered.

For one thing, he could do with a change, a break, a distraction before setting off. For another, he had argued strongly with Eddie about the invitation. The two of them had met the previous year, when the boy stole George's wallet. George shook his head as he recalled the trouble and danger which had resulted from that.

Another result was that, after their initial distrust of each other, they had become friends and Eddie Hopkins was staying in the spare room of the house that George had inherited from his father. Now, George was pretty much Eddie's surrogate father – though in age he was more of an older brother.

Sir William Protheroe had arranged the invitations and had suggested Eddie come too. But George was adamant that he should not. It was too late for the boy, who had to be awake and alert for school the next day. And it was hardly the sort of event where a recently reformed pickpocket and street urchin would fit in. Eddie had insisted he would behave and that he was interested. George wasn't convinced of either, and had eventually pacified Eddie

– slightly – by promising he would tell him all about the evening's events the next day.

So if he went back home now, and admitted he'd not bothered even going to the Unwrapping, he would be in serious trouble with Eddie.

Not to mention Sir William, who must have gone to some trouble to secure the invitations. Egyptology was not an area that Sir William specialised in. He was a curator at the British Museum, but his department was not like Egyptology, or indeed any other. Sir William's department – the department where George worked as Sir William's assistant – did not officially exist.

At this moment, George was standing in the middle of an enormous storage area which very few people knew was hidden in the cellars of the Museum. The main room was under the Great Court and the circular Reading Room. The walls were the foundations of the main Museum buildings round the court – rough unfinished stone. Where there were doorways above, so there were below. Doors that led to more rooms, many of which George had yet to explore. But they were not filled with artefacts and relics belonging to the better-known departments of the Museum. This was not a staging area for treasures yet to be displayed or awaiting a suitable exhibition space.

The crates and boxes and cupboards and drawers in

this huge area and the others were filled with things that – like Sir William's department – did not, officially, exist. That was what the Department of Unclassified Artefacts was for, what it did. It looked after, stored, preserved, and catalogued those items which did not fit into any of the other departments.

Sometimes that was because the object just didn't match any of the criteria the other departments used for cataloguing. But more often it was because of the very nature of the artefact itself. Anything deemed too strange or unusual, or *dangerous*, anything that defied analysis or which went against modern science or thinking – or which simply could not be understood – was sent to Sir William's department.

When George first joined Sir William, it was as he was investigating a dead man whose skeleton seemed to be made of dinosaur bones . . .

Thoughts of Sir William reminded George that his superior was certainly expecting George to attend the Unwrapping. But the most compelling reason, George knew (though he scarcely even dared admit it to himself), was that Miss Elizabeth Oldfield would also be there. George had first met Liz when she returned his wallet – the wallet that Eddie had stolen. And before long they had all of them – George, Liz, Eddie and Sir William – been caught up in the devilish plans of a madman.

'Are you ready for our evening's entertainment, young man?'

Sir William's voice brought George back to the present with a jolt. The elderly man was standing beside him, his shock of white hair erupting enthusiastically from his head. He was vigorously polishing his spectacles on a handkerchief. George put the invitation card back into his pocket, and closed the large notebook where he had been describing and sketching several unidentified items in the archive.

'Of course,' George said. 'I'm looking forward to it.'

As they made their way up the wide, stone staircase that led to the Egyptian Rooms, George realised that the invitation was considerably more of a privilege than he had imagined. Sir William seemed unperturbed by the number of people. Men in dark suits and women in long dresses and expensive jewellery conspired to make George feel rather under-dressed.

He ran his hand through his tangle of curly brown hair and tried to look inconspicuous. A man with an impressive handlebar moustache pushed past impatiently, a stick-thin woman with pinched, angular features followed in his wake. She paused just long enough to smile an apology at George. Or perhaps it was sympathy.

'Everyone is in such a rush these days,' Sir William said. 'But there's really no need to hurry. Brinson won't start without me.'

'Is he a friend? A colleague?'

'Good gracious no,' the older man announced loudly. 'Can't stand the fellow.'

'Then why would he wait for you?'

They reached the top of the stairs, and found themselves at the back of a short queue of people waiting to move on. Sir William paused to take a deep breath before he answered. 'Because it's my mummy he's unwrapping,' he told George. 'That's why.'

There were two men at the door checking invitations. Sir William produced his crumpled invitation and waved it at one of the men, barely turning to look. George showed his own invitation to the other man at the door.

'Thank you, sir,' the man said. 'Professor Brinson will be starting very soon now, I believe.'

Normally, there were display cases arranged down the middle of the large room where George found himself. For this evening, they had been moved to make space for a dais to be set up at the far end, and the guests to gather in the main part of the room. Being quite tall, George could see over the assembled guests that on the dais there was a sarcophagus. It was raised on trestles and George could see that the top of the gold, coffin-shaped box was sculpted into the form of a figure.

'Impressive,' he said out loud.

Beside him, Sir William sniffed. 'Rather indifferent, actually. But still a mistake. A violation.'

'You don't think Brinson should unwrap the mummy?'

'I do not,' Sir William said. 'Mummies have been unwrapped before, and by better men than Brinson, though I would always dispute the science of destroying that which one is charged with preserving. The only thing Brinson hopes to achieve by this evening's theatrics is his own aggrandisement.' Sir William turned to smile at George. 'But I have said my piece, for all the good it has done.'

'You said it was your mummy,' George reminded him.

'From the Department,' Sir William said. 'Been in the collection almost since Xavier Hemming established it. One of our oldest unclassified artefacts.'

'And why is it unclassified?'

Sir William shrugged. 'No idea. Perhaps Hemming just fancied having a mummy in the collection when he originally set it up. Who knows? Something he acquired perhaps and never passed on to another department. He was a formidable collector, you know. Maybe we should hunt around for another one after this evening's over.'

'Did you not give permission for it to be unwrapped?' George wondered.

'Overruled,' Sir William said. 'By some idiot from the Royal Society.' He gave a heavy sigh. 'At least I managed to persuade that fool Brinson to photograph . . . Ah,' he broke off. 'Here he is now.'

An insincere smile appeared on Sir William's face as a rather short, stout man pushed towards them through the mingling guests. He had a round red face, and dabbed at his damp forehead with a grubby handkerchief. In his other hand he held a glass of red wine.

'Sir William, thank goodness.' The man's voice was nasal and almost squeaky with nerves. 'Thank goodness,' he said again.

Sir William reached out for the wine glass. 'For me? How very kind, Professor.'

Professor Brinson hastily moved the glass out of Sir William's reach. 'Oh there is refreshment on the table over there.' He nodded into the distance. 'Have you seen Denning?'

'Denning?'

'Photographer. Dratted man's not turned up. You spoke to him after this afternoon's session. Did he say where he was off to? What his plans were? When he'd be back?'

'He did mention something about visiting a public house,' Sir William said. His mouth twitched slightly, and George guessed he was trying not to smile.

'A public house!' Brinson squeaked. His face seemed to grow even more red. 'Oh good grief. He's probably lying drunk in a gutter, or been arrested on a charge of being disorderly.'

'I'm sure he will turn up in his own good time,' Sir William said. 'He seemed to know his business.'

'Yes, well, I hope so.' Brinson had his handkerchief out again. 'Oh goodness, there's Sir Harrison Judd, please excuse me.' He thrust his way into a group of people nearby, and barrelled through towards a tall military-looking gentleman talking loudly in another part of the room.

'We are not, it seems, as important to Professor Brinson as the Commissioner of the Metropolitan Police,' Sir William said to George. 'Perhaps we should be grateful for small mercies. Now then, let's find that wine, shall we?'

The flow of people into the room had all but stopped. George and Sir William helped themselves to a glass of red wine each from the table and made their way back through the assembled guests to a space close to the dais where they would have a good view. But George's attention was focused on the door, waiting for Liz to arrive.

Or perhaps she was already here. He looked round, hoping to catch sight of his friend.

'That's Lord Ruthven from the Royal Society,' Sir William said, pointing out a pale, gaunt figure standing with a group of others nearby. 'He's the chap who eventually insisted I hand over the mummy. Why Brinson couldn't use some minor character from the Egyptian Department's own collection I don't know.' He took a sip of wine, looking round with interest. 'And unless I'm mistaken, that's the Prime Minister's special adviser, what's his name?' Sir William's forehead creased as he tried to remember. 'Bradford? Barford? Something like that.'

But George was not listening. His attention had been caught by another figure in the crowd. A woman. She was standing alone, close to the door, wearing a deep red velvet dress that seemed to cling to her body, the neck line plunging daringly low. Her black hair was tied up intricately and for a moment her dark eyes met George's across the room.

Then someone moved in between them, and he lost sight of her. 'Who is that?' he said out loud.

'Someone important, I'll be bound,' Sir William said, glancing without interest in the direction in which George was still staring. 'A gathering of the great and the good. Well,' he sniffed, 'the great anyway.'

Intrigued and captivated by the glimpse of the beautiful woman, George was edging away towards the door. 'I'll just go and see,' he said.

Sir William sipped at his wine. 'Don't be long,' he cautioned. 'Expect Brinson will give up on his photographer soon and start anyway.'

There was a general movement towards the dais, and George found he was pushing against the tide of people. 'Excuse me,' he muttered as he collided with a tall woman.

'Excuse *me*, George Archer,' the woman said, gently catching his arm.

George paused, all thoughts of finding the lady in red suddenly gone. 'Liz?'

'Don't tell me you were looking for someone else?' she joked.

'You look wonderful,' George said quickly, anxious to change the subject. But it was true. Elizabeth Oldfield was wearing a pale green dress that was distinctly more modest than the scarlet dress that had recently attracted George's interest. But her beauty was undeniable, with her lively face, fair hair, and cat-like green eyes.

'I do hope I haven't missed everything,' she was saying. 'I had the devil of a job to persuade Father I should come. I think he believed it was some sort of performance – you know how he cannot abide the theatre.'

George did indeed. He also knew that Liz was of a very different opinion on the subject. Her greatest ambition was to be an actress. But her frail, elderly father the Reverend Oldfield could not be more opposed to the theatre and all the sin – as he saw it – that was bound up with the profession of acting. So Liz was forced to sneak out to the theatre in secret. She was a member of a local acting company where she helped as much as her stolen time would allow. Which was, George knew, little enough. But she never complained at having to look after the old man. She never gave any sign that it was a chore rather than her devoted duty.

He smiled at the thought, and found that Liz was smiling back at him. 'I said, how is Eddie?' There was a hint of censure in her voice – she knew he had not been listening.

'Sorry. He is doing well, I think. School has been a bit of a shock to the lad.'

'And I imagine that Eddie has been a shock to the school.'

George laughed. 'I imagine so. He is rather older than most of the children there. But from what little Eddie tells me of what goes on, it sounds as if he is doing well.'

'Perhaps he is a reformed character,' Liz suggested.

George nodded. 'Perhaps he is.'

Any further discussion of Eddie's progress from

proven sinner to possible saint was cut short by a commotion at the door behind them. There were few people now at the back of the room as everyone pushed forwards to try to get a better sight of the events soon to unfold on the raised dais. So George and Liz were afforded a good view of the man arguing loudly with the two Museum staff at the door as he struggled to get past.

'I tell you I *do* have an invitation,' the man stormed. His face was bloodless with anger.

'Then perhaps I can see it, sir,' the larger of the two Museum men asked.

'I had it just a moment ago, I know I did.' The man was patting his pockets. He was tall and slim with handsome features, slicked-back dark hair, and dressed in an immaculate suit that looked decidedly expensive. 'Do you know who I am?' he demanded of the men blocking his way. 'This is intolerable.'

'Your invitation, sir,' the second doorman said calmly. 'No one is permitted inside without an invitation from Professor Brinson.'

Liz's voice was hushed with awe. 'I know who he is,' she said to George. 'Don't you see – it's Henry Malvern.'

The name meant nothing to George and he shook his head. As the man continued to argue, without effect, another smaller figure in a rather less expensive suit

made a point of flashing his own invitation at the doormen and pushing past. He kept his head down and
George was unable to see the young man's face.
Nonetheless, he felt there was something very familiar
about him. He felt his blood run cold as he realised who
it was.

Liz gave a gasp of astonishment as she realised too.

'Oy, guv'nor,' the new arrival said loudly to the closer
of the two doormen, 'I think that gentleman dropped
his invitation at the top of the stairs. Saw it come out of
his pocket I did.' He nodded to Henry Malvern. 'Didn't
realise what it was, but I'm sure that's what happened.
Just over there, it was.' He pointed, and all three men in
the doorway turned to look.

As they turned, the young man flicked the invitation
he was holding across the floor. It came to rest, unseen,
just outside the door. 'Oh, my mistake,' the lad
announced. 'There it is, look.'

One of the doormen picked up the card. 'Henry
Malvern?'

Malvern snatched the card. 'Indeed.' He straightened
his jacket, glared at each doorman in turn, and then
strode into the room. He paused as he passed the lad.
'Thank you,' he said curtly.

'Lucky I was here,' the lad replied. But Malvern had
already moved on.

'Very lucky,' George said, moving quickly to intercept the young man. 'Eddie.' He turned for moral support from Liz. But she was staring open-mouthed after Malvern.

'Henry Malvern,' she said.

'So I gathered,' George said, unimpressed.

'But, he's the manager and leading man at the Parthenon Theatre.' Liz hurried away – 'I must speak to him if I possibly can.' – leaving George glaring at the unrepentant Eddie.

'You are supposed to be at home,' George said through gritted teeth. 'You stole that man's invitation.'

'Wasn't stealing – I gave it back,' Eddie made a point of looking carefully at George's half-empty glass of wine. 'Is there anything to eat?'

'An important actor and a respected gentleman and you took his invitation to get in here under false pretences.'

'Yeah, all right, fair enough,' Eddie conceded. He nodded towards where Liz was standing with a group of people listening to Malvern. 'Liz seems to like him though.' Before George could react, Eddie grabbed his arm and dragged him further into the room. 'Come on, we need to get a better view than this. Look, Sir William's got a good spot, let's join him over there.'

George followed Eddie through the guests. He was

still angry, though he found it difficult to distinguish between the annoyance he felt with Eddie and his irritation at Liz's interest in Henry Malvern.

An expectant hush was falling as everyone began to perceive that the evening's events would soon start. Through it, George heard Liz's laughter, and the deep tones of Henry Malvern. He spared them a glance as he and Eddie passed close to their group. Malvern was holding forth as if he was on the stage – thumb hooked into his waistcoat pocket and free hand gesticulating earnestly. The people round him watched enraptured. Especially the ladies.

Especially Liz. Her eyes wide and fixed on the man. Her mouth open in awe. George felt Eddie tug impatiently at his sleeve, and moved on.

Professor Brinson had returned. He looked less flustered, and was accompanied by a short woman of about the same age. His wife, George guessed, from the way she had her arm linked with Brinson's. She seemed very thin next to her husband's ample form. Her skin was pale and delicate and her hair was piled up on her head – a mousy brown streaked at the sides with grey.

'Now don't fuss, dear,' Mrs Brinson was saying. 'I'm sure no one will mind if there isn't a photograph. I certainly shan't. You know I can't abide having my picture taken.'

'Indeed,' Sir William agreed. He seemed to be trying to stifle a yawn. He caught sight of George and Eddie. 'Ah, there you are. You're looking well, Eddie.'

'Is that where it's going to happen?' Eddie asked, pointing at the sarcophagus on the dais in front of them. There was a row of chairs arranged behind the sarcophagus, and several people were taking their seats there. George could see the imposing figure of Sir Harrison Judd settling himself into the seat next to Lord Ruthven.

'Yes, yes,' Brinson said, rubbing his hands together. 'I rather think we should start.'

'Can't see much from down here,' Eddie complained. 'Why do they get the best view?'

'You're right, Eddie,' Sir William agreed. 'We shall see nothing of consequence from down here. If I am to suffer the scientific indignity of having my mummy unwrapped, I do think I should be permitted to see it properly.' He strode after Brinson. 'I shall join you on the stage, sir.'

Brinson stopped. 'What?'

'Oh don't worry,' Sir William assured him, 'I won't steal your thunder. Just want to see what you're up to.'

Brinson's wife was encouraging the professor towards the dais again. 'Oh very well,' he agreed with a sigh.

'Excellent.' Sir William clapped his hands together and looked from Eddie to George. 'Shall we?'

'I'm not sure the professor understood you to mean us as well,' George said.

'My dear George, there is a lot the professor does not understand. But I can't help feeling that is his problem, not ours. Are you coming?' He did not wait for an answer, but hurried after Brinson, who was already stepping up on to the makeshift stage.

There were not enough chairs now on the stage for the number of people. Sir William took the last chair, leaving Eddie and George to stand beside him. Eddie seemed not to mind, but George felt embarrassed and uncomfortable as he looked out over the mass of people standing watching. He felt that almost everyone was looking at him, though he knew that could not really be the case.

Right at the front of the spectators was the woman in the red dress. George was sure she was watching him rather than Brinson. But he forced himself to look away, to pay attention to the professor who was now coming to the end of his short speech.

'His name seems to have been Orabis,' Brinson was saying. 'I'm afraid beyond that we know little about him. Judging by the ornate sarcophagus he was an important fellow.' Brinson paused to wave his hand across the carved figure on the top of the sarcophagus, despite the fact that only those on the stage had a good view of it.

'Look at this gold leaf. Very expensive, and not to be wasted on just anyone, you know. There is also a lot of silver, here in the details, which I am told is unusual. Perhaps in a moment we will find out more about Orabis.' Brinson stepped back from the sarcophagus. 'I shall now remove the lid, and we will see what lies inside.'

Sir Harrison Judd volunteered to assist Brinson in lifting the heavy lid. It was a struggle, even with the two of them, and Lord Ruthven rose to help. Together they swung the lid away from the coffin and set it down at the side of the stage, close to where George and Eddie were standing. The painted eyes of Orabis, long-dead Egyptian, watched George as closely as he imagined the woman in the scarlet dress had done.

Brinson stood at the head of the sarcophagus, looking down at the mummy. It was a crude man-shaped figure, wrapped tight in grey strips of linen. The wrappings were discoloured and stained with age, frayed and torn and ragged. The coverings over the face seemed to have sunk into the rough shape of the dead features beneath. There were shadowy indentations for the eyes, a bump of a nose. The strips of cloth over the mouth had torn and broken, as if to let out the cries of the figure within.

'Exactly as we would expect,' Brinson said to the hushed audience. 'Although there appears to be sand under the body, and I think the lining of the casket is perhaps rather unusual.'

'Unprecedented,' Sir William said, loud enough for everyone to hear. 'The sarcophagus is lined with silver.'

It made the inside of the casket seem to shine with reflected light. George moved slightly so the glare was not in his eyes. He could see the gleaming sides of the inside of the casket quite clearly, but the mummy itself still seemed wreathed in shadows as well as cloth.

The dignitaries on the stage were leaning forward in their seats to get the best possible view. Lord Ruthven and Harrison Judd stood beside Brinson.

'There is, I see, a chain around the neck. Is that also silver, would you say?'

'It is,' Lord Ruthven said. His voice sounded strained and nervous.

'And on the chain is a device, a piece of jewellery or adornment. A simple loop of what seems to be gold with a stem. The device is called an ankh, I believe.' Brinson cleared his throat. 'Sometimes, jewellery and precious stones were placed between the wrappings. We shall soon discover if that was the case with our friend Orabis.'

He produced a knife from where it had been resting on the end of one of the trestles that supported the sarcophagus. The blade gleamed as it caught the light, and

Brinson made a great show of holding it up for everyone to see.

'Oh do hurry up,' Sir William said quietly.

'I am now cutting, very carefully, through the outer wrappings,' Brinson announced, leaning into the sarcophagus.

George had a good view of the knife as it sliced through the decaying wrappings. Brinson started at the feet, cutting a straight line up between the legs and to the chest.

'We must be extremely careful when we fold back these delicate wrappings,' he said. 'I am now about to make a very careful cut across the head, and soon we will look on the ancient face of Orabis. The first people to gaze upon his visage in four thousand years.'

There was a collective intake of breath as Brinson again leaned into the coffin, stretching out with the sharp knife.

Beside the professor, Sir Harrison Judd cleared his throat. 'Perhaps I can help,' he said gruffly. 'Hold the chap's head still for you.' He stepped towards where Brinson was concentrating on his work.

And as he stepped, Sir Harrison Judd seemed to stumble and lurched sideways, clutching for support. He caught at Brinson's arm, almost regained his balance, then slipped again.

It was not much of a stumble, not much of an inconvenience. But from where they were standing, George and Eddie both had a good view of the result, though Eddie was having to stand on tiptoe to see into the sarcophagus. To see the knife knocked sideways and slicing into Brinson's left wrist as the professor held the side of the mummy's head.

Brinson cried out – first in surprise, then fear as he realised he was bleeding. He dropped the knife, which clattered into the coffin. Clutching his left wrist with his right hand, he raised it slowly. The blood was already welling up along the cut. It ran and dripped, falling after the knife. Splashing on to the bandaged face of the mummy.

The pale wrappings were spattered with red. Drips, then a trickle as the blood ran freely. Sir Harrison Judd was holding Brinson's injured wrist between both his hands, gripping it tight in an effort to stop the bleeding. But the immediate effect was to force out a rush of blood. A cascade falling into the open mouth of the wrapped figure.

Seeing the blood, the people on the stage were standing, gasping. Lord Ruthven produced a handkerchief and with help from Judd tied it tight round Brinson's wrist.

The guests standing in the room below were watching, hushed. The woman in the red dress licked her lips.

But George had no time to wonder at that. His attention was fixed once again on the sarcophagus. On the red-stained face of the figure inside. The wrappings seemed to dissolve. Steam was rising from the points where the blood had dripped, drifting away in a faint mist to reveal the weathered, parchment-like skin beneath. A face cracked and sunken with age.

A face that was moving, turning, looking up at the people above.

Then the wrappings seemed to tremble. George cried out in alarm and fright. Eddie grabbed his arm. Sir William took a step backwards knocking into his chair.

A brown, emaciated hand thrust out through the cloth, clutching at the side of the sarcophagus. Slowly, almost majestically, the ancient figure sat up. The wrappings split apart as it hauled itself out of the sarcophagus. A woman screamed. Then another. People were running, shouting.

In amongst them the ancient, long-dead, mummified figure of Orabis stepped heavily down from the stage and staggered towards the door.

CHAPTER 2

Eddie recovered from the shock first. 'Blimey,' he said, grabbing George's hand. 'Come on, quick – after him.'

'After him? Why?' George's eyes were wide with shock as he watched the nightmare figure disappear out of the back door of the room.

People were milling round, talking and shaking their heads. Professor Brinson had slumped into a chair behind the sarcophagus and was staring through unfocused eyes into space.

Sir William nodded encouragement. 'Best follow as Eddie says,' he told George.

'And then what?' George asked. But Eddie was pulling him to the side of the dais, and together they jumped down.

'What *is* going on?' a woman asked as they pushed past. 'Well, *really*,' she complained when neither George nor Eddie paused to answer.

'Actor was it?' a man with a full beard asked. 'Will there be any port wine later, do you think? Cheese, maybe?'

Again, George and Eddie did not answer. It seemed to take an age to get to the door. There was no sign of the mummy. But George could see a tattered strip of ancient cloth lying on the stairs – part of the wrappings.

'This way,' he told Eddie. 'I still don't know what we do when we catch up with him,' he said breathless as they ran down the wide staircase.

'Ask him what he's playing at,' Eddie said. 'That bloke was right – it must be an actor. Someone dressed up. Mustn't it?'

'I suppose so,' George conceded. But it seemed a lot of trouble to go to for a joke. And if it wasn't meant to be a joke, then why . . .?

Several of the guests were already standing confused and nervous at the bottom of the stairs, blocking the way back to the Great Court. Eddie pushed through the group and ran on.

George paused. 'Have you seen . . .' He broke off. 'Never mind.'

But one of the men pointed in the direction that Eddie had already taken.

'Thank you,' George said. 'Keep going!' he yelled after Eddie.

They cut through the courtyard and back into the Museum. Ahead of him, George could see Eddie at the main doors, which were standing slightly open. Wisps of fog were curling round the frame and edging into the Museum. George caught up with Eddie and helped him pull the doors open fully. Outside, the night was grey smudged with vague lights from the street and nearby buildings.

In the murk ahead of them, George could make out a figure – pale, lurching its way out of the Museum gates and on to the street outside.

'Come on!' Eddie shouted, haring down the steps. George was close behind him – they were almost there. 'We've got him!'

The carriage seemed to erupt out of the fog, clattering past George and Eddie and after the pale figure stumbling slowly along the pavement. A strip of cloth trailed from one leg. The carriage slowed, and the door on the pavement side swung open. Black in the grey fog. George could just make out a design painted on the door – a shape, a device. Like the gold ornament round the mummy's neck, only in scarlet. A cross, with the top bar replaced by a loop. An 'ankh', Brinson had called it.

'What's he doing?' Eddie muttered.

But no one got out of the carriage. Instead, the bizarre figure on the pavement turned and climbed inside.

'Quick!' George shouted, realising they were about to lose their quarry. But he was too late. The door was already closing. A fog-muffled whip-crack spurred the horses into motion and the carriage clattered away.

George and Eddie kept running. But the carriage was fading into the fog. Its shape was indistinct, then it was gone, swallowed up by the grey night.

'That settles it,' Eddie said. He slowed to a halt, head down and hands on knees as he gasped for breath. 'No one who's thousands of years old could have a blooming cab waiting.'

It wasn't until Henry Malvern clapped his hands together, laughed, and declared it was the most impressive piece of theatre he had seen for a long while that Liz realised it must all be an act.

She looked round for Sir William, and saw he was deep in conversation with a tall, important-looking man. There was no sign of either George or Eddie.

'Indeed,' she said, picking up on his earlier comment, 'a most impressive piece of acting even in my rather less experienced opinion.'

'You have some experience of the theatre?' Malvern said. 'I'm sorry, I do apologise, I did not catch your name – Miss . . .?'

'Miss Oldfield.' She felt her heart quicken at the attention.

Malvern's mouth opened slightly, as if in recognition. 'Of course.' He nodded. 'Tell me, Miss Oldfield, do you have a relative in holy orders? An uncle, perhaps? Or . . .'

'My father,' Liz exclaimed in surprise. 'He is all but retired now. You know him?'

'Not really. Our paths happened to cross some years ago. I doubt he would remember me.'

'Nevertheless,' Liz said, 'I shall remember you to my father.'

'Please do not bother yourself, or him.' Malvern's smile became a slight frown. 'We met only briefly. At a religious ceremony some years ago.' The smile returned. 'As I recall, he was somewhat disapproving of the theatre.'

'He has not mellowed in his opinion,' Liz confessed.

'But you mentioned that you have some interest in the art of performance. Can I take it that you do not share your father's feelings on the subject?'

'Indeed not.' Realising she had said this rather emphatically, Liz quickly added: 'I respect his opinions of course. But no, I do not share them. In fact, though my father would be somewhat annoyed if he found out, I very much enjoy the theatre and am a member of a small acting group that meets at the Chistleton Theatre.'

'Are you a good actress, Miss Oldfield?'

The boldness of the question, along with the scrutiny of Malvern's deep, dark eyes unsettled Liz. 'Goodness, that isn't for me to say. But Mr Jessop seems to think that I have some small talent. I haven't taken any leading roles, but that is partly because I need to look after Father and cannot always guarantee to be available.'

Malvern nodded slowly. 'I think perhaps you are unduly modest, Miss Oldfield. I pride myself on being a good judge and I would say that you most definitely have a stage presence.'

'Do you think so?'

Malvern laughed at her enthusiasm. 'I am sure of it.'

Liz took a deep breath. 'Thank you. You have no idea how much I value your opinion, just as I respect and envy your own talent, Mr Malvern.' Slightly over-whelmed by the way the conversation had gone, Liz needed some fresh air and she was aware of how late it must be. 'If you will excuse me, I should be getting back home to Father.'

'Indeed. I have much to do myself. We are rehearsing for a new production of *Camille*. Do you know it?'

'By Dumas,' Liz said automatically. 'I have seen it, yes. A very sad play.'

'About a woman who is full of life. And death.' Malvern rubbed his chin as he considered. 'There is something . . .' He hesitated, then went on: 'I wonder, Miss Oldfield, perhaps you would care to see a rehearsal at the Parthenon?'

'I would find that most instructive,' Liz said, surprised at the offer. 'And I should like it very much.'

'Then, please, feel free to visit. We rehearse every evening this week and next, from six o'clock. And I must be getting back to see how they have fared without me tonight.'

Without realising, Liz had allowed Malvern to take her arm and walk her to the top of the stairs.

'May I find you a cab?' Malvern was asking. 'Or do you have other arrangements?'

'No,' she said, her mouth dry and her face flushed. 'A cab will be fine. Thank you.'

When George left for work in the morning, Eddie left for school. But, whereas George always went to work, Eddie did not always go to school.

The teacher did not seem to mind when Eddie was absent. In fact, from the way Eddie was told off and shouted at when he was there, he imagined the teacher was as happy as Eddie on those days when he did not put in an appearance.

Eddie felt he had made an effort. After all he could

read (a bit) and write (just about) and do his sums (with money anyway). So there did not seem to be an awful lot of point in actually going to school, other than to keep George and Sir William happy.

Which was why he told neither of them that he rarely went. That just wouldn't be fair on them. Though if they knew how Eddie was helping them this cold, February morning, they would be impressed, he decided.

He met the others round the back of the workhouse. The workhouse children that weren't too old were supposed to go to school as well. Most of them did, but there were a few who avoided school, like Eddie. There were others who were skiving off whatever work the workhouse master Mr Pearce had set them.

The building was made of dark brick, with small arched windows covered with iron bars. Rising into the cold pale light of the morning and silhouetted against the weak sun, it looked like a medieval fortress. From what the children had told him, Eddie thought it was about as inviting and comfortable. Every time he saw it, he gave thanks for the series of events that had brought him to George Archer's house rather than here.

Certainly, Eddie had more in common with the workhouse kids than he did with most of the children in his class at the elementary school. Eddie could have been one of them as he leaned against the back wall of the building. There was Charlie, who was about the same age as Eddie with an untidy mop of sandy-coloured hair, and Jack who had stopped going to school so much when he got bullied. Despite that, Jack was always grinning, no matter what happened. Charlie said that Jack grinned even when Mr Pearce the workhouse master was beating him. Then there was Mikey who never said anything and was rumoured to be deaf too, though no one knew for sure, and Eve – the only girl. Her hair was cut just as short as the boys', which she hated. She was all right, was Eve.

In fact, they were all good mates, Eddie thought. There used to be more of them, but children seemed to drift away from the workhouse, often without any goodbye or even a hint they were thinking of moving on. Like Charlie's best mate Josh who just left one night. Or little Florence who had seemed to be such a friend to Eve – one morning she just wasn't there any more. As he spoke, Eddie looked round at his friends, knowing that tomorrow any one of them might have moved on to try their meagre luck elsewhere . . .

Mikey was sitting cross-legged on the ground, picking up bits of gravel and dropping them again. The others were listening intently to Eddie's story. He had just reached the part where the mummy escaped from the

British Museum and lurched off into the foggy night.

'So this mummy thing, what, came back to life?' Charlie said.

'You're making it up,' Jack muttered.

'I'm not,' Eddie assured them. 'Anyway, what we reckon is that it wasn't a mummy at all. Just someone pretending.'

'So, who was he?' Eve asked. She sounded like she wasn't that bothered, but her eyes were gleaming with interest.

'Yeah, did the peelers take him away and lock him up?' Charlie asked enthusiastically.

'No, because we *didn't* catch him. We gave him a good chase, but it had all been planned out, you see and there was a carriage waiting. I thought it was a cab, but then as the door opened and the mummy bloke got in, I saw there was this design on the door. Like you see a coat of arms on posh carriage doors sometimes. Only it was just a shape. Like this.' He crouched down and drew in the dust on the ground with his finger – the shape of the ankh engraved on the carriage door.

'Never seen anything like that before,' Charlie said.

'Me neither,' Jack agreed.

Even Mikey was shaking his head.

'You want us to let you know if we see a carriage with that on it?' Eve asked.

'I want more than that,' Eddie said. 'This could be really important.'

'So?' Charlie asked.

'So, I want you, and anyone else you can get to help, to go looking. Maybe we can find this carriage and discover who it belongs to. Maybe we can help solve the mystery of the mummy.'

Eve sniffed. 'What's in it for us?'

Eddie shrugged. 'Dunno. Thruppence. Sixpence maybe. Depends if we find the carriage.'

Eve nodded. 'Better get started, then.'

'Better get running, then,' Charlie said urgently. 'Pearce is coming.'

As he spoke a man appeared round the end of the building. He was a big man, broad-shouldered and with a large beer belly. His face was twisted into a malevolent leer and he was hefting a wooden cudgel in one beefy hand. When he caught sight of the children, his expression became even more unpleasant and he smacked the cudgel into the palm of his free hand.

'What are you lot doing hanging round here?' he

demanded. His voice sounded like the gravel that Mikey was playing with. 'Should be at school or working, not loitering.'

'Scarper,' Charlie hissed.

They ran, as fast as they could, as Pearce approached. Mikey reacted most slowly, getting to his feet at last and turning to follow his friends. But Pearce lumbered forwards, grabbed Mikey's coat and dragged him back. He raised the cudgel.

'I'll learn you to muck about here when you should be getting schooled.'

But as he tried to bring down the cudgel on the cowering Mikey, he found his arm held tight from behind.

'Pick on someone your own size,' Eddie told the big man, struggling to hold back the cudgel.

It was not a struggle Eddie could win. Pearce was twisting round and wrenching the cudgel free.

'Run!' Eddie shouted at Mikey.

Whether Mikey could hear or not, he understood – and he ran.

Eddie stepped away as Pearce walked slowly towards him. He felt the rough, cold brickwork against his back and knew he was up against the wall.

'Why should I pick on someone my own size,' Pearce said menacingly, 'when I've got you?'

'Have you?' Eddie was inching along the wall. As he

felt the corner of the building behind him, he turned on his heel. 'Got to catch me first, Fatso!'

With Pearce's shout of rage echoing off the brick buildings, Eddie ran full pelt after his friends.

'I wonder if I could presume on your time for a little while?' Sir William asked.

George had spent the morning finishing his cataloguing work from the day before. Sir William had already been at work when George arrived, sitting in his office leafing through a large dusty book with a faded cloth cover. He had spared George a glance and a 'Good morning' and George had left him in peace.

'Of course, sir.'

Without further comment, Sir William turned and led the way through the archive, past specimen cabinets and shelves and tables and through one of the doorless openings into the rooms beyond. For George, this was uncharted territory. Almost a third of the enormous space they entered was taken up with crates and boxes filled with items that Sir William or his predecessor had already catalogued and stored away.

At last they arrived in front of a large crate. It was open, and whatever had been inside had been removed, leaving only the crushed straw that had protected it.

'What was . . .?' George began to ask. But then he realised, from the size of the crate and the shape of the hollow in the straw packing. 'The sarcophagus.'

Sir William nodded. 'Came from this crate, yes. Lord Ruthven and his Royal Society colleagues were insistent, though I have no idea why. They maintain it is because the mummy was of no consequence, and would not be missed. Whereas it would be a shame to have to unwrap a specimen from the official collection. There might be complaints.'

'It was a shame to have to unwrap a mummy at all,' George said. 'If there ever was one. Before that prankster, whoever it was, took the mummy's place.'

'You think it was some sort of prank, then?'

'What else?' George laughed. 'A real, ancient Egyptian mummy is hardly likely to get up and wander off now, is it?' He hesitated, seeing that Sir William's expression was still as grave as ever. 'Is it?' he asked again, less sure now.

'It does seem most improbable,' Sir William admitted. 'And the fellow had a carriage waiting. I hardly think he could have arranged that while inside a sarcophagus that was itself first buried for thousands of years and then nailed up in this crate for the past few decades.' He reached inside the crate and pulled at the straw, as if to check that the real mummy was not still concealed inside. 'It is a shame the photographer did not come back.'

'You think photographs of the chap might help identify him?'

'By a process of comparison, perhaps. You see, when I opened this crate yesterday morning, there was most certainly a genuine mummy resting inside at that time.'

'So any substitution took place in the afternoon.'

'The evening,' Sir William corrected him. 'In the afternoon, I arranged for the photographer, Mr Denning, to photograph the mummy.'

'Before the Unwrapping?'

'It seemed sensible and prudent to keep a record of that which was about to be destroyed. Now, if we could compare the photographs Denning took with our memories of how the mummy appeared last night, we might be able to identify something from the photographs, some change.'

'If this Denning turns up.'

'Oh we shall find him.' Sir William turned, the light glinting on his round spectacles. 'But that isn't why I wanted you here.'

'Then, why?'

Sir William turned towards another crate that was beside the open one. This crate was also wooden, old and battered. It was smaller than the first crate, and square rather than rectangular – a cube about four feet along each side. Sir William patted the top of it with the flat of his hand, and was rewarded with a puff of dust that hung in the air like smoke.

'Now this crate is catalogued in the inventory as 57E2.'

'And what is inside it?' George wondered.

'I have no idea. There is a number in the inventory, and also on the top of the crate.' He pointed to where the number was stencilled. 'But that number is described as simply "Casket". My predecessor, the late Xavier Hemming, was meticulous in his records, so I find it odd that he entered such a vague description.'

'He was instrumental in establishing this department, wasn't he?' George recalled. 'Did you ever meet him?'

Sir William seemed not to hear. 'The crate with the sarcophagus was properly catalogued. That is how we found it. After some preliminary remarks about how Hemming came by the artefact, the description reads, as I recall: "Silver-lined sarcophagus from ancient Egypt c. 2000 BC. Contains mummified remains of Orabis (see document 56E19)."'

'And that document explains who this Orabis was?'

Sir William sniffed. 'That document does not exist. Not in the inventory, not on the shelves. No such number.' He turned back to the square crate. 'But the inventory number for the mummy and sarcophagus is 57E1. A connection perhaps? Related artefacts?'

'You think the missing document might be in that crate?' George wondered. 'It's very big.'

'There is only one way to find out what's inside,' Sir William said. 'Perhaps it is a document, perhaps a casket, perhaps something else. Perhaps whatever is inside will explain why the wise and clever Xavier Hemming believed that what seemed to be a perfectly ordinary and well-preserved Egyptian mummy deserved a place in the archives of the Department of Unclassified Artefacts.'

'Unless he knew Orabis was going to rise from the dead,' George said with a smile.

Again Sir William fixed him with a serious look. 'Don't think I haven't considered that,' he said. 'Now, I shall wait here while you find something to prise open this crate.'

There was a crowbar lying on top of one of the other crates nearby, and George assumed it had been left there from when the crate containing the mummy of Orabis had been opened. He eased the end of the crowbar beneath the wooden lid of the square crate and pushed down heavily on the other end. He could feel the wood straining against the nails. Then with a squeal, several of the nails pulled free of the wood and the lid lifted.

'Well done,' Sir William said, as George moved round to prise open the other side.

Before long, the lid was propped against the side of another crate, and George and Sir William were staring into the open box. It was filled with straw, but there was obviously something inside the straw. George could see the glint of metal – of gold?

'I had several chaps from Egyptology help lift the sarcophagus from its crate,' Sir William said. 'Not ideal as they were more than a little intrigued to know what we get up to down here. But in this case, I think we need to remove one of the sides. Since there are just the two of us, you agree?'

George nodded.

'I don't,' another voice announced before George could say anything. 'There's three of us.'

George almost dropped the heavy crowbar as he turned sharply to see who had spoken. He sighed with relief as he saw who it was. He should have guessed.

'So, what's going on here?' Eddie asked. He had his hands jammed deep in his trouser pockets and was leaning against the empty mummy crate. He had a piece of straw sticking out of his mouth while he chewed on the end, like a music-hall farmer about to burst into comic song.

Sir William was still sifting through the straw inside

the square crate. 'Nonetheless,' he said, apparently unsurprised at Eddie's arrival, 'I feel removing one of the sides would be the best course of action.'

As the side of the crate fell away, straw spilled out across the floor. Sir William reached in and pulled it away until they could see what was beneath.

'It's another box,' Eddie said, disappointed. 'I've never seen so many boxes as you've got stashed down here.'

George was rather more impressed. The box was made of a pale ceramic-like material that had an almost translucent quality. The glint of metal that George had seen was part of the mass of hieroglyphs that covered much of the sides and top of the box, in brilliant gold and deep blue. Tiny pictures and symbols that meant little to George – figures and birds and shapes . . .

'Old, is it?' Eddie wondered.

'Very,' Sir William assured him. 'Now, let's see if we can get the top off, shall we?'

The lid was heavy and felt like fragile stone. Sir William described it as 'calcite' but it wasn't a material that George was familiar with. The closest he had seen before was alabaster.

They laid the lid carefully on the ground and looked inside the box. It was divided up into five – a square area of two pairs, and at the end a single double-sized compartment. This larger space was empty, but in each of the others was what looked like a statue.

'A canopic chest,' Sir William announced, as if this was entirely to be expected. He lifted out one of the statues.

It was about two feet tall, cylindrical but widening to a top that was carved in the vague shape of a head. There were more hieroglyphs down the front, with the top painted into the face of an ape.

George and Eddie lifted out the other statues and set them down in a row on a nearby shelf of a bookcase. They were similar, but the head of each figure was different.

'Are they just decorative?' George wondered.

'They are canopic jars,' Sir William explained. 'As was the tradition, they are in the shapes of the sons of Horus. I forget their names, but as you can see, we have an ape, a falcon, a jackal and a human figure.'

'Jars?' Eddie said. 'You mean they open and there's stuff inside?'

'I wouldn't,' Sir William warned as Eddie reached for the dog-like jackal-head of the nearest canopic jar.

'Why not?'

'Well, I was right. These jars and this chest do indeed belong with the mummy of Orabis. In fact, you could say they are part of the mummy. Part of the ancient process of mummification involved the removal of bodily organs. They were placed in these jars.'

Eddie's hand came away from the jar. 'That's just . . . disgusting,' he said, screwing his face up. 'What bodily organs?' he asked after a moment.

'Liver, lungs, stomach and intestines, I think.'

Eddie nodded, looking no happier. 'That's *really* disgusting.'

Sir William was looking into the casket again. He reached down into the larger compartment, feeling round. 'Seems to be empty,' he announced.

'What should be inside it?' George asked.

'Well, nothing. We have the four canopic jars. So far, so ordinary and entirely as expected. But why have a compartment if there's nothing to go in it?'

'Something's been taken out?' Eddie asked.

'Or perhaps the casket was a little too big, so there was space left after they divided it up for the jars,' George said.

Sir William drummed his fingers on the narrow dividing wall. 'Possibly. Perhaps the inscription explains it.' He crouched down in front of the casket, inspecting the hieroglyphs.

'So, what do all these symbols mean?' George wanted to know.

'Mmm?' Sir William straightened up, rubbing his chin as he considered. 'I'm afraid I have no idea,' he said at last. 'Perhaps someone in Egyptology will be able to enlighten us. We should make a copy.'

Eddie whistled. 'Take a while for George to copy that lot in his sketchbook.

'Which is why,' Sir William said, 'we shall have photographs taken. If that photographer ever turns up.'

'Oh yes,' Eddie said. 'I knew there was something I had to tell you. There's a man up in your office. I said I'd let you know. Anyway, he said something about photographs.'

'Anything else?' George asked, sarcastically.

Eddie nodded. 'Murder.' He grinned. 'Photographs, and murder.'

CHAPTER 3

Liz was unable to get away from home until she was sure her father was settled and asleep. He was frail and weak, and retired early so she was hopeful that the rehearsal would not yet have finished.

Leaving a note for her father explaining that she had gone out and not to worry as she would be back soon, Liz made her way to the Parthenon Theatre. Her heart was pounding and she felt more nervous than she could remember. She tried to convince herself that it was better to arrive late than to be at the theatre on the stroke of six and watch the whole rehearsal. Of course, she wanted to see how the actors worked, how Henry Malvern organised and ran the session. But she did not wish to intrude.

The theatre was large and imposing, built in the early 1850s. It dominated the small street in the West End of London where it was situated. It was not a theatre that

Liz had been to, but she could imagine the audience spilling on to the narrow pavement at the end of a performance – talking about the play they had just seen, the experience they had shared . . .

There was no sign of life from inside, though posters proclaimed: 'Coming Soon – *The Lady of the Camellias*', giving top billing to Henry Malvern and Marie Cuttler. Even more prominent posters announced: 'Traditional Music Hall – Late House. This Week Only'.

The door was heavy but opened easily to allow Liz into the dimly lit foyer. She stood on the dark red carpet and looked round. It was all far more ornate and splendid than the small Chistleton Theatre where she helped with productions whenever she could.

A uniformed attendant was standing beside the ticket booth at the side of the foyer. 'Late house isn't till ten,' he said gruffly, handlebar moustache twitching as he spoke. 'Doors open nine-thirty.' He sniffed and checked his pocket watch. 'That isn't for over two hours.'

'I'm sorry,' Liz said nervously. 'But I'm not here for the late house.'

'Advance sales from eleven till five,' the man responded, still examining his watch.

'Mr Malvern invited me – to watch the rehearsal.'

The watch disappeared, and the moustache moved slightly to reveal a toothy smile. 'Then you must be Miss

Oldfield. This way, please.'

He led her through to the auditorium and then left Liz to fend for herself. She was at the back of the enormous theatre and the stage seemed miles away. She was impressed at how clearly she could hear Malvern and the other actors as they went through a scene of the play. Liz settled herself into a seat at the end of the centre block about halfway to the stage.

The scene was played out between just two people. The other actors stood in front of the stage or sat in the front row as they watched, and occasionally Malvern asked them what they thought about the clarity of diction or the blocking of the action on the stage. Despite the constant stopping and restarting as they refined their performance, Liz was soon caught up in it all.

It was a moment in the play where Marguerite Gautier tells her lover Armand Duval that she cannot see him again. Liz knew the story from Dumas's novel, *La Dame aux Camélias*. She knew that Marguerite was still in love with Armand, but had been persuaded by the man's father that it was best if she broke off the relationship. Marguerite was a well-known courtesan – based on a woman that Dumas had himself loved.

And like Dumas's own lover, Marguerite was destined to die a slow, wasting death from consumption. But that was not for many scenes yet. The spark of love between

Marguerite and Armand would still be there, tragically, as she died . . .

Malvern was of course playing Armand Duval, combining fury and disappointment with his passion as Marguerite dismissed him. As Marguerite, Marie Cuttler was cold and aloof but with an underlying depth of emotion that brought tears to Liz's eyes. The actress was pale, but with a slight blush to her cheeks that heightened the emotion of the scene still further. Watching them act, Liz was sure that this was what she herself wanted to do. And inside, she despaired at ever aspiring to the levels of talent displayed in front of her.

As the scene closed, Armand turned on his heel and left. The door closed behind him, and Marguerite collapsed to the floor in tears she had not been able to cry while the man she loved was present. As one, the actors in front of the stage applauded, and Liz found that she was clapping with them – laughing and crying at the same time.

Malvern returned to the stage, smiling, and took a short bow before helping Marie Cuttler to her feet. The actress dabbed at her eyes with a handkerchief and smiled her own appreciation. Liz marvelled at how she could turn such passionate emotion up and down like a gas lamp.

'I think that will suffice for this evening,' Malvern

announced. 'Thank you to those who stayed when they did not need to. I certainly value your comments, your support, and your appreciation and I imagine Marie does too.'

'Oh, I do. My colleagues are always my best critics,' Marie said.

Everyone laughed politely, and the company slowly dispersed. A couple of the actors nodded to Liz as they walked past, heading for the front of the theatre. The rest disappeared backstage.

Malvern put his hand gently on Marie's arm. 'Could you spare me a moment longer, do you think?' he asked.

'Of course I can. Anything for you, Henry.'

Malvern led her to the edge of the stage and helped her down into the auditorium. Then he nodded towards where Liz was still sitting. 'There's someone I'd like you to meet.'

Charlie had been looking at carriages all day. He'd seen dozens of them, but none with the sort of pattern that Eddie had mentioned on the door. He did feel that he was getting close, though. Nellie the porter's daughter at Waterloo had told him she thought she saw the carriage picking up at the station the previous day. Or maybe setting down.

'It was smoggy,' she admitted. 'Didn't see too well. Just, like, the shape of it. There was something on the door, but the driver got shirty when I got close.' She sniffed. 'I was hoping for a tip. Carry a bag or something. But he put his whip up to me so I hoofed it.'

'Where did it go?' Charlie asked.

She shrugged. 'Towards Charing Cross, so far as I could tell.'

There was a lamplighter called Nick at Charing Cross who was about the same age as Charlie and used to be at the workhouse, before he upped and left. Charlie saw him sometimes, round the town. And yes, he reckoned he'd seen the carriage with the pattern on the door.

'Try down Albernum Street,' he said. 'You know, round the back of the posh clubs and that, up west. I've seen it there a couple of times, I'm sure, when I've been covering for Josiah Cooper.' The lad grinned, showing off broken teeth. 'You'd better be getting back though or Pearce'll have you.'

'He won't know,' Charlie said. 'He never checks who's in and who's out.'

'That John Remick still there?' Nick asked. When Charlie nodded, the lamplighter's grin got wider. 'He'll tell Pearce. Or duff you up himself.'

Charlie swallowed. Remick was a nasty piece of work who'd thump the smaller kids just to hear them squeal.

With Pearce the workhouse master, Remick was helpful and polite. With any of the other kids, he was a violent bully. Which was probably why Pearce liked him. Remick kept the children in order better than Pearce himself ever could.

Despite his anxiety about being late back and incurring the fist of John Remick or the strap of Master Pearce, or both, Charlie decided to take a diversion and walk down Albernum Street. It was a mile away, so it took him a while. The cold damp evening was heavy with fog, and the lamps were vague glows in the hazy air.

Albernum Street ran parallel to a larger road where there were several imposing town houses and a couple of gentlemen's clubs. Charlie didn't really know the area. But he remembered the street as one he'd hidden in from a policeman when he was trying to make a living lifting watches and wallets. He'd not been any good at it and almost got caught more times than he could recall. Not like Eddie, Charlie thought as he turned into the narrow street – now Eddie could lift anything from anyone and they'd not know for ages. Soft and quick as a butterfly, were Eddie's fingers . . .

There was a carriage at the side of the street. The fog was so deep here that Charlie nearly walked into it. The dark outline loomed out of the gathering night, and he stepped off the pavement quickly. His heart was beating faster as he peered through the gloom. He could see the door handle, but no design. Just a cab. He sighed with disappointment and walked quickly on.

There was another cab further along, outside the back of one of the clubs. Maybe gentlemen used the rear exit if they didn't want to be seen leaving. Charlie knew some gentlemen – and some clubs – were like that. He barely glanced at the cab as he walked past.

And froze in mid-step. Colour in the grey of the fog. Brilliant red, burning through the colourless air around it. The shape that Eddie had drawn in the dust. Charlie almost called out in triumph, and took a step closer to the carriage, staring intently at the shape. No doubt about it – this was the carriage Eddie wanted.

'You – boy!' The voice was clear and commanding, cutting through the fog from above.

The driver of the carriage was leaning down towards Charlie, whip in hand.

Charlie stepped back, ready to run. But something about the man's deep dark voice made him hesitate, as if his feet did not want to obey his fear. 'Sorry,' he stammered. 'Just looking.'

'Who are you?'

He answered despite his fear. Like his voice was not his own. 'Charlie Frankham. From the Kenton Workhouse. I didn't mean no harm.'

As the Coachman raised his whip hand, a door at the back of the building opened. Light washed through the swirling fog, illuminating the Coachman's face for a moment.

A face like a pale skull.

In that moment, the spell was broken. Charlie's legs began to feel like his own again. And he ran.

'I sometimes think,' Marie Cuttler confided in Liz, 'the only time that man feels emotion is when he's on stage. Perhaps that's why he does it.'

They both turned slightly to watch Malvern as he paced the stage, occasionally adjusting a piece of furniture or an ornament in Marguerite Gautier's room.

'I hardly know him, I'm afraid,' Liz said.

'I hardly know him myself,' Marie said quietly. 'And we've been appearing together here for over five years.' She smiled. 'I mustn't be too down on him. Many years ago, he gave me my first real chance on the stage. And you've seen yourself, he's an accomplished actor.'

'That scene between you was incredible,' Liz told her.

'Thank you, dear.'

The words sounded quaint and odd coming from such a beautiful young woman. Though now that Liz was close to Marie, she could see that her face was thick with make-up and her cheeks were pink with rouge. Beneath it, Marie Cuttler was not so young as she would like to appear. But then, that was true of many of the women in the theatre. Experience came with the greatest price of all . . .

'Henry tells me you've some little acting experience yourself.'

'Little is right,' Liz said, feeling her cheeks redden without the need for rouge.

'That's lucky.'

'Why?'

'I need a maid,' Marie said. She laughed as she saw Liz's expression. 'I don't mean I *really* need a maid, dear. But little Beryl who was playing Marguerite's maid didn't turn up this evening. Henry says he always worried about her and doesn't expect to see her again. He's usually right. Good at judging character. What do you think?'

Liz felt her face was burning now. 'Me? But, what if Beryl does come back? What if she's been ill or something?'

'What if she doesn't?' Marie countered. 'It isn't a big role. Not many lines. But lots of time on stage with Marguerite. I need someone I can get on with, and just between the two of us, Beryl was such a . . .' She stopped and laughed. 'Well, I won't say what she was, but I'm sure you get the idea. She wasn't someone I could easily talk to. Be a friend.'

'I, well . . .' Liz was blustering. 'My father, he doesn't really . . . That is, I'm not sure if I could – if I'd be able to . . .' Her voice faded as she ran out of words, still without saying what was on her mind.

'But would you do it?' Marie asked. 'For me? And for Henry? Actually,' she lowered her voice, 'it was Henry who suggested I might ask you. He's such a treasure, isn't he?'

'I . . .' Still no words would come, and Liz looked from Marie to Malvern and back again.

'Do you want to?' Marie asked.

'Yes!' she blurted. 'Yes, of course.'

'Then we'll make it work.' Marie held up her hand to quell any protest. 'I know your father doesn't really approve. But we'll sort it out, you'll see.' Before Liz could protest further, Marie put her hand to her forehead and sighed.

'Are you all right?'

Marie nodded. 'I felt a little dizzy, just for a moment. It'll pass. Such an emotional scene.'

Beneath her make-up, the actress seemed suddenly frail and tired.

The young man was sitting patiently in the chair opposite Sir William's desk. He had a battered briefcase on the floor beside the chair. As Eddie, George and Sir William arrived, he stood up, rubbing his hands together nervously.

'It's good of you to see me, Sir William. And at such a late hour.' His voice was nasal and oily. He stopped rubbing his hands, and instead ran one of them over his thin, greasy, black hair. His jacket was a shade too small, and there were pale dots across the front of it where something had splashed.

'Good evening,' Sir William said. 'And how may I help you? Eddie said you mentioned something about photography.'

'And murder,' George added quietly.

The man sat down again and buried his face for a moment in his hands. When he looked up, Eddie could see how tired he seemed.

'I'm afraid so. My name is Gilbert Pennyman,' the man said. 'I work as an apprentice and assistant to Mr Denning. Or rather, I did until today.'

'Mr Bernard Denning, the photographer?' Sir William said.

Pennyman nodded. 'The same.'

'So what happened?' Eddie asked. 'He give you the boot?'

George glared and Sir William waved him to silence.

'I was at work early this morning at Mr Denning's studio. That is, it's his house but he has a room there specially adapted as a dark room where he can develop his photographs. I have a key, as on occasion I have to work there when he is out. We had a lot on this week and I needed to make an early start, so I was there by eight o'clock. And so it was me who discovered the burglary.'

'Burglary?' George echoed.

Sir William leaned forward. 'Was Mr Denning not at home?'

Pennyman seemed to go pale at this. 'You mean, you don't know?' he said. 'I thought, when this gentleman mentioned murder, I just thought . . .' He pulled out his hanky again. 'Oh my goodness,' he said into it, his voice muffled. Slowly he lowered the handkerchief. 'Mr Denning was killed last night. Not three streets away from here.'

There was a shocked silence for several moments. 'Murdered?!' Eddie whispered.

'Run down it seems by a carriage. The police said they thought it must be deliberate from the position of the body on the pavement. An accident, and surely the carriage would have stopped.'

'And his house – his studio – was last night broken into,' Sir William said thoughtfully.

Pennyman nodded. 'It was a mess. Photographs removed from their files and strewn about the place. Some were taken, but most were not. I did wonder . . .' He reached down for the briefcase at his feet.

'Yes?' Sir William prompted.

'I did wonder if the thieves could be after these.' He took out a large brown envelope and held it out to Sir William. 'Mr Denning had his camera with him. It was under his body, and miraculously was not badly damaged. It holds a magazine of dry process plates, a dozen in all. He had saved several plates of course for the evening, but the photographs I know he took for you in the afternoon were on the earlier plates, and ready to be developed.'

'And you have developed them?' Sir William asked. He reached out and took the proffered envelope.

Pennyman nodded.

'What do they show?' George asked.

Pennyman shrugged and blinked. 'Nothing,' he said. 'They show . . . nothing.'

Sir William frowned and pulled several photographs from inside the envelope.

'You mean they're blank?' George asked. 'The plates were not exposed properly?'

Pennyman shook his head. 'They show an empty box. Except for the last one, look.' He reached across and pulled out the last of the photographs.

'Here – give us a look,' Eddie said, pushing past George and leaning over the desk to see.

The photograph that Pennyman had selected was a fog of darkness. There was a shape barely visible, square and box-like with what looked like wooden prongs jutting forward from it.

'There was insufficient light for a good photograph,' Pennyman explained. 'It looks like it was taken outside, at night. Perhaps by accident. The shutter of the camera is automatic, it exposes the plate for just a fraction of a second. Not like the old days with wet process where you needed to hold the shutter open . . .'

'I think it's a carriage,' George said suddenly. He pointed to the dark, square shape. 'This is the front of the carriage, and here are the shafts for the horses,' he went on indicating the wooden prongs.

'Maybe it's the carriage that ran him down,' Eddie exclaimed with excitement. 'A picture of his own murderer taken in his dying moments.'

'Yes,' said Sir William, 'well, if there were any horses I might agree.'

'Runaway carriage,' Eddie said eagerly. 'Rolling downhill with no one to stop it. Rolled right over him – wallop!' He clapped his hands together by way of demonstration. 'Didn't stand an earthly. No?'

'There were . . .' Pennyman swallowed. 'Hoof prints.'

He took the photograph from Sir William and stared at it. 'No coachman, either. It's a mystery, I'm afraid. But I assume these other pictures were taken for you in the afternoon, Sir William. I thought they might be important. Though as you can see . . .' He let the comment hang in the air as Sir William spread the photographs out on the blotter.

'How very extraordinary,' Sir William said. He looked pale.

There were five photographs in all, and each and every one showed the same box. Eddie recognised it at once as the casket the mummy had rested in at the previous night's ceremony. The flash the photographer had used reflected as a flare off the silver lining of the sarcophagus. The sand strewn across the bottom of the casket looked more like salt as it caught the bright light. Each photograph was taken from a different angle, some closer and some further away. One showed just the top end of the sarcophagus, where the mummy's head had rested.

George picked up one of the photographs. 'Seems normal enough.'

'Bit boring,' Eddie said. 'I mean, why did you take pictures of an empty box?'

George was nodding. 'I'm inclined to agree, sir. I thought you had photographed the mummified remains, not just the sarcophagus.'

Sir William took off his spectacles and pinched the bridge of his nose between his thumb and forefinger. 'Photographing the empty sarcophagus would indeed be something of a wasted effort,' he said. 'Which is why I had Mr Denning photograph the *mummy*. We did not take it out of the sarcophagus. The mummy was there, in the casket, when these photographs were taken.'

'So where's it gone then?' Eddie said. 'Where's the mummy? Why doesn't it show up in the pictures?'

'That is precisely the question,' Sir William said, replacing his glasses, 'that is troubling me.'

CHAPTER 4

It was not yet light when Sir William arrived for work the next morning. The remnants of the previous night's fog still swirled and drifted. Making his way briskly along the corridor that led to his office, Sir William's mind was on the events of the previous days. He had given George the task of examining the photographs of the sarcophagus to see if there was some way they could have been tampered with, but he suspected the truth was not so simple or mundane.

Head down, deep in thought, he did not see that the door to his office was ajar until he had the key ready. Warily, Sir William pushed the door gently open. A tall figure was standing at the window close to the desk. A tall, slim man, silhouetted against the first grey of the morning.

'It will be light soon,' the man said as he turned. His face was a dark shadow, but Sir William had recognised the cultured voice.

'Indeed it will, your grace.' He made his way to his desk and gestured for Lord Ruthven to be seated the other side. 'Tell me, did I neglect to lock my door last night?'

'I have been given carte blanche to go where I wish in the Museum. But please forgive the intrusion, Sir William. I was not sure how long you would be. I have another appointment soon, so allow me to come quickly to the point.'

'Please do.' Sir William clasped his hands together over his waistcoat and leaned back in his chair, staring intently at his uninvited guest.

Lord Ruthven was past middle age, but not yet old. He might have been in his fifties or even his early sixties. His eyes were an alert blue and his hair was steel grey. His moustache, by contrast, was almost white. The man's prominent cheekbones and slightly hooked nose gave him an aristocratic bearing and he exuded self-confidence. If anyone else had broken into Sir William's office he would have taken them to task for it. But Lord Ruthven deserved respect. Not just for who he was, but for what he was. The Department of Unclassified Artefacts answered not to the trustees of the British Museum, but to an oversight committee appointed from its own ranks by the Royal Society.

Lord Ruthven was a prominent member of that committee.

'This unfortunate business the other night,' Lord Ruthven said.

'The walking mummy?' Sir William kept his tone matter-of-fact and calm.

'Walking prankster, more like. But be that as it may, the Committee feels it is important to be cautious.'

'In what respect?' Sir William smiled. 'All Egyptian caskets to be kept locked shut henceforth perhaps?'

Lord Ruthven's eyes glinted sharply as he glanced towards the window. 'This is hardly a matter for levity.'

'My apologies. But my question stands – in what respect should we be cautious?'

'In respect of your department, sir,' Lord Ruthven said sternly. 'The press are all over this incident, as you can well imagine. We cannot afford for it to become known where the mummy originated. Is that plain enough for you?'

'We are in a museum full of mummies and relics,' Sir William pointed out. 'Why would the press, or anyone else for that matter, take it upon themselves to wonder about the exact provenance of the long-dead gentleman in question?'

'Why indeed? But the ways and thoughts of Fleet Street are a law unto themselves.'

'We will be discreet, if that is what you are suggesting. Myself and my assistant are the only ones who know where the mummy was supplied from. Even Brinson knows only that it came from a secondary collection linked to the Museum's Egyptian Department.' That was not strictly true, of course. But Sir William was not about to try to explain Eddie to Lord Ruthven and he was wary of mentioning the photographs to anyone.

'More than that.' Lord Ruthven said. 'We, that is, the Committee, feel it would be sensible if all connected artefacts were removed from your department. If we need to produce them at a later date for whatever reason, they can be seen to be stored elsewhere.'

Sir William frowned. 'Connected artefacts?'

'The sarcophagus, for example.'

'I hardly think it is likely that the newspapers will find their way into hidden vaults, which they are unaware even exist, to look at an empty sarcophagus.'

'Nevertheless, we feel it is best if the sarcophagus is taken into safe-keeping elsewhere.' There was an edge of impatience in Lord Ruthven's voice.

'And where might that be?'

The impatience became annoyance. 'That is no concern of yours, Protheroe.'

Sir William leaned across the desk. 'Forgive me, but I think it is.'

Lord Ruthven stared back at him for several seconds. Then he looked away. He stood up, gathering his hat and gloves from a side table. 'Very well, if you must know, and I suppose it is only right and proper, I am having the sarcophagus taken from the Egyptian Rooms to my club.'

'Your club?' Sir William echoed in disbelief.

'Where it won't attract unwanted attention and the interest of sensationalists. Can't have people coming from all over London to stare at the thing.' He turned towards the door.

'This is the British Museum, sir,' Sir William said sharply. 'Its very purpose is to attract people from all over London, and indeed further afield, to stare at things.'

Lord Ruthven turned in the doorway. 'I think perhaps, on this matter, we must agree to differ. Let us not fall out over it though.' He put on his hat and began to pull on his gloves.

'Very well,' Sir William conceded. 'You have my permission, though I am sure you do not need it, to take the sarcophagus into protective custody. I really cannot see the point of removing something from one secret location and hiding it in another. But, as you say, it is hardly worth arguing about.'

'Thank you. You know,' Ruthven went on, 'I believe there is a vacancy at the Club. They don't come up very often and of course membership is by nomination only. I was wondering if I could put your name forward?'

Sir William blinked in surprise. 'Forgive me, which club is that?'

'More than just a club, you know. I believe the correct title is "the Society of Diabolic and Mystic Nominees". We are very . . . exclusive.'

'And very secretive,' Sir William said. 'I am flattered and honoured, your grace. But I am quite happy with my own club and would hardly have the time or the stamina for two.'

'The Atlantian Club?' Lord Ruthven smiled thinly, his moustache twitching. 'You could resign.'

'Dear Julius would never forgive me. As I say, I am grateful for the honour, but I am afraid I must decline.'

Lord Ruthven shrugged. 'Very well.' He seemed about to leave, but then he paused, and turned back. 'Oh, and the casket of canopic jars. Best we look after that too, away from prying eyes. Have it brought up from the vault, will you? I'll send someone to collect it this morning.'

Sir William stared at the closed door for several moments, the tips of his fingers tapping out a steady rhythm on the blotter. So the sarcophagus and the jars – and how did Ruthven know about them? – were to be taken to Lord Ruthven's club. In a way that seemed strangely appropriate. For Sir William was aware that the Society of Diabolic and Mystic Nominees was better known by another name.

It was more commonly called the Damnation Club.

Eve had gone to work, which Eddie felt was a minor betrayal. Especially on a Saturday. She should have been out looking for the carriage like the rest of them, not weaving wicker baskets with the older girls and the women. Although actually they were meeting as before, not searching. Except Eve.

And Charlie, who hadn't turned up. Knowing Charlie, he might be out with the mudlarks – the kids down on the muddy banks of the Thames looking for anything that might have washed up. Anything they could sell or pawn or use.

'He said he'd be here,' Jack pointed out. 'He don't let you down, Charlie. If he says something he means it. Unless Pearce has got him cleaning out the kitchens or something. Pearce was waiting for him when he got in last night,' Jack went on. 'He hardly had time to say anything to us before Pearce came and yanked him out the dormitory. But he said he'd be here. Seemed excited.'

'What about?' Eddie asked. He felt a twinge of excitement himself – had Charlie found something?

'Dunno,' Jack confessed. 'He was talking to Mikey, wasn't he, Mikey?' He raised his voice and nodded vehemently to make Mikey understand. But the other boy stared back at him blankly.

'We need to know if he found anything, and where he's been looking,' Eddie decided.

'He might be in the kitchens,' Jack said. 'Want me to go and look, Eddie?' he didn't sound enthusiastic.

Eddie could imagine what would happen to him if he got caught bunking off school. 'All right,' he said. 'But just a quick look. Any chance you might get seen, come straight back. Don't want you feeling the rough side of Pearce's belt like Charlie. If that's what's happened to him.'

Eddie watched Jack hurry off, round the side of the forbidding building.

'Eddie.'

The voice was hesitant and nervous. Eddie spun round. But there was no one there. No one but himself and Mikey – and Mikey never said anything.

'Eddie.' Firmer and more confident this time. Eddie's mouth dropped open.

'You can talk,' he said to Mikey.

The other boy shuffled his feet and looked away. 'Don't tell,' he said. 'Charlie knows. He's the only one. But if I can't hear or speak, well – they leave me alone.'

'Who do?' Eddie was outraged. Who frightened a kid so much he pretended to be deaf and dumb?

'Me dad. Years ago, before I came here. If you can't talk you can't answer back. I used to answer back. But then . . .' He shrugged. 'I stopped. Don't get hit so much then. Don't answer back, he said. So I didn't. Not ever.' He looked up at Eddie, eyes wide and scared. 'Don't tell,' he said again.

'Course not,' Eddie promised. 'But, why talk now? Why to me?'

'Cos of Charlie,' Mikey said. 'I don't think he's in the kitchens. I don't think he got extra chores or nothing. I think they sent him away.'

'Why?'

Mikey looked round, as if afraid that he might be overheard. Eddie felt unnerved by the boy's fear, and he looked round too. But they were completely alone. A sudden shaft of sunlight cut through the misty morning air and cast their shadows against the dark wall of the workhouse.

'Why d'you think they sent Charlie away?' Eddie asked again. 'What did he tell you, last night before Pearce came for him?'

Mikey took a deep breath, and his answer came out in an unpunctuated rush: 'He said he found the carriage up west somewhere. A lamplighter's boy he knows told him where to look and there it was.'

Eddie put his hand on Mikey's shoulder. He could feel the boy trembling beneath his threadbare jacket. 'Where? Did he say where the carriage was?'

'In a side street. Back of some buildings. Posh clubs and stuff. Charlie said . . .' Mikey paused, looking over his shoulder before going on: 'He said it was round the back of the Damnation Club.'

It took them several journeys. Since Sir William was not prepared to allow Lord Ruthven's men down into his archives, he and George carried the heavy casket between them. They struggled up the stone stairway that led from the vaults to the ground floor of the British Museum.

They left the large, rectangular casket in Sir William's office, where it took up most of the empty space in front of the desk. Then they went back for the canopic jars.

'I was going to examine those photographs this morning,' George said. 'See if I can discern anything unusual about them. I mean, about how they have been developed and printed up.'

'It's a good thing we were able to get Pennyman to photograph this casket and the jars last night,' Sir William said. 'At least we shall have a record of them.'

Sir William was tapping his finger thoughtfully against his chin. 'There are some other photographs that might be of interest,' he said.

The Department's catalogues were kept in the workroom, shelved in a heavy, glass-fronted bookcase. Each of the leather-bound volumes had a number written on the spine in dark ink. The first of the books was an index which Sir William consulted.

'Ah yes. Volume 17 is listed here as *Artwork, Paintings, Photographic.*' He replaced the index and removed volume 17 of the catalogue, which he handed to George.

George opened the book on the workbench so they could both look at it. He turned through the heavy parchment pages until he reached a section headed 'Photographic Items'.

'Lens of polished glass that focuses light as if for a camera or camera obscura,' he read aloud from the first entry. 'Discovered amongst artefacts dating from early Rome and showing signs of sophisticated machining.'

'Fascinating,' Sir William said. 'But not what we are concerned with at the present.' He turned the page. 'This, I think, is more like it. Photographic Pictures . . .' He turned a few more pages, running his finger down the lists of catalogue numbers. 'We have pictures of things that should not exist, pictures that were taken before the photographic process was invented. Sketches of some shroud in a church in Italy . . . And a section here of pictures that have apparent problems at the detail level. I would think that is where we should start.' He pointed to a complicated reference code made up of numbers and letters.

Sir William closed the book and replaced it on the shelf before hurrying back towards the stairs to the vault.

'Did you know Professor Hemming?' George again asked as they made their way back down to the cellars.

'Went to his funeral. But sadly I never met the man, though he was by all accounts a genius. Eccentric, but a genius. The Department was formed at his suggestion and most of the initial set of artefacts, including our mummy, came from his own collection. Ah, here we are.'

Sir William stopped in front of a dusty bookcase stuffed with envelopes and cardboard files.

There did not seem to be anything at all amiss with the photographs in the file. There were about twenty of them, spread out on George's desk as he examined them in his small office. Some were very old and faded. Others looked as if they might have been taken just a few days before, though they must have been ten years old at least if Xavier Hemming had put them there.

George was grateful for the arrival of Pennyman, who brought the printed photographs of the canopic casket and jars. Since the photographer's assistant had already learned that there was something distinctly odd about the photographs his erstwhile employer had taken for Sir William, George couldn't see there would be any harm in showing him the pictures from the archive file.

Pennyman was rather more self-assured and confident than he had been the previous evening. He was evidently getting over the loss of his employer, and he was happy to look at the photographs for George.

'Well, process-wise they seem fine,' he said. 'But dear oh me – who took these then?'

'Does it matter?' George asked. 'Lots of people, I expect. Is there a problem?'

Pennyman sniffed. 'I'll say there is. I mean, I'm no expert, not on composition and such. But look at this one.'

He reached for a picture of a group of people. It had been taken in a garden. A large hedge formed the background, and about twenty people were standing in a group. Or rather, they were standing in two groups, a narrow gap between them.

'Why's he done that, then?' Pennyman asked, tapping

each of the groups of people in turn. 'Makes no sense. They should all be standing together. And look here.' He pulled another photograph from the untidy pile. This one showed three children and a large chair. There was a girl standing beside the chair and two younger boys sitting on the floor in front of it. 'What's the chair for?'

'It's like there's something missing,' George said slowly. 'Something or someone.'

Pennyman dropped the photograph back on the pile. 'I don't know, maybe they're practice shots. Like a rehearsal for a play. Mr Denning does that sometimes, to check the lighting and arrangement and everything. Not usually with people though. But some photographers might. Then they take the real photograph when all the parties are present, knowing the conditions are right and favourable.'

'Maybe,' George said, but he wasn't convinced that was the answer.

'As for the process used and whether there's anything odd about that . . .' Pennyman gave an exaggerated shrug. 'I know what to do, but I don't understand how or why it all works. You need to talk to an expert. Mr Denning would have known. Or –' He broke off and clicked his fingers. 'You need to talk to Nathaniel Blake,' he said.

Nathaniel Blake's voice was as stretched and cracked as his ancient face. 'I worked with him back in the forties,' he said. The skin was baggy and lined and the flesh of his neck was bulging out over the top of his collar. What little hair he had was a white wisp that stirred in the chill breeze. He huddled deeper into the blanket draped over his shoulders.

'So you understand the photographic process?' George prompted. He was feeling the cold himself, despite his heavy coat.

The two of them were sitting on a bench away from the main house. The gardens were well kept, with many narrow paths through the lawns and flower beds. Several of the guests at the home for retired and infirm gentlepeople were walking slowly round the grounds. One old man had a nurse steadying his elbow as he shuffled past the bench.

'Grandson, Nathaniel?' the old man asked in a husky voice.

Blake didn't answer. 'He was working on his book,' he told George. '*The Pencil of Nature*. That was how Fox Talbot saw photography. Everyone called him Fox. He hated that. William Henry Fox Talbot.' Blake broke off so as to let loose a cannonade of rasping coughs. 'Yes, I understand the silver process. Helped him refine it. He saw it as a tool, a mechanism. Not an art. Not like these fancy boys now who pose everything. You had to back then, with such long exposure times. No need now. You can catch nature in the act. So why don't they? Eh?'

'Well,' George said. 'Er, quite.'

'Exactly.' Blake nodded. 'Exactly. What did you say your name was?'

'Archer, sir. George Archer.'

'Sir George Archer?' Blake seemed impressed.

'Um, no. Just plain Mr.'

'Oh,' Blake said, disappointed. 'Never mind. Maybe one day . . . What do you want, anyway?'

'I wondered if you would look at some photographs for me,' George said. 'There may be something strange about the way they have been created. The process.'

Blake gave a grunt and adjusted his blanket. 'Suppose I could,' he muttered. 'You said you are from the British Museum,' he added, with a hint of suspicion in his tone.

'That's right. I'm afraid the photographs have to stay at the Museum, but perhaps you could come and look at them there. I can send a carriage,' he added, hoping that this would indeed be possible. 'Tomorrow?'

'Trip out, eh?' Blake seemed interested. 'British Museum. How grand.' He nodded slowly. 'So long as that harpy Mrs Eggerton lets me escape for a day.'

'I'm sure it will be fine,' George said, though he did not relish speaking with Mrs Eggerton. The large, severe woman who ran the home had met him at the door and subjected him to a loud, intense questioning before allowing him to see Blake.

'Strangest thing I ever saw,' Blake said, 'to do with weird photography . . .' His voice faded and he stared out across the grounds.

'Yes?' George said.

'I've seen double exposures, where you get two pictures all muddled up together. Fogged plates where the light got in. Even a picture of a séance where there's spirits above the medium, though I expect that was faked up in the processing. There's always an explanation, a technical explanation. But the strangest thing was when I was with Talbot, all those years ago. When he was refining the process, looking at using silver and taking his first photographs.'

'And what was it?'

Blake seemed lost in his memories, and George had to prompt him again before he went on. 'There was a man. Came all the way out to Lacock one night to see us. From London. Well, to see Talbot. Offered him money.' Blake laughed, but his mirth turned to coughing and it took him several moments to recover. 'Tried to talk Talbot out of it. Told him the process would never work, though we could show him it did. Then he offered Talbot money. A lot of money. Just to stop, do something else, abandon his work. Most peculiar.'

'Indeed,' George agreed, wondering whether the man was just rambling now.

'But Talbot would have none of it. Stubborn, was Fox. He said he'd prove to the gent – and he *was* a gent. Very highly placed, I remember. Fox said he'd show him it worked, and he had me set up a camera in the next room. There was an adjoining door, and he opened it just a little. Just enough for me to point the camera into the room without being seen. And this fellow was sat in a chair by the window, while Talbot said he had to go out for a minute and would he wait. That's when I did it. I took the photograph, with that man sitting plain as daylight, nice and still, in the chair by the brightest lamp. Fox was going to post it to him afterwards, just to make the point.'

'And did he?' George wondered.

Blake's watery eyes widened slightly and the flabby skin at his neck shivered. 'Did he what?'

'Send the photograph.'

'No,' Blake said. 'And you know why? Because when I developed that photograph, when I printed it up, it showed the lamp and the chair plain as anything. But the man, the man who wanted Talbot to cease his work . . .'

Blake shuddered, perhaps with the cold. He pulled his blanket tight round him.

'The man,' he went on, 'wasn't there. The chair was empty. I took his photograph, I know I did. But he just didn't appear in it. Like he was invisible to the camera. Darnedest thing I ever saw,' he said. 'Or didn't see. British Museum,' he added, nodding. 'Yes, I'd like that.'

But George hardly heard him.

CHAPTER 5

The morning was as cold and bleak as their mood. Eve was pale, and Mikey wouldn't look at any of them. Jack, for once, was not grinning. He wasn't even smiling, and that seemed to Eddie to be the most poignant expression of grief from any of them.

'Did anyone say what happened?' Eddie asked.

'They just found him,' Eve said. 'Down by the river. Reckon he fell in.'

'Once a mudlark, always a mudlark,' Jack said. 'Wouldn't let us see him. Poor Charlie lying dead and they wouldn't let none of his friends go and look.'

'So, what happened – he drowned?' Eddie asked. It seemed so unreal. He could remember laughing and joking with Charlie just the other day. Could remember the lad's cheeky grin and mop of tangled sandy hair. Charlie was about the same age as Eddie, and that just made it so much more unfair.

'Connie says they don't know how it happened,' Eve was saying. 'She was there when the peelers found him on the bank. She says he looked just like he was asleep or resting. Only pale – so pale.' Eve swallowed and blinked back her tears. She was staring down at her feet as she spoke. 'Connie says the man with the peelers, the man they took to see Charlie, said he'd been dead all night, maybe longer. And something else too, though I think Connie made it up.'

'What?' Eddie asked. 'What did she say?'

Eve looked up, and she was crying properly now. She wiped the back of her hand across her face, smearing the tears away. 'Connie says Charlie's body was drained of blood.'

There was silence for a moment, then Jack laughed. It wasn't the sort of laugh that meant he thought it was funny. It was nervous and incredulous. 'Connie's been listening to those stories,' he said. 'She's been sneaking in the Dog and Whistle again and listening to the gin-talk and the gossip. Everyone's been talking about it.'

'About what?' Eddie demanded. 'First I've heard.'

'Bloodless bodies,' Jack told him. 'There's a bloke down the market swears it's Spring-Heeled Jack back for revenge.'

'I heard it was a plague brought on a ship from

China,' Eve said. 'But it don't matter what it is,' she went on impatiently. 'Just gossip, probably.' She shook her head. 'Time we was going.'

'Going where?'

'To church,' Eve said. 'We're all going. It's Sunday. Going to pray for Charlie's soul. And you should too, Eddie Hopkins.'

'And what do you think you lot are doing hiding round here when it's time for church?' a voice demanded.

Eddie swung round to find another boy leaning on the corner of the wall a few yards away. He was tall and lanky – older than Eddie by a few years. There was a sneer of utter contempt plastered across his face. 'Mr Pearce ain't going to be too happy with you if you're late,' he said. 'Reckon he'll learn you a lesson.' He pushed himself away from the wall and walked slowly towards them. 'Reckon I'll learn you a lesson first.'

Jack was shuffling nervously. Mikey was cowering with visible fear. Only Eve seemed unperturbed – Eve and Eddie.

'Get lost, John Remick,' Eve said. 'We were just coming anyway.'

Perhaps because he didn't seem at all scared, Remick glared at Eddie. 'And who are you?'

'Who wants to know?'

'We don't want no trouble,' Jack assured Remick as the lad took a step towards Eddie. 'We'll be right there.'

'You'd better be, or I'll find a use for my belt you won't like.' He raised his hand. 'Go on, get along with you.' He cuffed Jack across the ears.

'Want a use for your belt?' Eddie said defiantly. 'I'll give you one. Belt up!'

Remick's eyes were blazing as he walked slowly towards Eddie. Eddie stood his ground, hands bunched into hard fists at his sides.

'Eddie!' Eve warned.

'It's all right,' Eddie assured her as he squared up to Remick. 'You get off to church, all of you. Pray for Charlie. And pray for this lout too.'

Remick launched himself at Eddie. But Eddie wasn't there. He stepped neatly out of the way and the larger boy's fists pummelled the air.

As he moved, Eddie's hand brushed against Remick. Just lightly, just a little. Just enough. 'What have we got here, then?' Eddie wondered as he held up the things he'd so easily and gracefully lifted from Remick's pocket.

'How did you . . .? Give that back!'

'Ooh look – hanky.' Eddie waved the grubby handkerchief. 'Bit snotty, but then that's one heck of a hooter you've got.' He tossed the handkerchief at Remick as the boy advanced.

'What else?' Eddie wondered, sidestepping another punch. As well as the hanky, Eddie had pulled out a faded piece of paper. 'What's this?'

'Give that back.' Remick snatched at it – and missed.

'Now now, easy does it, mate,' Eddie chided. He unfolded the paper.

And Remick hurled himself at Eddie with a shout of rage, grasping desperately for the paper.

Eddie held it away from the clutching fingers and tried to push Remick away. 'Keep your hair on,' he shouted above Remick's angry cries. 'It's just a letter.' He got only a glimpse before Remick managed to snatch it away. He saw only as few words, a signature. But it was enough. There was one word there that Eddie could read easily.

'Miss your mummy, do you?' Eddie asked. 'Keep her letter in your pocket all the time?'

Remick stared at him, lip quivering. 'You . . .' He seemed to struggling to speak. 'You shut up.'

'Think she'd be proud of you?' Eddie said quietly. 'Proud of the way you beat up the smaller kids? What about when you belt 'em – she proud of that?'

'It's time for church.' Remick's voice was shaking, and so were the hands clenched at his sides. 'Get along – all of you.'

'See you, Eddie,' Jack said quietly. Mikey was already running. Eve glared at Remick for a moment, then followed.

Remick was still staring at Eddie. 'If I see you round here again . . . If I see you *anywhere* again,' he said, 'then I'll kill you.'

And there was something in the way he said it, something deep in John Remick's eyes that made Eddie shiver.

Sir William had listened patiently to Eddie's brief description of how Charlie had gone missing and turned up dead.

They were in the workroom at the end of the corridor that led past Sir William's and George's offices. The room was lined with cabinets and cupboards, and dominated by a heavy wooden table. Eddie hadn't been surprised to find Sir William at work, even though it was Sunday. He knew George was showing photographs to some old bloke in his own office a short distance away.

Sir William paused to dip what seemed to be a piece of dirty glass into what appeared to be a dish of water. The water began to steam and bubble and Sir William watched intently.

'He was a mudlark for a time,' Eddie said. 'Up to his knees pulling bits of coal out of the river bank, was

Charlie. Rags, shards of metal, copper nails too, he said, if they were repairing a big ship down the docks.'

Sir William lifted the glass that wasn't glass from the water that wasn't water. The liquid stopped steaming and bubbling at once. He carefully put down the fragment of glass and turned to look directly at Eddie. 'Oh, Eddie,' he said. 'I am afraid that death is a part of life. Especially for the young and the vulnerable. Fever, poverty, violence, bad luck. Whatever the cause, it is sad, but it happens.' He reached out and put his hand on Eddie's shoulder. 'And I am sorry for your loss, I truly am.'

Eddie shook off Sir William's grip. 'Weren't fever or plague or nothing,' he protested. He hadn't realised it until now, but: 'It was my fault. I asked him to find that carriage and he did. And then he turns up down by the river, with the blood drained out of him like all the others.'

Sir William was shaking his head sadly. But as Eddie finished speaking, the old man was suddenly still and alert. 'What did you say?' he demanded.

'I said it's my fault.'

'No, no, no. Drained of blood? Like all the others?'

'That's what I said. But you're not interested, not in Charlie. He's just another poor kid who died of bad luck to you, isn't he?'

Sir William was staring intently at Eddie. 'This may

be very important,' he said seriously. 'Tell me everything you know, right from the beginning.'

Bodies mysteriously drained of blood were exactly the sort of thing that Sir William Protheroe thought his department should be investigating. But the hearsay and gossip passed on by young Eddie was hardly reliable evidence and probably stemmed from unsubstantiated rumour.

Nonetheless, Sir William wrote a short note to the duty sergeant at Scotland Yard and asked Eddie to deliver it. Eddie was less than impressed, until swayed by the promise of a ha'penny.

Sir William expected to hear nothing for several days, perhaps even a week, and then a reply probably by third-class post denying any knowledge of such things. So when the Commissioner of the Metropolitan Police himself turned up that same evening to tell Sir William that there was absolutely no truth whatsoever in these stories, he suddenly became much more interested.

'So, forgive me Sir Harrison, but you came all the way here – on a Sunday no less – to tell me in person that these rumours are not worth my time?'

Sir Harrison Judd's eyes narrowed. 'There have been some unexplained deaths recently,' he admitted. 'But no more than usual.'

'And some of these poor unfortunates have been drained of blood?'

'One always expects some blood loss when there is murder involved.'

'Not with poisoning,' Sir William pointed out. 'But the murders were committed with a blade then?'

'That is yet to be determined.'

'And how many not-at-all unusual murders involving the loss of blood are we discussing, Sir Harrison?'

'*I* am not discussing any,' the Commissioner said sharply. 'If and when we need the help of your rather unorthodox methods, Sir William, we will ask for it.'

Sir William smiled. 'And I shall of course be delighted to oblige. Just as soon as that time comes.' He stood up and reached across his desk to shake Sir Harrison's hand. 'I appreciate you taking the time to come all this way not to ask for my help.'

'Yes, well, that wasn't the only reason,' Sir Harrison admitted.

'Oh?'

'I also came to see a member of your staff. Mr George Archer.'

This was a surprise. 'Really? And may I ask why?'

'I would like him to identify a body. Someone he knows, or rather knew, quite well I understand.'

George visibly paled when asked to attend the mortuary. Sir Harrison would say no more, and Sir William told George to take as long as he needed – certainly he did not expect George to return to the Museum today.

'I shall look after Mr Blake and make sure he gets back to the redoubtable Mrs Eggerton,' he assured George. 'Now, off you go. And I pray this episode will not be too traumatic.'

The elderly Nathaniel Blake was wedged uncomfortably into George's desk chair, a blanket over his shoulders like a shawl, examining the photographs from the archive through a magnifying glass. He seemed happy to be left to his work, confessing that so far he had found nothing untoward about any of the photographs.

'Let me know at once if you do,' Sir William said.

'No idea, these young whippersnappers,' Blake rasped in reply. 'No idea at all how to compose a picture. Bad as Fox Talbot himself. Might as well be photographing a window.' His grumbles lapsed into mutters.

Sir William returned to his own office, leaving the door to George's room half open so he could easily glance across the corridor and make sure Blake was all right.

'No peace for the wicked, it seems,' he said to the tall

figure that stood waiting for him.

'Indeed not,' Lord Ruthven replied. 'Forgive me, but I shall not disturb you for long.'

'Your men came for the canopic chest,' Sir William assured him. 'As you can see.' He described the scratches on the floorboards with the toe of his shoe – the scratches the men had made ineptly manhandling the heavy casket.

'Indeed. I am told that it is now safe and sound at the Club, together with the sarcophagus. And four of the canopic jars.'

'Then I trust you are satisfied.' Sir William held open the door, but Lord Ruthven made no effort to leave.

'I will be,' he said. 'Just as soon as I have the fifth jar.'

Sir William frowned. 'The *fifth* jar? There is no fifth jar.'

'Oh I assure you there is.'

'No.' Sir William shook his head. 'I opened the casket myself. Four jars only. As is usual I believe.'

'But there is a fifth compartment in the chest.'

Sir Williams' eyes narrowed. 'The chest that, from your words just now, I think you have not yet seen. So how can you possibly know there is space for a fifth jar?'

Lord Ruthven hesitated. 'I – it was described to me.'

'Well, I can assure you again there is no fifth jar. Or if there is, I have no idea where it might be.'

Lord Ruthven stared back at Sir William for several moments, his expression unreadable. 'Then I am mistaken,' he said at last. 'But should you happen to find a fifth jar or discover evidence of one, you will let me know?'

'Of course. Good day to you.'

'And to you.' Lord Ruthven walked briskly away, leaving Sir William alone with his thoughts in the doorway of his office.

Before he could arrange those thoughts into a shape, he was aware of a figure standing in the corridor, just outside George's office. Nathaniel Blake.

The blanket had slipped from one of Blake's shoulders so it hung across him vaguely like a toga. The man was staring down the corridor, past Sir William, slack-jawed. The flesh of his neck wobbled where it bulged over the collar and Sir William realised that the man's whole body was trembling. Blake raised a hand, pointing down the corridor in the direction Lord Ruthven had just gone.

'That man . . .' he said, voice hoarse and throaty.

'Lord Ruthven, what of him?' Sir William walked quickly over to Blake, worried he might be about to have a seizure he was shaking so much.

'That man,' Blake repeated. 'That was *him*.'

'I don't understand.' Sir William gently took Blake's

elbow and led him back into George's office.

'I told Archer about him. Came to see Fox Talbot, tried to stop his research. Over thirty years ago.'

'Lord Ruthven? I suppose it's possible.'

Blake was clutching at Sir William's sleeve. 'But – I photographed him. And then when we developed the plate, he wasn't there. Just didn't show up.'

Sir William let go of Blake, allowing the man to sink into the chair beside the desk. 'You're sure?'

'It's haunted me ever since. Of course I'm sure.'

Sir William could tell Blake was sincere, yet this was extraordinary. 'Can you be certain it's the same man? I mean, after more than thirty years.'

Blake looked up at him, his flabby features pale. 'But that's just it. I remember him so well. Etched into my memory if not the photographic plate. It was the same man. The very same. Even after all these years, the very same. Don't you understand – he hasn't aged or changed at all.'

CHAPTER 6

Liz's father had planned to spend Sunday afternoon at the local church. Usually she accompanied him, but today she had other plans. She walked with him to the church.

'Not staying this week?' her father asked.

'I thought I might get some air. If you don't need me.'

'Goodness me no, you please yourself. It'll be cold air, mind. Rather brisk out today. Though I expect I feel it in my old bones rather more than you do.'

'I have a coat,' Liz pointed out. 'If I get too cold I shall go home and make up a fire.'

'Your mother always felt the cold,' Oldfield remembered. 'Especially in her feet. I hope you have sturdy soles.'

'I shall be fine.'

Her father smiled and patted her gently on the shoulder. 'In search of sturdy souls – that could be the story of my life. Perhaps I shall write a book of my life.' He stared off into the distance. 'Used to keep a journal. But that was a long time ago.'

'You must show me it one day,' Liz said. He had never mentioned a journal before, but perhaps it would be something they could read together. All too often the house was silent as they both sat and read.

'Oh, I'm not sure it is really for your eyes,' her father said quietly. He was still staring off into the distance, into his memories. 'In fact, I fervently hope that no one ever has cause to read it.'

Liz smiled and kissed him gently on the cheek. 'It can't be that bad.'

'Some things in this world are very bad,' her father replied. He shivered. 'Evil.'

'Like the theatre?' Liz suggested with a small smile, unable to resist the temptation to tease him just a little.

He smiled thinly, sadly. 'Oh, you mock me, my girl. Though nothing good ever came out of the theatre. It breeds decadence and vice. It appeals to man's baser instincts. And woman's too, I think. No,' suddenly he was as serious and solemn as Liz had ever seen him. 'Take it from me, while God watches over us all in his infinite wisdom, so do others who wish only evil and destruction.'

Slightly unsettled by the exchange, Liz left her father

in the vestry with the rector and church wardens. She would have liked to stay, to make sure he was all right. But she had promised – or almost promised – Henry Malvern that she would try to get to the afternoon rehearsal at the Parthenon Theatre. She shuddered to think what her father would say, especially in his current mood, if he knew where she was going.

Liz arrived early for the five o'clock rehearsal, and Marie Cuttler greeted her as though they had been friends for years. The actress still seemed a little tired, and her eyes lacked some of the depth and energy Liz had seen in them before.

'I am having such trouble sleeping,' she confided in Liz after they had spent a while going through their short scenes together. 'Tell me, do you find it easy to learn lines?'

'Oh, I shall have no trouble,' Liz assured her quickly. 'The maid says very little. I am sure I know her lines already.'

Marie smiled. 'I am sure you do. But Henry has not yet appointed an understudy. I'm sure I won't need one, but being so tired, I wonder if it might be a good idea . . .'

'Understudy?' Liz echoed, scarcely able to believe what she was hearing. 'Understudy the role of Marguerite? Me?'

'Well, it's up to Henry,' Marie said. 'But he mentioned

the idea to me yesterday, depending how well we felt you managed the part of the maid.'

Henry Malvern was indeed delighted to hear that Marie thought Liz up to the role of understudy for the leading part. He arrived on the dot of five o'clock and spent a few minutes talking to each and every member of the cast. Liz could almost feel their awe and respect.

Liz's own feelings were mixed. What if she was actually called upon to perform? She was nervous enough about how she would be able to play the maid, but at least she could arrive late and leave immediately after the performance each night.

But put against that was the opportunity, the experience and the excitement of rehearsing a leading role opposite one of the luminaries of modern theatre. To be asked, and after such a short time involved with the production, was such an honour it was almost humbling. Could she really turn down the offer?

Malvern sensed her uncertainty. He took Liz's hand in his and held it so tight she could feel the seams in the leather of his gloves.

'Let me talk to your father,' he said.

'I really don't –'

'Please,' he insisted. 'Let me try.'

'You think he may remember you?' Liz asked.

Malvern blinked in surprise. 'You told me that you had met before.'

'So I did. But that was a long time ago. Whatever the outcome, whatever happens, I should very much like to meet your father. As I remember, and I do remember our meeting well, he was an extraordinary man.'

Still not sure that this was the best course of action, Liz eventually agreed, and Malvern insisted in coming home with her after the rehearsal. He hailed a cab outside the theatre and before long they were standing in the hallway of the house Liz shared with her father. Elizabeth Oldfield standing with Henry Malvern – it seemed incredible to Liz.

There was no sign of her father in the drawing room. 'He may not be home yet. Or he might be in his study,' Liz told Malvern quietly.

Sure enough, at that moment her father's voice called out: 'Liz – is that you?'

'It is,' she replied. 'And I have brought someone to see you.'

Malvern held up a finger. 'Please, allow me to speak with him alone. Just the two of us.'

'But surely, I should introduce you.' Liz made for the door.

But Malvern stayed her. 'No. Alone. I really do think that would be best.'

Liz nodded. 'Very well.'

Malvern knocked at the door. Without waiting for a reply, he opened it and stepped inside, pushing the door shut behind him.

Liz waited nervously outside, straining to hear what was said. But almost at once, she heard Malvern cry out:

'Liz – quickly!'

She tore open the door and ran into the room. 'What is it?'

Malvern was still standing just inside the door. But Liz hardly noticed him. All her attention was on her father – slumped forwards upon his desk. She ran quickly over.

'He was barely conscious as I came in,' Malvern said, hurrying to join her. 'He tried to say something, but he must have used the last of his energy calling out to you for help just now.'

'He has a pulse,' Liz was relieved to find. 'Very weak. He looks so pale.' The old man's eyes were closed and his breathing was shallow. 'Father – Father, can you hear me?'

'I'm sorry,' Malvern said when there was no reply. 'It took me a moment to realise he was in trouble. Something of a shock.' He wiped a handkerchief across his pale brow. 'Let me get a doctor.'

'Yes,' Liz agreed. 'Yes, thank you. But, do you think we should move him?'

'I really don't know. I could carry him up to his bed. He would be more comfortable there. I don't think he is in any immediate danger – he seems to be asleep.'

'He has had a busy week, and he is quite frail at the best of times,' Liz said. Perhaps she was clutching at straws, but it could be that the old man was simply exhausted. 'Yes, please,' she decided. 'If you will help me carry him up to his bed, and then I shall sit with him while you fetch the doctor.'

There was a sudden movement from behind them, which startled Liz. But it was just the curtains blowing in a breeze through the open window.

'He must have felt unwell,' she said as she closed the window. 'He so rarely opens the window. He feels the cold.'

She helped Malvern lean her father back in the chair. Then Malvern got his arms under the old man and hefted him gently over his shoulder.

If either of them noticed the two small splashes of red that had seeped into the blotter beneath Horace Oldfield's head, they thought nothing of it.

George slept badly that night. His thoughts were full of memories of his apprenticeship and of the offer that Sir Harrison Judd had made him.

When he was first out of school and learning his trade as an engineer, he had been apprenticed to one of the chief engineers of the London and North Western Railway. There were several apprentices, but the chief engineer had recognised George's enthusiasm and aptitude and taken him under his wing. By the time that George left for another job, his apprenticeship complete, the two of them were firm friends with a mutual respect for each other's abilities and talents.

The chief engineer's name was Christopher Kingsley. And George had last seen him that evening, stretched out pale and dead on a mortuary slab.

'Sorry to ask you to do this, but he had no family,' Sir Harrison explained. 'His wife died of influenza years ago.'

'He had a daughter,' George recalled. 'Little girl with dark hair. Lucy, was it?'

The commissioner of the Metropolitan Police shook his head sadly. 'Not any more. Scarlet fever, apparently, a few years ago. You can confirm this is Christopher Kingsley?'

George nodded. 'It is.' The man looked so pale – almost as white as the sheet that covered most of his body. He looked younger than George remembered. Strange how one always assumed more experienced people must be so much older. But Kingsley could only have been in his forties looking at him now.

He could recall his first day working for the man. George had cut himself on a lathe – not badly, but Kingsley had been all sympathy. 'You're bleeding, George,' he had said, genuinely concerned. 'That's bad.' George had learned a lot from Christopher Kingsley.

'Why did you come?' George asked Sir Harrison Judd.

'I'm sorry?'

'Why did *you* come – in person. Why not send a constable. This must be very routine.'

Sir Harrison Judd nodded. He looked down at the dead man for a moment, then drew the sheet back over him. 'I suppose,' he said slowly, 'that I could have identified him formally myself. But that didn't seem proper.'

And suddenly George understood. 'You knew him. He was a friend.'

Sir Harrison sighed. 'More of an acquaintance. But I knew from our brief conversations that he held you in very high regard, Mr Archer.'

George was surprised. He had venerated Kingsley. But while they had become good friends, George and Kingsley had lost contact after George left the railway company.

'Oh yes, he spoke of you often. We were members of the same club. In fact, that is partly why I came to find you. I took the opportunity to see Sir William too, but it was you I really wanted to speak to.'

'About Kingsley?'

'In a way. I said we were members of the same club. Membership is strictly limited, but there is now, sadly, a vacancy. I think that Christopher would like nothing better than for me to propose you as the man to take his place.'

'I . . .' George was astonished. 'I don't know what to say.'

'No need to decide now.' Some of Sir Harrison's military bearing and brusqueness was back as they left the mortuary. 'You have a think about it. Let me know. But I'd be delighted to propose your name. Doesn't mean you'll be accepted, of course. Though I do have some influence. One thing though, we are a close-knit lot. I would appreciate it if you would tell no one of this invitation. Not least because they might be jealous. It's quite an honour even to be considered.'

'Thank you. I am honoured, truly. And I'll think about it,' George promised. 'I'm sorry – all this. Seeing Christopher like that. Well, it's a shock.'

'Indeed it is.'

'This club,' George asked as Sir Harrison bade him farewell. 'Which club is it?'

'It is really a society,' Sir Harrison told him. 'But it is more usually called the Damnation Club.'

When he woke the next morning, George's mind was full of railways and trains and memories of Christopher Kingsley. He was surprised to find it was already after ten, but remembering Sir William's advice to take some time and get over the shock he did not worry about hurrying in to work.

When George did eventually make his way to the British Museum the afternoon was drawing in and it was almost dark. George cursed the heavy smog, clutching his handkerchief over his mouth in an effort to keep out the worst fumes. He did not go first to his office. Instead he made his way across the Great Court to the Reading Room. The large, round building wrought out of dark brick dominated the courtyard. Inside, the single circular reading room with its high domed ceiling was equally impressive, if slightly daunting.

The librarian looked down his nose at George when asked to find the latest edition of the *Gentleman's London Journal*. But he produced it a few minutes later without comment. The reading desks curved with the shape of the walls, and George found an empty area and set down the book. As he had hoped and expected, an appendix provided a brief description of all the London clubs. He soon found the one he was looking for.

Of all the Gentlemen's Clubs registered in London, the so-called *Damnation Club* is possibly the most exclusive. Its real name is *the Society of Diabolic and Mystic Nominees*, the rather melodramatic nickname by which it is usually known being taken from the initial letters DaMN. It is also referred to in its induction papers, which it is claimed date back to 1457, as *The Parliament of Blood* though there is no known explanation for this title.

It is not clear that members have to demonstrate any aptitude for mysticism or indeed any interest in the Occult. But certainly, membership is exclusive and by nomination only. There are rumours of complicated and bizarre induction rites, but it is likely that these are fostered by the Club itself to bolster its esteem and exclusivity, and to add to the mythos.

There is little point in applying to join the Damnation Club, though the legend that the third Earl Aldebourne actually went to the Club and demanded to be admitted the very night that he disappeared in 1723 seems to have no historical basis.

At various times, the Home Secretary, the Governor of the Bank of England, and many other prominent people – including even Sir Harrison Judd Commissioner of the Metropolitan Police – have been linked to the Damnation Club.

As Sir Harrison Judd had told him, it did indeed seem to be an honour – if an unexpected one – to be nominated for membership. George closed the book. It thumped shut more loudly than George had intended, and he glanced round nervously hoping he hadn't disturbed anyone.

His eyes immediately met those of the woman sitting next to him – just a few yards away. A woman he recognised at once. A woman who was sitting alone, with no books or papers in front of her. A woman who was turned slightly towards George and staring at him intently as he sensed now she had been for quite some time.

It was the woman from the Unwrapping. She was wearing a heavy, dark coat, her black hair spilling over the fur collar. Her full red lips curled into a smile and she pressed her index finger against them warning George to be quiet.

'Sorry,' he mouthed.

The woman stood up, still looking at George. The finger to her lips moved to point at George, then curled to beckon him. She walked slowly from the reading room, pausing once to look back over her shoulder, to make sure that George was following.

'Who are you, what do you want?' he gasped as soon as they were outside. A cold mist hung in the air between them, so that her features seemed slightly smudged and if anything even more perfect. 'You were here the other night.'

'For the Unwrapping of Orabis,' she agreed. 'It was quite a night, was it not, Mr Archer.'

'Yes. I'm sorry, you have me at a disadvantage. I don't know who you are.'

'Clarissa.'

'Clarissa?' he repeated.

'Just Clarissa.'

'And did you wish to speak to me?'

Her mouth twitched as if she was suppressing a smile. 'I was wondering if you had made your decision.'

George felt suddenly cold. 'Decision?'

'About whether to join us.' She laughed at his expression. 'To join the society, as Sir Harrison Judd suggested.'

George was struggling to understand. 'You are a member of the Damnation Club?'

'We are all damned, one way or another. Have you decided yet?'

'I, um, no,' George admitted.

'A shame. But I can help you perhaps.' She took a step towards him.

George backed away, suddenly nervous, and she laughed again. Clarissa reached out her finger, the one with which she had beckoned to him. She drew it slowly down George's cheek and he felt how cold it was, even through her glove.

'There is a ball this evening. Only members are invited. Members and their guests. I would be delighted if you would be my guest.'

'Me?'

'Meet me there at eight,' she said. She didn't wait for his reply, but turned away and continued across the courtyard.

'At eight,' George called after her.

She did not turn back, but her voice drifted to him out of the gathering mist. 'At the Damnation Club.'

CHAPTER 7

Liz had sat by her father's bed all night. By midnight he seemed to have settled into a fitful sleep. She held his hand, aware of how cold it felt. The skin was slack and wrinkled, and his fingers were bony and brittle. As the old man's breathing became gradually more regular, Liz felt herself drifting into sleep.

At one point, Horace Oldfield cried out. A sudden, startled sound that jolted Liz immediately awake. In the light of the moon filtering round the curtains, she could see her father's eyes were open. He was staring at her, though he seemed to be focusing somewhere behind her.

'Box,' he gasped weakly. He tried to sit up, raising himself from the pillows 'Get me . . . Box!' Then he slumped back, eyes closed and breathing ragged.

'It's all right.' Liz held his shoulders for a moment, feeling the bones trembling through his nightshirt. But he seemed to be asleep again. 'Just a dream,' she murmured, tucking in the bed sheets.

Before long, despite her concern, Liz was asleep again too. Her head rested on the bed covers, her hand on the pillow beside her father's head.

Dawn came and went, and it was mid-morning before Liz woke. She sat up, blinking in the pale light and still feeling the press of the blankets against her cheek. She stood up, taking a moment to awaken fully, then gently, quietly opened the curtains.

'Goodness me – what time is it?' her father asked.

'Quite late, I think.'

He looked pale and weak and confused as he pulled himself up. 'I must make a start,' he announced. 'I was hoping to index some of my sermons today.'

'You are doing nothing of the sort,' Liz told him. She was smiling, which made it difficult to sound strict. But she was so pleased he seemed to be improving. 'You are ill.'

'Am I?' He seemed surprised. 'I do confess I feel rather tired.' He slumped back into the pillows. 'Perhaps just a few minutes to get my strength back then.'

'You are staying in bed all day,' Liz told him firmly. 'You collapsed at your desk yesterday – don't you remember?'

He frowned and shook his head. 'No, I don't. I was . . . The door opened and . . . Darkness.'

By midday, Oldfield was once more asleep. His breathing seemed regular if shallow, and his face was pale and waxen. But Liz was far less worried about him now, and he seemed to improve further after a small bowl of vegetable soup for late luncheon.

Liz took a nap herself after lunch. She was awakened by the sound of knocking at the front door. She hurried downstairs, hoping the sound had not woken her father.

Outside, the afternoon was drawing in and a smoggy mist was blotting out the sun – the edges of the heavier smog that George Archer was at the same time cursing as he made his way to the British Museum. The figure at the door turned from his inspection of the street and smiled at Liz. It was Henry Malvern.

'How is your father?' he asked. 'I was passing, I thought I would enquire.'

Liz invited him into the drawing room. 'Passing?' she said.

'In the area. It's getting quite thick out there now.' He coughed, and apologised. 'Oh dear, not good for the lungs at all. I don't suppose I could bother you for a cup of tea to wash away the smog?'

'Of course.' Having just woken, Liz's own throat was dry. A cup of tea seemed very welcome. 'I will not be long. Make yourself at home.'

'You're very kind.' Malvern made to sit down, then

changed his mind. 'May I look in on your father? I promise not to upset or tire him, but I should like to know he is on the mend.'

'He is sleeping,' Liz said. 'But please do.'

'I know the way,' Malvern assured her, having helped carry Oldfield to his room the previous evening.

When Liz returned with the tea, Malvern was back in the drawing room.

'He seems to be sleeping peacefully. Let's hope it was nothing too serious.' Malvern sipped appreciatively at his tea. 'Now, I do have a confession to make.'

Liz set down her own cup. 'Oh?'

'I was not just passing. I came here quite on purpose. To see you.'

'Oh.' Liz could feel the blood in her cheeks as she blushed. 'Father will be fine, but it is kind of you to –'

'No, to see *you*.'

'Oh,' Liz said again. 'Er, would you like some more tea?' It was all she could think to say.

Malvern laughed at her expression. 'Thank you, but no. I'm sure it is inconvenient, and that you are concerned about your father, but I wonder if you could spare me a couple of hours this evening?'

'A rehearsal?' Liz asked. 'I'm not sure I should leave him. I mean, he seems to be much better now and sleeping, but . . .'

Malvern was shaking his head. 'Not a rehearsal. I have been invited to a . . . function I suppose you might call it. This evening. Very exclusive. I wondered if you might join me.'

'Me?' Liz was astonished.

Malvern laughed again. 'I admit I had invited Marie, but she is so tired after this afternoon's rehearsals that she has had to cry off. Then I thought it would do *you* good. It would take your mind off things.'

Looking into Malvern's deep, pale eyes, Liz felt herself longing for this moment to continue, to stay in the man's company . . . But still Liz hesitated. 'I don't know. Father . . .' She turned away.

'Please – don't decide now,' Malvern said. 'Let me call for you at eight, and see how he is then. If he seems well enough to be left, then two hours – I promise. If not . . .' He sighed, disappointment heavy in his voice: 'Well, another time perhaps.'

It was the 'perhaps' – the thought that this was an offer that might never be repeated – that made Liz catch her breath.

It was dark by the time Sir William's cab drew up outside Lord Ruthven's imposing residence. It was a large house, perhaps a hundred years old, set back from the main road and with some small grounds of its own. The place was a black silhouette against the grey of the smoggy evening. The blank windows were like the eye sockets of an old skull. The pale, chipped stone steps that led to the door were its broken teeth . . .

The cab driver shivered and drew his cloak close about him. His horse whinnied nervously and dragged an impatient hoof through the gravel.

'I shan't be long,' Sir William assured them.

The door opened even before he pulled the bell. A thin, almost emaciated man with jutting cheekbones stood in the doorway. He said nothing, staring down at Sir William through deep, dark eyes.

'Sir William Protheroe. For Lord Ruthven.' Sir William smiled. 'Please let him know I am here.'

The manservant hesitated long enough to show he was deciding what to do rather than being told. Then he led Sir William through to the drawing room. Heavy curtains were drawn across the bay windows, and the lamps were turned down so low that the middle of the room was a black pool.

In the blackness, something stirred. A shape, a darkness moved slowly towards Sir William. It gradually coalesced into a figure. Sir William let out his breath in relief as he recognised Lord Ruthven.

'To what do I owe this honour?' Lord Ruthven asked.

'Have you perhaps found the missing canopic jar?'

'I am afraid not.'

'Pity.' Lord Ruthven turned up the nearest lamp and the shadows shrank away. 'Forgive me, I was asleep. So, is this a social call? It is too late for tea and too early for dinner.' He moved to the next wall lamp.

The room seemed almost as dark even with the lights turned up. The carpet was a deep but faded red. The furniture was dark oak, the fabrics all burgundy and scarlet. A clock on the mantelpiece above the dying red embers of a fire stood on a raised wooden plinth that looked as though it had once been covered with a glass dome. There was no dome now. No glass anywhere, except hidden behind the heavy curtains.

'I came to ask your advice,' Sir William said.

'How flattering.'

'There are some things which recently have disturbed me. Scared me, even.'

'Such as?' Lord Ruthven asked cautiously.

'Oh, I don't know.' Sir William stood up, walking slowly round the room and noting the layer of dust over everything. Aware of his host's eyes following him. 'The business with the mummy.'

'A harmless prank.'

'I admit that seems likely, but we really don't know do we? Then there is the unfortunate death of the photographer, Denning.'

'An accident.'

Sir William nodded. 'Perhaps. Again, perhaps. He took some very strange photographs, you know.'

Sir Ruthven seemed to straighten in his chair. 'I did not.'

'No. Nor did whoever killed him.' He hesitated, waiting for Lord Ruthven to express surprise. But there was only silence. 'I did wonder if he was killed to prevent him taking photographs of the mummy of Orabis.'

'And why would anyone want to prevent that?'

'Ah, well, if we still had the mummy we could photograph it and find out.'

'A pity then that it is lost.'

'As you say.'

'And what,' Lord Ruthven asked, 'do you think photographs of the mummy would have shown?'

Sir William turned to look directly as Lord Ruthven. 'Nothing,' he said. 'And I mean literally nothing. You see, I had the mummy photographed that afternoon, before Denning died.'

'And you have seen the photographs?'

'I have.'

Lord Ruthven sank back into his chair. 'Then you know,' he said softly.

Sir William took three rapid paces towards Lord Ruthven. 'No, sir – I do not know!' he declared. 'But it seems that *you* do. You know why the mummy cannot be photographed. And I think you know because you yourself do not show up in photographs.'

Lord Ruthven's mouth opened in surprise.

'Oh yes,' Sir William lied, 'I have spent the best part of two days looking for a single photograph of you. And there is not one. Not even,' he went on more slowly, more quietly, 'the one that Fox Talbot's assistant secretly took of you all those years ago in Lacock.'

The door creaked slightly as it opened. The gaunt figure of the manservant stood framed in the pale glow from the hall outside.

Lord Ruthven stood up. 'I have to go now,' he said. 'If you will excuse me.'

'Of course,' Sir William muttered, disappointed at the interruption. He sensed that he had been about to discover something important, but he feared the moment was gone.

Lord Ruthven reached out to shake Sir William's hand, and his own was ice cold. 'But,' he said quietly, 'we must talk again. Soon.' He nodded, and Sir William could again see the worry in the man's dark eyes. 'And I shall tell you what scares me.'

The headstones looked as if they had been pushed up

through the mist. Eddie was sitting on the low wall at the edge of the graveyard, swinging his feet and hugging himself against the damp cold of the evening. If Charlie had been some rich kid – or even someone with a family – he'd not have been rushed into the ground.

As it was, he was in the coffin and under the earth in a couple of days. If there had been an inquest it was probably over in minutes. It didn't seem fair. But then Charlie's death was hardly fair. Eddie had only discovered that afternoon from Eve that there had been a short service on Sunday evening. She and Mikey had been there. Just them and the priest.

If he'd known, he'd have gone. But the best Eddie could do now – the least he could do – was sit and keep poor Charlie company in the cold of the night. The evening had drawn in and the mist was getting thicker. Eddie realised he could no longer see the low mound of earth that covered his friend. No headstone yet, of course. You needed to wait for the ground to settle. And who'd buy a headstone for a kid like Charlie anyway? Who'd even know he was there . . .?

He pushed himself off the wall and stuffed his hands into his pockets. There was a scraping, creaking sound from somewhere in the fog. Another grave being dug, maybe. Or someone else visiting a dearly departed. Eddie didn't really care. The cold was numbing his thoughts and emotions as well as his fingers and toes.

Then suddenly he was alert again. Staring into the murky evening at the mound of earth – at the ragged hole in it. Someone had been digging at Charlie's grave. Eddie was running, skidding to a halt on the muddy ground at the edge and looking in. He could just make out the splintered wood of the coffin. He looked round – angry, afraid, shocked.

And somewhere in the fog he could hear laughter. Mocking, high-pitched laughter, like a young woman. Or a child. There was a shape, barely more than a shadow, moving away into the gloom. Slipping and sliding in his haste, Eddie followed, desperate not to lose whoever it was in the foggy night.

He had almost caught up with the figure when they reached the gate to the main road outside. If they knew they were being followed, they gave no sign. Despite being almost close enough to catch hold of the figure, Eddie could barely see it through the gloom. A small man hardly bigger than Eddie. But more than that he could not tell.

It looked as though he would never find out, because in the street outside the graveyard was a carriage. Eddie could not see it. But he could hear the slam of the door, the stamp of the horses' feet and the rumble of the wheels on the cobbles.

Then the carriage clattered past him, horses pale as ghosts in the smog. Eddie leaped back out of the way. He almost fell. His breath caught in his throat as he saw the blood-red emblem on the carriage door – the ankh.

He stirred at her voice. Liz had sat beside her father since Malvern had left. He was sleeping deeply, peacefully, and she had convinced herself that she could leave him. Not for long. Just for an hour or two.

'I have to go out,' she murmured, kissing him gently on the cold cheek. 'I won't be long, I promise.'

He stirred, eyes flickering. His irises were wide and dark as he tried to focus. 'Elizabeth?'

'It's all right. I'll stay if you want me to. But . . .'

'I'm . . .' He was still half asleep, still confused. 'I need . . .'

'Do you want a drink? There's some soup left if you'd like.'

He shook his head. 'Don't know,' he admitted drowsily. 'Need . . . something.'

'A book?' Liz wondered. 'Your sermons?' He was still shaking his head slowly, rolling it on the pillow. She remembered how agitated he had been the night before. 'You mentioned a box.'

Her father was still. His brow wrinkled and his eyes

seemed more alert for a moment. 'My box. Yes. Yes – my box.'

'I don't know what box you mean. Is it in your study?'

'Silver box,' he said, slipping back into sleep even as he was speaking. As if just the thought of it was a comfort. 'Don't open it. You mustn't . . . Bottom left drawer of my desk . . .' Then he was asleep again.

Liz sat with him until it was almost eight. Then, satisfied that he was once again calm, she changed quickly into her best dress. She felt she ought to thank Malvern in some way for his concern and the invitation. But all she could think to give him was a jar of her father's home-made raspberry jam.

As she took a jar from the pantry and put it on the kitchen table, Liz remembered the silver box and went to look for it. The desk drawer was locked, but her father kept the small key tucked into the edge of the blotter.

The silver box was the only thing in the drawer. It was about six inches square and four inches deep and looked very old. The silver had tarnished, and some of it came off black on her hand. There was a simple clasp holding the lid shut, and a cross stood proud of the top. It reminded Liz of the box her father had used to keep communion wafers in, only larger. Did he really want this old silver box with him? It was cold and stained . . .

The sound of knocking at the door startled her. She

put the box back in the desk drawer and started to close it. Then she stopped. She was going out, leaving her father on his own. He had asked her to do just one thing – to bring her this box.

'I'll be there directly,' she called down the hall as she hurried upstairs to kiss her sleeping father gently goodbye.

There was a line of carriages. Eddie could see the one with the red ankh symbol on the door. He'd been lucky to find a cab so quickly, and even luckier he had a few coins in his pocket.

His cab had followed the carriage through London, and was now on the other side of the street from it. Eddie climbed out and gave a handful of coins to the driver.

From further along, Eddie was able to angle himself to see the carriage as the door finally opened. But the person who got out was certainly not the person he had seen at the graveyard. It was a woman with long, black hair and pale delicate features. She was wearing a heavy, dark cloak that opened slightly as she climbed down from the carriage, to reveal a long scarlet dress.

Eddie waited, but no one else emerged from the carriage. The door slammed shut and the carriage pulled away.

With a sigh of annoyance, Eddie ran after it, wishing

he'd stayed in his cab. Luckily the carriage did not go far. It turned at the end of the street, then again almost immediately – doubling round to the back of the same building.

As it drew up again and once more the door swung open, Eddie realised where he was. He recognised the building and he knew instinctively that this must be where Charlie had seen the carriage.

A small figure climbed out and walked slowly towards the back door. Eddie drew back into the shadows as the Coachman called out to the boy – because Eddie could see now that it was a boy. Dressed in a dark jacket and trousers that were caked in mud. A boy whose pale face was also smeared with grime, and whose unruly fair hair was stained brown by the earth.

The boy turned as the Coachman spoke to him. Eddie couldn't hear what the Coachman said, couldn't make out the shadowed features of the man's face. But he could see the boy clearly now in the light spilling out of the building. It was Charlie. Charlie, who had climbed out of his grave to get into a carriage that had brought him here. To the Damnation Club.

CHAPTER 8

Liz stood at the side of the ballroom with Henry Malvern, watching the couples dancing, the people drinking. Everywhere she looked, men in smart dinner suits and women in beautiful gowns talked and danced and drank red wine. She felt underdressed and out of place. She was grateful for the mask.

Malvern wore a plain black mask, a single red teardrop painted beneath one of the eye holes. The mask reached from his mouth to his hairline, so Liz had to judge his expression from his mouth and his eyes. He had brought a smaller half-mask for Liz. It covered just the area round her eyes. It was brilliant green, matching her dress, with thin black whiskers painted over the lower part and almond-shaped eye holes so that with her fair hair tied up behind her head she looked like a cat.

The variety of masks was amazing. A horned devil danced with an angel – small wings attached to the side of the woman's mask. A grotesque gargoyle was talking quietly to a woman whose face was covered by a blue butterfly. A woman with a totally blank white mask was standing with a man in a dark cloak whose entire face was a skull . . .

Several waiters were carrying trays of drinks. The trays were made of a dull metal, perhaps pewter. The glasses of red wine looked heavy and misty with age. The waiters themselves were wearing grinning golden cherub masks that covered their entire faces. They were no bigger than children – perhaps they were children.

One of the gold-faced waiters brought a tray over to Liz and Malvern. There were two glasses on it – one of red wine, one of white. Henry took the glass closest to him – the red wine. Liz was happy to take the white. It was sweet and viscous and she could immediately feel it going to her head. There did not seem to be anything to eat, and she hoped that food would be served later.

Later . . . how long should she stay? Liz felt out of place already and she had only just arrived. And then there was her father . . . she should never have agreed to leave him. What had possessed her?

Sensing Liz's discomfort, Malvern raised his glass to her and his mouth smiled. 'Your father will be fine,' he assured her. 'We need not stay long, then I will take you home. There are, I'm afraid, people here that I need to see but I can return and talk to them later.'

'Thank you.'

'Enjoy yourself. Just for an hour. Forget your troubles and worries and make the most of the company and the dancing and the wine.'

'I think the wine is a little strong,' Liz admitted.

'Then do not drink it. The red is . . . interesting.' Malvern took Liz's glass from her as a waiter walked past. 'I'm not sure it's really to my taste either.' The waiter paused for him to place the glasses on the tray, then continued on his way.

'The trouble with a masked ball,' Malvern said after a few moments' uncomfortable silence, 'is that it is so difficult to recognise people you actually wish to speak to. Though I think I see Sir Harrison Judd.'

'The police commissioner? He was at the Unwrapping the other evening.'

'As was Lord Ruthven,' Malvern said. He nodded towards a tall, thin figure who was handing his coat to one of the waiters at the door. His mask was divided in two down the middle. On one side, the face was white and smiled with an upturned cut-out mouth. On the other side it was black, the mouth turned down in misery.

'How clever of you to know it was him,' Liz said. 'Do you come to many events here?' She was not entirely sure where 'here' actually was.

'I confess I saw Lord Ruthven putting his mask on. And no, I wouldn't say that the Damnation Club is one of my frequent haunts.'

'Damnation Club?'

'Oh, just a nickname. It's actually called, I believe, the Society for Mystic Nominees or something of the sort. The invitation is something of an honour.' He leaned closer to Liz, and added quietly: 'Though between you and me I can't say I'm mightily impressed.'

But Liz hardly heard this last comment. She was watching a figure arriving behind Lord Ruthven. A figure adjusting a plain black eye-mask similar to Malvern's and dressed in a suit that looked decidedly shabby compared with the others on show.

'George?' she murmured. 'What's George Archer doing here?'

A pale, thin-faced man greeted George at the door to the Damnation Club. He seemed to know who George was, and ushered him in with several other guests. If he thought that George looked a little down-at-heel compared with the others, he did not comment.

'Mask, sir,' was all he said as he took George's coat.

'Er, sorry.'

'That's quite all right, sir. The Society can provide. Please wait here.' He returned a moment later without the coat, but with a small black mask that would cover George's eyes and nose. He led George through a hallway to a large ballroom, and waited while George put on the mask before entering.

The room seemed to be filled with dancing, talking people – all dressed more expensively than George and with more impressive masks. No one spared him a glance. He looked round, hoping to catch sight of Clarissa's distinctive red dress.

A woman was looking back at him, from the other side of the room. All he could see was her face, over the shoulder of the man she was with. The woman's hair was tied up behind her head so George could not see it, and the face was hidden behind a green cat-like mask. But even so, George felt a sudden shock of recognition.

'Liz?' he said out loud.

Then a couple on the dance floor between them obscured his view. A pig-faced man danced with a fox-headed woman. When their dance moved them on, the woman with the cat's mask was gone.

A hand came down on George's shoulder and he turned, startled.

'Mr Archer. I am so pleased you could come.' The man wore a simple black mask like George's. Seeing George's confusion, he lifted it for a moment so George could see his face.

'Sir Harrison,' George said. 'I'm sorry, you startled me. I was . . .'

'Overwhelmed? It's to be expected.' Sir Harrison still had his hand on George's shoulder and steered him further into the room as he spoke – away from where George thought he had seen Liz. 'An impressive evening, though sadly our patron and benefactor – the man in whose honour we are holding this ball – is indisposed and cannot be with us. A great shame.'

'I wish him a speedy recovery,' George said.

'As do we all. Let me introduce you to some of your fellow society members – or rather, future fellows. But we are all friends here.' He paused to take two glasses of red wine from a passing waiter – a child in a golden cherub's mask. 'You will soon be a part of all this.'

George sipped at the wine. It was heavy and slightly rough on the tongue with a strange, bitter metallic taste. It was certainly an impressive gathering. But George didn't feel as if he fitted in at all. He was conscious of how awkward and out of place he must look in his old suit and scuffed shoes.

He was barely aware of the people that Sir Harrison

was introducing. With their masks, he was not sure he could recognise them again anyway. And he was constantly looking round for the woman with the cat mask – had he imagined it? Or was Liz here somewhere? Could she be a member of the Damnation Club?

Sir Harrison steered George round several people who were laughing together in a corner. 'And I think you already know this lady,' he said.

The woman with the cat mask was standing in front of them, as if she had been waiting for George. She wore a long, pale green dress trimmed with white lace. It looked simple compared with so many of the other women's gowns, but that made her seem even more beautiful.

Liz had murmured an apology to Malvern and hurried to find George. She pushed past people, apologising and smiling politely. But when she got to the door, the figure in the shabby suit was gone.

She looked all round and thought she caught sight of him. She hurried towards the man, saw him pause to sip at his wine, and walk on.

Eventually Liz managed to reach him. 'George – it is you,' she said. She felt surprised and relieved and slightly excited. 'What are you doing here?'

'I'm sorry,' the man in the shabby suit said in a voice that was not George's. 'I think you have me confused with someone else.' And when he slowly lifted his mask to reveal the pasty, flabby features beneath, it was not George's face either.

'I'm so glad you came,' the woman in the green dress said to George. She turned her head slightly, watching Sir Harrison leave, and George could see that her hair was midnight black.

Taking his arm in hers, Clarissa led George through the room to an open door that led out on to a balcony looking out over a small lawn and a high wall beyond.

'You changed your dress,' George said. He was confused – had he seen Liz? No, it must have been Clarissa all along.

'I prefer red,' she told him. She still had hold of his arm, and was standing very close. She moved even closer and their bodies were almost touching. She reached up a gloved hand towards George's face.

George tried to answer, but no sound came from his mouth as Clarissa pressed her cold finger to his lips.

'Red is quite my favourite colour,' she said. 'And very soon it will be yours too, I think.' She lowered her hand

and leaned towards George, still holding him tight by the arm.

Her masked face filled George's vision, and the rest of the world seemed to stop. Her eyes were so large, so beautiful, so deep and dark . . . He was falling into them. Any second he would feel her breath on his neck.

'Clarissa!'

The voice was a deep rasp. Clarissa at once stepped back, and George took a deep breath. The world was back, his vision clearing. It was as if he was waking from a heavy sleep.

'I am sorry to interrupt,' the voice said. 'But Sir Harrison Judd was looking for Mr Archer.'

The man was standing close to them on the balcony, though George had not heard him arrive. He wore a black cloak and his mask was a skull that seemed to cover his whole head. It made George shiver just to look at it.

'My apologies,' the skull-faced man said. He took a step back and gestured for George and Clarissa to return to the main room.

'That's fine. Thank you.' George forced himself to glance at the man and smile as he stepped back through the door. The eyes of the skull were as dark and empty as Clarissa's had been.

A few minutes after Charlie disappeared into the back of the Damnation Club, the coach moved off. Eddie was left alone in the street, wondering what he should do. The more he thought about it, the more he became convinced that he should talk to Charlie.

Either the boy had somehow faked his own death, or he'd been revived. Eddie shuddered as he remembered the last time he had met a man supposed to be dead. But that man had been very different – he'd *looked* dead. Even from a distant glimpse, Eddie had seen that while Charlie was muddy and pale, he had a spring in his step, an enthusiasm . . . He had looked *happy*.

'What's the trick then, eh?' Eddie murmured.

Another figure was coming down the street – another boy about the same age as Eddie and Charlie. He was dressed in a smart dark suit, and like Charlie he looked pale but full of life. Eddie shrank back into the shadows to let him pass by. Then he hurried after the boy to catch him up.

'You going to the Damnation Club, then?' Eddie asked.

The boy looked at him with large, dark eyes. He seemed to be sizing Eddie up, and Eddie didn't like it.

'It's all right,' Eddie reassured the boy – as a joke to

break the sudden tense atmosphere as much as anything. 'I'm dead too.'

The boy's eyes narrowed slightly. His voice was strangely flat and without emotion. 'Who are you? Are you here to serve?'

'Oh yes,' Eddie said quickly. 'My name's Eddie. It's my first time though. So I'll stick with you if that's all right. You can show me the ropes.'

The boy was smiling as they reached the door. He pulled his collar down, and in the light from the Club, Eddie could see a thick raw red line across his neck. To one side there were scratches and scars.

'I'll show you the ropes all right,' the boy said. 'They hanged me, you know.'

Eddie hesitated, his own smile frozen on his face. He had probably gone as pale as the boy. By the time they had reached a small room at the back of the Damnation Club, Eddie was wondering if he shouldn't have legged it when he had the chance.

The only furniture in the oak-panelled room was a low table. From it, several golden faces stared at Eddie. Masks – cherubs. The boy he was with picked one up and put it on. When he turned to look at Eddie, it was like a statue had come to life.

'You have no suit,' the boy said. 'The Coachman won't be pleased.'

'He'll have to lump it then, won't he,' Eddie said. He dusted himself down and buttoned his threadbare jacket over his grubby shirt. 'This'll have to do.' Then he put on one of the masks.

The boy led him along a dimly lit corridor to a foyer at the front of the building. Several of the cherub-masked boys were taking trays of drinks through to a large ballroom and returning with trays of empty glasses, which they took down another corridor – perhaps to be washed.

Without waiting to be told, Eddie took a tray and went into the ballroom. There must have been a hundred people or more dancing or watching, or talking, or drinking. All of them were wearing masks. In amongst them, boys in golden masks carried their trays, and Eddie fixed on each in turn as he made his way slowly through the room. Fortunately, while the mask came over the top of the head like a hat, it did not reach far down the back. Eddie was looking for a cherub with a shock of dishevelled fair hair under his mask.

He was distracted from his search by a figure beckoning him over. Eddie changed course to carry his tray over to a woman wearing the face of a bird of prey and a wolf-faced man. Eddie let them take drinks, and then turned away.

His path took him close to a corner of the room

where two men were talking heatedly. One of them wore a mask that was half black and half white, divided down the middle. The other wore a cloak and his face was a skull – the Coachman who had brought Charlie here.

Eddie edged closer, trying to look as if he was just going about his business with his tray while getting near enough to listen in on their argument.

'They should not both be here together,' the Coachman was saying. 'You approved the guest list.'

'I did not know that Malvern would bring her,' the other man retorted. 'How could I?'

'We need the man alone, isolated. With no one to turn to for advice. Least of all *her*. With her connections. Clarissa and Harrison did well to keep them apart.'

'I wasn't aware that they even knew each other,' the man with the black and white mask said.

'Then you should have been,' the Coachman rasped. 'I will not tolerate this incompetence. And neither will . . .' He broke off, and seemed to gather himself. 'We must move quickly now. To distract the girl, and to protect ourselves.'

The skull-face swung round, and Eddie quickly moved away. But as he did, he caught the Coachman's parting words:

'It is time I went. While she is here, I can complete

what should have been done years ago. It will be a fine story to tell my sister when she wakes.' He gathered his cloak about him and swept past Eddie. A woman wearing a cat mask and a pale green dress was waiting for the Coachman on the other side of the room.

On his way across to meet her, the Coachman passed another waiter, and patted him on the shoulder – an almost affectionate gesture. The boy turned to watch the man go, and Eddie could see the mass of fair hair under the back of his mask.

There were still several full glasses of wine on the tray, so Eddie put it back with the other trays of wine ready to be taken into the ballroom.

Then, walking with a confident stride which he hoped made it look like he was doing something he was supposed to be doing, he followed the fair-haired boy. He was sure it was Charlie, though either he'd brushed the dirt from his clothes or had changed into a clean suit. He was carrying a tray of empty glasses.

Charlie headed out of the foyer down a passageway. The passage was empty apart from the two of them, and as soon as Charlie was passing a doorway, Eddie called out to him.

'Charlie!'

The boy stopped, and slowly turned to face Eddie. 'What do you want?' It was Charlie's voice, and yet it wasn't – again it seemed flat and empty.

Eddie walked right up to him before he pulled off his own mask to reveal himself. 'Remember me, do you?' he said quietly.

'Eddie? What are you doing here? You're not . . .' Charlie turned to go – perhaps to tell someone there was an intruder.

But Eddie was quicker. He flung his arms round Charlie before the boy could move, and bundled him through the door, kicking it shut behind them.

The room was not very large. It was dimly lit by flickering wall lights. There was a small reading table with two upright chairs, and several bookcases against the walls. The windows at the end of the room were unshuttered and the panes of glass were like black mirrors against the night outside.

Charlie stumbled and fell as he staggered back from Eddie. The tray went flying and a glass shattered loudly on the surface of the table. Eddie was off balance too, and collapsed close to Charlie. His hand came down on a shard of broken wineglass, and he gave a cry of pain and surprise.

Above him, Charlie had got up again and was pulling off his mask. He glared angrily at Eddie. 'Why are you here?' he hissed. 'You'll spoil everything.' Then he blinked and his expression changed. 'You've cut yourself,' he said quietly. 'You're bleeding.'

'Like you care.' Eddie pulled himself to his feet and wiped his wounded palm down his jacket. More blood welled up along the cut, but it wasn't too deep. It would soon stop. 'What's happened to you, Charlie? We're mates, right?'

Charlie walked slowly towards him. 'You're bleeding,' he repeated. He lunged suddenly at Eddie, who darted behind the table – keeping it between the two of them.

'What have they done to you? So what if I'm bleeding?'

The boy's lips curled into something like a smile, and he slammed his own hand down on the fragments of glass on the table. Eddie winced just watching, but Charlie's smile did not falter. He lifted his hand, and several of the pieces of glass were sticking out of it. Not taking his eyes off Eddie, Charlie pulled them out.

'I can't bleed,' he said quietly. He held his hand out to prove it. 'Why don't you come over, join us, Eddie? You'd like it. I've never felt so alive.'

Eddie continued to work his way round the table, seriously rattled now. If he could get to the door, he could make a run for it. The sooner he got away from this place, the better.

'I shouldn't have come,' he said. If he could keep Charlie distracted he might yet make it. 'Forget I was here, all right? Whatever you're up to, I won't tell no one. You make the most of it. I'm pleased for you, Charlie. Really I am.'

Eddie had his back to the door. Charlie was leaning over the table, facing Eddie. Beyond him, Eddie could see his own reflection staring back at him from the dark window. He looked pale and flustered. And he saw his eyes widen in fear as he realised that while he could see the room – the table, himself – there was no sign of Charlie. The boy opposite him cast no reflection. More than the blood and the grave and the change in character, that frightened Eddie.

'It's all right,' Charlie said. 'You'll enjoy it. Once it's done.'

There was the sound of people from the corridor outside.

'Just let it happen, Eddie.' He made it sound so simple. 'Just die.'

Eddie didn't ask for an explanation. There was definitely someone in the corridor, and he was trapped. The only other way out was the window.

So he put his head down and charged. Eddie slammed into Charlie as the boy moved to intercept him. Eddie wrapped his arms round Charlie and carried him along by the sheer force of his momentum. He could see his reflected self hurtling towards the window, arms wrapped round . . . nothing.

Despite the reflection, two bodies slammed into the window. Wood and glass exploded outwards. The noise was deafening. Eddie and Charlie were thrown apart by the impact and Eddie found himself rolling across grass, bruised and numbed. He was in a small garden beside the building, bounded by a high wall.

He was on his feet again immediately, ready to run for the wall before Charlie or anyone else could stop him. He could easily climb the rough stonework. But Eddie glanced back – and saw Charlie lying where he had fallen in the middle of a sea of broken glass. A wooden strut from the window was poking up through the boy's shirt. His hand was stretched out towards Eddie, fingers clutching the air.

The broken glass reflected broken images of the scene as Eddie hurried back to Charlie. He took the boy's cold hand. But Charlie himself did not appear in the reflections.

'I'll get help,' Eddie said. 'It'll be all right, Charlie. I promise.'

'No it won't,' Charlie gasped. 'It's too late. But you done the right thing, Eddie. Don't let them get you.

Don't listen to their promises.' He gripped Eddie's hand tight. His voice was barely a whisper: 'Thank you.' Then Charlie's hand was limp, falling back across his body.

Blood welled up round the wooden strut in his chest. The reflection of a dead boy faded into the broken glass. Shouts came from inside the Damnation Club, and Eddie ran for the wall.

CHAPTER 9

There was a chill breeze coming from the window. The curtains had blown slightly open and the light of the moon fell across the blankets on Horace Oldfield's bed.

He struggled to sit up, wondering what had woken him. It might have been the draught, or perhaps a sound from outside. From the bed he could see the back wall of the tiny garden behind the house. Built into it was an old outhouse. The brickwork was pitted and scarred and the roof was missing more than a few tiles. But the door was securely fastened and locked – and never opened. Even Oldfield himself had not been inside for years. Not since . . .

His mind was wandering, and he made an effort to bring it back to the present. He had been ill. Collapsed or fainted. Liz had said so, though all he remembered was the blackness. Blackness so intense it made him shiver. Blackness and shadow and darkness and death.

On an impulse, he reached back under his pillow. But the movement made him suddenly aware of the deepest shadows just inside the door.

'Who's there?' Oldfield called. He could just make out a shape – the silhouette of a young woman. His throat was dry and his voice was cracked and weak. 'Liz – is that you?'

'Your daughter had to go out,' a voice replied from closer to the bed. A dark figure stepped forward, into the moonlight shining through the window.

Oldfield turned back towards the door. 'Then – who?' He gave a gasp of astonishment as a dark-haired woman in a pale green dress stepped into the light.

'She's abandoned you,' Clarissa said quietly. 'Just as you abandoned me.'

'Never!' Oldfield insisted. 'Why have you come back to me? What have you done with Liz?'

'Nothing. Not yet.' The second figure was wearing a dark cloak. But it was his face that now transfixed Oldfield.

The face of a skull.

'Who are you?' the old man demanded.

The skull-faced figure's reply was a rattle of dry laughter. 'You know who I am. And whose coach I drive. You met my sister Belamis many years ago – can you ever forget?'

Oldfield struggled backwards, pressing against the head of the bed, the pillow tight at his back. 'No,' he gasped. 'No – it can't be!'

'That is what I said when they told me about you,' Clarissa told him, walking slowly towards the bed. 'After all these years. All these unkind years. You could have stayed so young.' She was beside him now, reaching out a pale hand and stroking down Oldfield's trembling cheek. Wiping away the single tear.

'Clarissa,' he murmured. He closed his eyes, remembering.

The woman sighed. 'But now you will have to be old. For ever.'

Oldfield's eyes snapped open in horror. 'You can't . . .' he stammered.

Clarissa smiled sadly. 'Oh, Horace. We already have.'

'But – my daughter!'

The Coachman was standing beside Clarissa. 'Your daughter will be very well looked after, I assure you.' He leaned over the bed.

The skull all but filled Oldfield's world. That and the hard edge of the box under the pillow. He grasped it tight, pulling it free.

'We owe you that, at least,' Clarissa's voice said from the darkness.

'You owe me nothing but death,' Oldfield said.

Clarissa sighed. 'I'm afraid it will be a long time before you go to heaven.'

Oldfield brought the silver box from behind him. His fingers were trembling as he struggled to undo the clasp. 'Then it's time you both went to hell!'

The skull drew back. The broken, discoloured teeth opened. But the sound that came out was brittle laughter. A bony hand pointed to the silver box with its embossed crucifix on the lid. 'A cross? How very quaint. You threaten us with symbols?'

'And silver,' Oldfield said. He was relieved and pleased to see that the skull-faced man drew back slightly. 'And faith.'

The laughter had stopped. But the dark figures did not withdraw. The Coachman and Clarissa stood motionless, framed against the pale moonlight from the window.

Oldfield had finally undone the clasp. 'And this,' he said, as he opened the lid.

Clarissa's scream joined the Coachman's cries of fury and fear as the contents of the box were revealed.

The man was hurrying along the pavement. His dark cloak spread out behind him as he staggered towards a carriage waiting further down the street. A woman was already climbing quickly inside, slamming the door shut behind her. Liz could see the two pale horses waiting patiently as the man clambered with some difficulty up to the driving seat.

'Do you think we should help?' she asked Malvern, who was checking his watch.

'Probably spent too long in the nearest public house,' Malvern said, but he did look concerned. Their carriage was drawing up opposite Liz's house.

The other carriage moved quickly off, disappearing into the night. Liz caught sight of the woman inside, framed at the window, staring back at her.

'Whoever they are, they'll be fine.' Malvern smiled. 'Just late for an appointment, I expect. May I walk with you to your door?'

'Thank you.'

The driver opened the carriage door and Malvern climbed out before helping Liz down to the pavement.

'I do hope Father is all right,' she said. 'I had not intended to stay out so long.'

'I'm glad you did.'

As they approached, Liz saw that the front door was standing slightly open. She couldn't have left it like that – Malvern had been with her, and one of them would have noticed. Suddenly afraid, she ran to the house.

She hurried up the stairs and into her father's room.

Gasping with relief, Liz saw that her father was still there, in the bed. But as her eyes adapted to the dim light, she saw that he was sprawled back against the pillows and headboard. The blankets and sheets were in disarray, as if he had struggled to be free of them. The curtains were blowing in the breeze from outside.

And a dark shape lifted from the pillow close to Horace Oldfield's head. Black wings beat the air, propelling the creature towards the moonlight outside.

Liz gave a startled shriek and jumped back as it flapped past her and through the open window. She saw it flying rapidly across the garden, heading for the back wall, for her father's old outhouse and the gardens and streets beyond . . .

There were heavy footsteps on the stairs behind her, but Liz hardly heard them, was hardly aware of Malvern hurrying into the bedroom.

She was hugging her father's lifeless body, her tears dripping on to the bed, her hand fumbling for his wrist to check for a pulse. She could feel nothing.

'Let me.' Malvern gently eased her back, and bent his head to listen to the old man's chest

'There was something . . .' She could barely get the words out.

'I don't think he's breathing,' Malvern said anxiously.

'On the pillow. Black. Horrid. A bird.'

Malvern looked up abruptly. 'A bird? You think there was a bird in the room?'

'No, not a bird,' Liz realised. A part of her mind was analysing what she had seen. A dispassionate part of her had picked up her father's shaving mirror from the dressing table by the door.

'Then – what? What did you see?'

'It was a bat,' Liz told him. But she was too upset, too distracted as she approached the bed to see the fear in Malvern's eyes. She saw only her father's immobile body, drained of life.

CHAPTER 10

It was not George Archer who came for him the next morning. Nathaniel Blake regarded the tall, gaunt stranger with suspicion. But the man assured him that Mr Archer was already waiting for them at the British Museum.

'He said he'd come himself if he needed anything else,' Blake said. 'Got some other mysteries he wants cleared up, eh?'

The tall man's voice was loud and confident. 'There is something to be cleared up, yes.'

'Well, it has to be more stimulating than sitting around here,' Blake admitted.

The carriage was certainly impressive. Blake settled his more than ample form into the plush red seat. There had been a symbol on the door, like a coat of arms. But he had not caught the detail of it as the early morning light was filtered through a heavy smog.

There was a chill in the air, and the driver of the carriage had been visibly shivering inside his heavy cloak. Coming down with a chill, perhaps, Blake thought. It didn't do to hang about out in the cold and damp for too long.

It was difficult to see anything of the journey through the heavy air, and Blake settled back and closed his eyes. His mind drifted back to younger days – to his time at Lacock with Talbot; making his own way as a photographer; his wife Sarah – God rest her soul . . .

He jerked awake as the carriage stopped. Bleary-eyed, he squeezed himself out and followed the tall man to the door of the large imposing building where they had stopped.

'This is not the Museum,' he said, confused.

'Please – Mr Archer is waiting.'

Blake hung back. There was something forbidding about the place that made him feel uneasy. 'You said Archer was at the British Museum.'

'He was. But he wants to meet you here. This is where the mystery is. This is . . .' the man smiled. 'This is his club.'

Blake grunted. 'Rum sort of place, if you ask me.'

Inside, the building seemed cold and empty. Dust hung in the air and the lights were turned down low. Behind Blake, the driver in his cloak and hat stepped into the entrance hall.

Immediately a young woman appeared in a doorway opposite. She was dressed in a scarlet evening dress, and hurried to greet the driver.

'You are no better?' she asked, concerned.

'I'll recover. You were lucky to escape unharmed.' The driver's voice was scratchy and cold. Blake shuddered as he caught sight of the man's face beneath his wide-brimmed hat. It was like staring at a skull.

'I was nearer the door. We'll make him pay for what he did,' the woman said. 'It's lucky you have not drunk for so long.'

'Look, what is going on here?' Blake demanded. 'I was brought here to see George Archer, not to discuss this coachman's ailments.'

'Don't worry about his ailments,' the tall man who had brought Blake here said.

'Better to worry about your own,' the driver snarled.

'Anno Domini is the only ailment I suffer from, young man,' Blake snapped.

There was silence for a moment, then the woman laughed. She turned from the driver and walked slowly over to Blake, still laughing.

'Old age?' she said, standing right in front of him.

'You have no idea what that is,' the driver said.

'And you never will,' the woman added. Her eyes

were deep, dark pools that seemed to get bigger and bigger as she leaned towards Blake. Then he felt the tall man grab him from behind, holding him immobile. Over the woman's shoulder, Blake could see another man – tall and thin with pale features. A man he knew. A man he had seen at the British Museum, and before that in Lacock – the man he had tried to photograph.

The man was slowly shaking his head, his expression a mixture of sympathy and horror.

As the woman opened her mouth.

Eddie ran for longer than he could remember. Even when he was absolutely sure that no one was following from the Damnation Club, he kept running. By the time he stopped – too exhausted to be frightened any more – he had no idea where he was. Dawn was breaking through the usual layer of smog that hung over London, turning the air from black to grey.

Eddie needed to talk to someone about the events of the night, but would George believe him? Or would he berate Eddie for being out all night? In any case, it was too late to get home in time to see George before he left for work. Eddie could try to catch him at the Museum, but the last thing he needed now was a lecture about how he should be in school. No, he had a better plan.

The workhouse was already a bustle of activity when Eddie arrived. Breakfast had finished, and men and women were heading for the areas where they would work. Eddie had no idea where he would find his friends, but he knew roughly where the dormitories were. He turned a corner, and came almost face to face with John Remick.

Quick as lightning, Eddie turned and ran. He sprinted to the nearest corner and found himself in a yard full of men pulling old hemp ropes apart. Through that, and he was in another where women were making wicker baskets. They all worked in silence – grim-faced and emaciated. Eddie did not loiter. He could hear Remick yelling for Pearce. Maybe he'd be better hiding inside, he thought and headed for a doorway across the next yard.

There was a trestle table set up close to the door that Eddie was aiming for. Several old men sat on stools, chopping small logs into kindling with hand axes. One of them glanced up at Eddie, his face cracked like old stone.

'Pearce is in there,' he warned, his voice tired and husky with age. 'And it sounds like John Remick isn't too happy with you neither.'

'Thanks.' Eddie looked round for somewhere to hide until Remick had gone and the Workhouse Master was well out of the way. As the door started to open, he dived under the table.

He had a good view of Pearce's legs as the man strutted out of his workhouse. The legs paused in front of the table, and Eddie could hear him picking over the bits of wood.

'Shoddy,' Pearce rasped. 'But it'll have to do. Buck your ideas up, or you'll get short rations come supper time.'

A second set of legs arrived hurriedly – Remick. Eddie could hear the boy whispering urgently to his master.

'Then you'd best find him,' Pearce replied quietly. 'Sounds like the brat who gave me lip the other day. I reckon he'd be just what the Coachman wants. Yeah, I reckon he'd pay handsomely for that lad. And sure as hell is hot, no one will miss *him*.'

The legs moved off, followed almost immediately by a splash of throaty spit. Eddie waited a few moments, then emerged from under the table. 'Thanks for the warning,' he said to the man with the crazy-paving face.

The man nodded. 'Reckoned you'd need a bit of help if you're not to end up like Charlie and the others.'

'You know what happened to Charlie?'

The man shrugged. 'I know it was nothing good. Kids disappear. Always the ones Pearce thinks won't be missed. Fat lot he knows. He thinks us old 'uns are all deaf as well as dumb here.' He glanced round. 'Anyway, he's gone now. Dragged poor Remick off by the ear, though there's not many will feel any sympathy for him. Best you leg it while you can. Mood he's in, Pearce'll flog you to within a farthing of your life.'

Mention of a farthing made Eddie pat his pockets with sudden embarrassment. 'I ain't got nothing to give you,' he apologised.

The old man laughed. 'That's all right, lad. I'd have no use for it anyway.'

Eddie thanked the old man and his friends at the wood-chopping table again, then made a hurried escape from the workhouse. He ducked into the shadows by the side of the forbidding building as he caught sight of Pearce in the road outside. He was with a younger man – little more than a boy. They were standing beside a coach.

A coach with a distinctive red symbol on the black door. The driver was muffled inside his cloak, his face hooded. He climbed down from the coach to speak to Pearce.

Keeping to the shadows, Eddie crept closer, straining to hear what was being said.

'Oh yeah, I got one for you,' Pearce was saying. 'Thought we'd found just the one, but he gave us the slip. So, we'll have to make do.'

'With this one?' The Coachman's brittle voice

reached Eddie as he peered round the corner of the building.

As the Coachman spoke, Pearce grabbed the boy, twisting his arms viciously up behind his back. 'Go on, quick. He's strong this one – use your 'fluence. Put the spell on him. *Mesmerise* him like the others so he'll quit squirming.'

The boy was struggling and shouting. But a single look from the Coachman, and he lapsed into docile silence. Then, as Eddie watched, Pearce opened the door and the boy climbed inside without protest.

'He will do,' the Coachman said.

'He'll more than do. He's just what you wanted. Full of fire and he certainly won't be missed.'

'You expect thanks?'

'I expect money.'

The Coachman said nothing, but turned back towards his carriage.

Pearce grabbed the man by the sleeve. But as the Coachman turned, Pearce backed away. 'Sorry, sir. Didn't mean nothing by that. I just – well, I reckon I deserve what's mine. What you promised.'

'You mean money?'

Pearce looked round as two men turned the corner of the street, on the other side from the carriage. 'Not here,' he hissed. 'Not with people watching.'

'You are scared?' The Coachman seemed amused by Pearce's nervousness.

'I'm careful. That's why I can still help you. But it can't go on much longer.'

The Coachman walked slowly away – heading towards where Eddie was hiding. 'Indeed it can't,' he said. 'And it won't. It will all be over soon.'

Eddie did not wait to hear any more.

Life was a dull haze that went on around her. People spoke to Liz, and she answered. But she had little idea of what they said or how she replied. The doctor that Malvern sent for; the neighbours; the rector from St Bartholomew's and the undertaker's assistant . . .

The rehearsal at the Parthenon was a welcome relief. It was a set sequence of actions and words that she could lose herself in. For a few precious hours she could let her mind be still and not feel guilty for leaving her father to die alone in an empty house.

'You mustn't blame yourself,' Marie Cuttler said quietly to Liz through a deadening fog as the other actors left. 'Sit with me for a moment.'

Marie looked more pale than ever. Even in her distracted state Liz could see the woman was not well. She seemed tired and weak, though she laughed off any sympathy or suggestion she should rest.

'Tell me about him,' Marie said as they sat together in Marie's dressing room. The words were simple, but they unlocked an unexpected rush of emotion, and Liz turned and cried into the older woman's shoulder.

'He was so very private,' she said at last, wiping her eyes. 'My own father – yet I feel I didn't really know him at all. I always thought that one day we would talk. When he was better – he was frail for so long. Not ill health so much as a tiredness of life. I know he loved me, but he missed my mother more than he could ever say. He blamed himself, somehow, for her loss. And for the death of his sister before that, I think.'

'And was he to blame?'

'Of course not,' Liz said sharply. 'How could he have been?'

Marie nodded and smiled sadly. 'And you are not to blame either. How could you be?' she echoed.

Liz turned away. 'Oh but I am. If only I had been there . . .'

The woman took Liz's hands between her own. 'You're grieving, upset, confused. You're angry with yourself because when your father died you were enjoying yourself. But there's no shame in that. It's how he would want you to be. However little you think you know about him, you must know that.'

Liz nodded, biting back the tears. 'There was so much I *wanted* to talk to him about, and yet so little I *could* talk to him about.'

'Like your work here?'

Liz nodded.

'Like Henry Malvern?' Marie asked quietly. Liz looked at her sharply, but Marie simply laughed. 'Something else that confuses you, I fancy.'

Liz looked away. Thinking of her father. Thinking of Henry Malvern.

Thinking of George Archer, whom she had not seen at the ball – had not seen for days. Was he somehow so lodged in her mind that she saw his face when he wasn't there?

'You must take life as it comes, seize the moments you have. Nothing lasts for ever,' Marie said sadly. 'Not even actresses.'

The carriage door opened easily. Inside, the boy was sitting in shadow and Eddie could not make out his face.

'You all right?' he hissed. 'They'll be back in a minute.'

There was no answer. Eddie glanced quickly in the direction that the Coachman and Pearce had taken before climbing into the carriage. 'What's he done to you?'

'I must wait for my instructions.' The voice was flat and lifeless. The boy's eyes stared unfocused into space.

Eddie sighed. 'Why the heck did it have to be you?'

John Remick turned slightly to look at Eddie. But his eyes were still glazed. 'Instructions,' he said again.

'You want instructions? Right then. You get out of here and go to this address I'm going to give you and you make sure you see George Archer. No one else. And you tell him what's happened, what's going on. Everything you know. Which has got to be more than I know.'

'George Archer,' Remick echoed.

'That's right.' Eddie gave him George's address. 'Tell him Eddie sent you. And tell him . . .' Eddie hesitated. Was this really a sensible thing to do? He looked into Remick's staring eyes, and he thought of how Charlie had looked at the end. 'Tell him I've taken your place. Tell him I'll find out what the Coachman and his mob are up to if it's the last thing I do.'

Sir William looked up in surprise as his office door swung open. 'To what do I owe this honour?' he asked as his visitor closed the door behind him.

'When you came to see me last night,' Lord Ruthven said, 'I was not sure that I could help you. Not sure that

I *should* help you.'

'And now?' Sir William waved him to a chair.

'Circumstances change. Things are getting out of hand. I think you are right. We need to talk.'

'Really?' Sir William leaned back in his chair. 'And what should we talk about? Photographs, perhaps? Ancient Egypt, maybe? The real significance of certain artefacts until recently in the care of my department?'

'All of these and more,' Lord Ruthven conceded. His voice was barely more than a whisper. 'But, most of all, we need to talk about vampires.'

CHAPTER II

There was silence for a long time. Sir William sensed that Lord Ruthven needed a while to gather his thoughts and to summon up his courage. Eventually, Ruthven nodded slowly and sat down, as if he had come to a momentous decision. His voice was low and Sir William leaned forward, listening keenly.

'There are so many stories. So very many. I'm sure you have heard a hundred and that doesn't even begin to scratch the surface. From the ancient Egyptian Book of the Undead to the *Necronomicon*, from the Forbidden Tablets of Myrkros to the writings of Thomas Prest just a few years ago . . . So many stories.' He lapsed into silence again, eyes unfocused.

'Do you mind if we draw the curtains?' Lord Ruthven said at last.

The smog of the early morning had burned off and

the sunlight was falling across the desk. Sir William got up and closed the curtains.

'You were talking about stories,' he prompted as he sat down again. 'I take it that you have a story to tell me? About vampires?'

'Ah, but that's the point. They are just stories. They may have a basis in fact, but the whole notion of vampirism is a fiction. There is no such thing as a vampire – how could there be?'

'How indeed?' Sir William waited a while, before clearing his throat and continuing. 'As you say, a fiction. Stories and myths. A popular idea with little basis in fact. An age-old legend of a creature that looks like a man – that was once a man – who now survives by drinking the blood of others. A parasitic creature that shuns sunlight . . .' He let the last comment hang in the air.

'You can understand how the stories started,' Lord Ruthven said. 'They sprang from tragic but ordinary circumstances, of course. Attempts to rationalise the effects of plague. A way of explaining the preservation of a dead body. Even to mitigate the horror of premature burial. How can we believe that a loved one we sealed in a coffin below the earth was not actually dead – that they scratched and scraped and screamed inside what became their tomb.'

'A self-fulfilling prophecy,' Sir William agreed. 'Better

to believe they were possessed or infected, no longer human, than to admit you condemned them to such a fate.'

'Anaemia,' Lord Ruthven went on. 'The inhumanity of man to man – an excuse for brutality that we would rather had a different explanation from simple sadism.'

'And so the legends and myths built up,' Sir William said. 'Is that your thesis? You came here to tell me that vampires do not exist. That it is absurd to believe the stories.'

'There are absurdities,' Ruthven admitted. 'How can a man turn into a bat, for example?'

'But there are also aspects that are rather more plausible. Don't you think?'

'Oh yes.' Lord Ruthven's tone was matter-of-fact, as if he were discussing the most mundane of subjects. 'But that is simply because beneath the façade and behind the stories, hiding in shadows and masked by legend and deceit, vampires *do* exist.'

Sir William sat back in his chair, and breathed a heavy sigh. 'Now, at last, we are getting somewhere.'

'As I said, the stories have a basis in truth. All stories do. They have been exaggerated and embellished until they seem absurd and ridiculous to the rational mind. But it is the trappings and the details that are the fiction. Little lies to overstate the truth. The great lie to conceal one fact.' He waved a hand in the air, as if to dismiss them all. 'A conspiracy that has lasted for centuries – millennia even – with precisely the intention of making it seem that vampires are a myth, a story, a fiction.'

'A way of drawing attention away from the truth,' Sir William realised. 'Not by trying to conceal it, but by making it so public, making it seem so far-fetched, that it cannot be believed.'

'While the terrible truth lurks in darkness and shadows.' Lord Ruthven hesitated for a moment before going on: 'Of course, we could never hope to hide our existence entirely. And so we chose a different path. We publicised accounts of our lives, exaggerating them. We encouraged the theatre and music-hall performances. Even wrote some of the penny dreadfuls ourselves. We created an obvious fiction wherein we could hide the truth.'

'A clever plan.'

'It worked,' Ruthven conceded. 'It worked to conceal the facts from the masses, and to mislead anyone who did stumble across the truth. And it continues. Even now, one of us is feeding ideas fit for a sensational new play to Mr Stoker at the Lyceum Theatre.'

'You spoke of the great lie,' Sir William said quietly.

'Do you realise how much I am risking just by speaking to you at all?' Ruthven countered. 'There have been so many lies. So many embellishments to hide the central truth.'

'And yet, at its core, you would have me believe that vampires do exist. That creatures of the night drink the blood of the living for sustenance. The undead walk among us.'

'Just as it has always been. And Man is so introspective, so selfish that he does not notice. Our victims – and yes, I choose that word deliberately – can fade and pale and waste away as we drain them dry. And no one notices. No one wants to notice. Is that ignorance, or wilful self-deceit?'

'Perhaps,' Sir William said slowly, 'there is a part of all of us that wants to live for ever. No matter what the cost.'

'Perhaps,' Ruthven conceded. 'For centuries we have existed alongside ordinary mortals. You described us as parasites. Perhaps you are right. A whole second civilisation that feeds off the first. Parallel and unsuspected, dependent on humanity for the blood that sustains us.'

Sir William listened carefully, making the occasional note on a sheet of paper. He felt detached and cold – as if he was indeed listening to a story rather than learning a terrible secret.

'We have a healthy, growing society. Too healthy perhaps as our numbers continue to increase. We have had to limit our activity in order to remain hidden and unknown.'

'So as not to draw attention to yourselves,' Sir William said.

'Indeed. While we are awake, we need a constant supply of fresh blood. And even here in London, there are only so many unfortunates who can disappear from the streets and the workhouses and never be missed. We take them from wherever we can find them. Anyone whose blood we can drink. Anyone who won't be missed.'

Sir William's throat was dry. He ran a finger round the inside of his collar to loosen it as Ruthven went on:

'But even so, there are too many of us now.'

'Then how do you stay hidden?'

'By sleeping. At any time only some of us are awake and active, while the rest sleep. We have resting houses all over London where they wait for their turn at life.' Ruthven gave a sudden snort of laughter. 'Life! I have seen so much death. Even today. What a cost, what a way to live. Oh, to sleep and never wake up.' He sank back into the chair and closed his eyes.

'Are there many of you who feel this dissatisfaction?' Sir William wondered.

Lord Ruthven shook his head. 'A few perhaps. There is a dissatisfaction, but not with our fate itself, more with the way we handle it. There is growing dissent among both the waking and the sleeping.'

'I can imagine.'

'Really?' From his tone, Ruthven did not believe him.

'It is a system that cannot be sustained,' Sir William said. 'The attraction, as I understand it and if I can use that word, of your condition is longevity. How appealing can it be to have everlasting life and yet be asked to sleep through it? How amenable are those already awake to giving up their lives and sleeping for – how long? Decades? Centuries?'

'Those of us who attain positions of power and wealth within society tend to want to maintain that,' Ruthven agreed. 'Others spend far longer than they would wish asleep. They argue that those in the public eye must be seen to age and die. The way of the world is change, yet we remain constant. Those of us awake must make way for the sleepers, but those with power want to keep it. At any cost.'

'Quite a dilemma. But with an obvious solution. An unacceptable solution.'

Ruthven nodded. 'Increasingly it is argued that the status quo must change. That what worked once is no longer the best way. As our numbers grow, so do the arguments that we should step out of the shadows. Announce our presence. That we are now strong enough to take over. We don't need to govern from hiding, shaping the destiny of the world while remaining forever shrouded in darkness. Why should we limit ourselves? Why feed only on the dross of society, on those who will not be missed – the children from the workhouse, the women on the streets, the drunks asleep in the alleys?' Lord Ruthven leaned forward, fixing Sir William with a dark, piercing stare. 'There are so many of us now in positions of power that we could take over and rule.'

'And will that happen?' Sir William asked quietly.

'A few years ago, I would have said no.' Lord Ruthven looked away. 'But circumstances have changed. Until now those of us who favour the status quo have been able to argue that the current system works. That it is best and safest not to change our strategy. It has served us well for centuries. But now . . . it is becoming a different world and things are happening that may expose us.'

'Expose?' Sir William smiled. 'You mean, as one might expose a photograph?'

CHAPTER 12

In his room across the corridor, George was examining one of the photographs from Xavier Hemming's files. It showed a man standing in a stiff pose on the sea front. A pencilled description on the back of the photograph read:

Brighton, 1864
Michael Adisson and unknown

The man in the picture – Adisson – had one arm hanging by his side. The other arm was held out, curled round. As he might have stood if he was holding someone with him in the photograph – his wife, or child, or . . .

'Unknown indeed,' George thought as he looked through his magnifying glass. The obvious explanation was that the man was just standing oddly. But the pose would have been held for a while. It was not an accidental posture.

The next possibility was that it was a trick. The person Adisson was holding had somehow been removed from the picture. George knew from his discussions with Blake and Pennyman that such things were possible. But they were complicated, they needed planning. If anyone had removed a figure from this picture, they would need an identical photograph taken from the same position to replace the background. And there was no sign of any trickery.

The only other possibility was the one that George kept rejecting. Despite Blake's assertions about Lord Ruthven.

It haunted him again as he gathered together his things and left his office. How could someone simply not show up in a photograph?

'We have a special relationship with various elements,' Ruthven said. 'Light, silver, water.'

'I have heard as much,' Sir William agreed.

'Running water is not in and of itself an obstacle. Another fiction,' Ruthven explained. 'But yes, we can drown. We need blood, and that blood needs air just like yours. More than yours.'

'And photographs?' Sir William prompted.

'The new technology. One that might yet force us to

act. As photography becomes more popular we cannot hope to remain hidden.' He stood up and walked slowly to the window, pulling back the curtain slightly. The afternoon was drawing into evening, and the air was heavy with grey fog.

'Sunlight,' Lord Ruthven said quietly. 'Not just daylight, but the rays of the sun itself. A filter of smog is sufficient for us, but it is helpful that the legends suggest all light is anathema.'

'You mentioned light, you mentioned silver . . .' Sir William stood up and joined Ruthven by the window, looking out into the grey. He saw himself in the glass, and beside him – nothing. 'You cast no reflection,' he said quietly.

'Not even in a mirror,' Ruthven admitted. 'That much is true. Light and silver – the principal elements of the photographic process. Like a mirror, the photograph ignores us.' He turned and looked directly at Sir William. 'We cast no shadows. I sometimes think that, if even the light of the sun can't see me, perhaps God himself is so ashamed he is trying to ignore us.'

'You think the advance of photography might force your fellows to act?'

'I fear so. But there are other reasons. Other things that are happening. Other matters that are coming to a head. Unspeakable things.'

She looked so pale and tired, propped up against the pillows on the bed in her hotel room. Marie Cuttler smiled at Liz, but her smile was as frail and thin as she had become.

'Thank you so much for coming.'

Liz sat on the edge of the bed and took her friend's hand. It was ice cold. 'Oh Marie, you look so . . . tired.'

'It will pass, I am sure. But, if it does not . . .' Her eyelids flickered over her eyes as she struggled to stay awake. 'Do something for me?'

'Of course. Anything.'

'A story based on truth, remember. Do it justice – our story.' Marie fell back, exhausted. 'You will be such a brilliant Marguerite, Miss Oldfield.'

The Coachman paid Eddie barely a glance when he returned, and the coach clattered through the foggy streets with Eddie alone inside.

It stopped outside the Damnation Club for a while, and Eddie shivered at the memories that brought back. Then the Coachman returned and they were off again.

At each of the several stops during the afternoon, Eddie was tempted to escape. But each and every time he decided that if the Coachman had not noticed the substitution then he would soon find out what was going on – where Charlie and the others had been taken, and what had happened to them.

Except, he wasn't sure he wanted to know. He was stuck now, just as Charlie and the others had been. Except they had probably been mesmerised like Remick. Eddie still had all his wits about him, and at the first sign of trouble he was out of here.

Even so, he felt suddenly cold and incredibly alone as the coach drew up outside the British Museum. The Coachman climbed down from the carriage, and walked purposefully towards the main entrance. This could be his last chance to escape, Eddie thought. Should he slip away now? Or should he stay and see what more he could discover?

There was a boy standing outside George's house when he got home. He thought at first it was Eddie, but as he approached he saw that the lad was taller and thinner. His dark hair was greased across his head and he was staring into space.

'Can I help you?' George asked.

'Help,' the boy echoed, his voice dead and flat.

'Are you looking for Eddie?' George wondered.

Perhaps he was a friend from school.

'Eddie sent me,' the reply came in the same mono-tone.

'If he's not here, I'm afraid I don't know where he is.'

'Eddie sent me to tell you all about it. About Mr Pearce and the Coachman.'

'Are you all right?' The lad looked blank-faced and dis-tracted. George unlocked the door and let himself in. The boy followed him.

'Look, I told you, Eddie's not here,' George said irrita-bly. He wasn't sure what to do – he couldn't throw the boy out. And the lad was just standing in the living room, eyes unfocused. He had lapsed into silence. In the better light George could see he was lean but well built. His hands were bunched into fists at his sides.

'Yes,' George said uneasily. 'Well, perhaps you'd like to wait?'

The boy did not answer, but stared blankly into the distance. George was not sure quite what to do with him, but before long he heard a coach pulling up out-side. Moments later, there was a knock at the door.

It was Sir Harrison Judd. 'Mr Archer, I bring good news. Your application has been accepted.'

George blinked. 'Accepted? Already?' He had been meaning to talk to Sir William about the strange masked ball and his night at the Damnation Club. But a suitable moment had not come. When George left the Museum, Sir William's door had been shut, the sound of voices coming from within. Now it seemed it was too late to ask for advice.

'We would very much like to have you as a member,' Judd said. 'Congratulations.'

George was surprised. He had imagined there would be an interview or meeting or some such formality at least. 'Thank you, sir.'

Sir Harrison turned to go. Then he stopped as he realised that George was not following. 'Well, come on then, man. Can't keep them waiting. This evening you will be initiated as a full member of the Damnation Club.'

George glanced nervously back towards the living room door. Could he safely leave the strange friend of Eddie's here? And where was Eddie, confound the boy?

The door slammed shut behind George and Sir Harrison. At the sound, John Remick shuddered and rocked back on his heels. As he regained his balance, he looked round in surprise. His mind was a fog every bit as thick as the air outside. But slowly his memory of the last few hours returned. He remembered Pearce's betrayal, the Coachman. And Eddie. He remembered George – how he had been supposed to tell him everything but his mind had blanked out.

He slumped down into an armchair, his head in his hands.

They talked about the myths and the legends, the fiction and the fact.

'Oh, it's true that we have some affinity for our home soil,' Lord Ruthven said. 'For the land where we last lived a full and proper existence. Perhaps it is just home-sickness and all in the mind, or perhaps there is indeed something stronger that binds us to that soil.'

'Literally binds you to it?' Sir William wondered.

By way of answer, Lord Ruthven undid his shoelaces. He slipped off first one then the other shoe. 'I was in Scotland when I was initiated. It's almost like joining an exclusive club.' He held out one of his shoes for Sir William to see the thin layer of soil sprinkled inside. 'A constant reminder. With every step of my life I can feel where I used to belong, who I used to be. Perhaps the others find that liberating and rejoice in the transition.' He put his shoes back on and retied the laces slowly and deftly. 'But I find I long for the things I no longer have.'

'Such as sunlight?'

'And love . . . And death.'

'Which is why you have come to see me, I imagine.' Sir William leaned forward across his desk, elbows on the blotter as he tapped his fingers against his chin. 'An exclusive club,' he said quietly. Then louder as he realised: 'Of course, the Damnation Club!'

Lord Ruthven was nodding. 'We have an initiation there this evening. A very special candidate, I'm afraid.'

'Who?' Sir William demanded.

Before Lord Ruthven could answer, the door to the office was hurled open. Sir William jumped to his feet, staring angrily at the cloaked figure standing in the doorway.

The man's voice was dry and cracked. 'I hope you have not been telling Sir William *all* our secrets. *All* our lies.' He pushed back the hood of his cloak.

Sir William backed away, staring in horrified disbelief at the skull where the man's head should have been. Somewhere deep inside the empty eye sockets there might have been a flicker of life. Or death.

'I have not drunk blood since our Lord was taken from us,' the Coachman said as he advanced on Sir William. 'Not for over four thousand years. My sister Belamis and I abstained from blood until his return. Have you any idea how I ache for it? How I hunger for it?' His bony fingers reached out for Sir William. 'But soon, he will walk among us once more, and so will she. Then – only then – will I allow myself to feed.'

Sir William's back was to the wall. The fingers of a

skeletal hand clamped on his throat, the other pushing his head back to expose his neck.

'I offer you a last chance to redeem yourself, Ruthven,' the Coachman rasped. 'To put right what you have done, before our Master hears of it.'

The room was shimmering and swaying as Sir William struggled to breathe. The skull stared back at him – an image of his own mortality. Then it was replaced by another image – by the pale, frightened face of Lord Ruthven.

'I'm sorry,' Ruthven said quietly. 'Truly sorry.' He leaned forward.

The pressure on Sir William's neck was released. But immediately replaced by the sharp pain of something hard slicing into his flesh. He could feel the warm blood pumping out and running down. The world was a misty red as Sir William sank to the ground.

The last thing he heard was the Coachman's brittle voice. 'Welcome to Damnation.'

Chapter 13

The pale, nervous man who got into the carriage before they left the British Museum looked familiar, but it took Eddie a while to recall where he had seen him. It was at the Mummy Unwrapping. The gaunt, grey-haired man with a white moustache had been there. Eddie kept his expression blank and hoped the man wouldn't remember him.

Eddie could see snatches of the journey through the fog. The streets were lined by warehouses and storage buildings rather than houses now. He could hear the clanking of machinery and the sound of steam engines.

A train was passing them, dragging a long line of trucks. Behind it Eddie could make out the dark shapes of engine sheds and huge piles of coal. They were approaching one of the sheds. The double doors were open ready, and the carriage clattered inside without slowing at all.

Eddie braced himself, afraid they were going to crash. But instead the whole carriage tilted downwards and he almost fell forward off the seat. The carriage charged on into the sloping darkness – far further than was possible inside an engine shed. A gas lamp sped past the window, then another. They were in a tunnel, Eddie realised, racing down into the earth.

It was a struggle for Eddie to keep his face blank and betray no feeling as the coach clattered through dimly lit tunnels for what seemed like an eternity. Eventually, it slowed to a halt.

'You know what you must do, Lord Ruthven,' the Coachman said as soon as the grey-haired man had climbed out.

'Of course.' He turned and beckoned for Eddie to follow him.

The carriage had stopped in the middle of a great cavern. It was like an enormous cave, but the roof and walls were held together by intricate stonework. The place was lit with sputtering lamps that made the walls glow a dull, moist red.

The vaulted roof sloped down at one end of the cavern. There was then a huge area where the roof was much lower and flat. The carriage had arrived under this flat area, the top of the Coachman's hood almost touching the roof as he sat on the driver's bench.

Lord Ruthven led Eddie a short distance away. 'We will watch from here,' he said quietly, without looking at Eddie.

More people were arriving in the cavern, from the various passageways and tunnels leading off. They walked with a formal, measured gait, dressed in black and red. Men and women, even a few children. Pale, emaciated figures that grouped themselves round the carriage. Dozens, perhaps even hundreds of them.

Despite the gathering crowd, Eddie still had a clear view of the carriage. When it seemed that everyone was present, the Coachman reached down beside the bench seat. Then he straightened up abruptly, raising a sword above his head so that its point was touching the roof. The blade was stained bronze, flashing as it caught the sputtering light.

'The age-old ceremony,' Lord Ruthven said quietly. He glanced at Eddie, and smiled. 'Not that you know or care.'

Eddie kept looking straight ahead, though he dearly wanted to see Ruthven's expression. Dearly wanted to ask him what was going on.

But it seemed Ruthven was going to tell him anyway. 'The cemetery is so close above us that I sometimes wonder if the gravediggers might excavate too deep and discover us.' There was a tremor in the man's voice. Was he nervous? Afraid? 'But of course, they are well paid to put the right bodies in the right places.'

As his eyes grew accustomed to the flickering light, Eddie could see something else. The stones that lined the flat ceiling – some of them were engraved. He had thought it was just the natural texture, but Ruthven's talk of grave digging made Eddie realise that they looked almost like tombstones.

The Coachman was dragging the sword along the edge of one of the large, engraved roof slabs. It bit deep into the ground above, dark, damp earth showering down and rattling on the roof of the carriage.

When he had cut all round the large slab, the Coachman lowered the sword and the coach moved forward a few yards. The horses were so pale they almost glowed. They were so thin that it seemed as if their ribs were standing proud of the sides of their bodies. There were black plumes attached to their skull-like heads, like those on undertakers' horses.

The Coachman held the sword in both hands for a moment, then swung it suddenly upwards like a club.

The sword smashed into the slab above, shattering it into fragments. Lumps of stone fell and bounced off the carriage roof. There was a tearing, wrenching, groaning that seemed to come from the ground above Eddie's head. Then something crashed down through the hole where the stone slab had been. A long wooden casket thumped on to the roof of the carriage.

A coffin.

The carriage was moving again now, heading for one of the wider tunnels leading from the cavern. The figures in their red and black finery followed it. Ruthven and Eddie joined the back of the procession as they walked slowly, stiffly, formally through the crimson gloom. Like a funeral procession.

The red mist was clearing, but Sir William could feel the fire burning in his neck where Lord Ruthven had bitten. He clutched at the arm of his chair and dragged himself to his feet.

At the side of the desk was a carafe of water. He grabbed at it, and with a shaking hand poured some into the glass. Then he splashed it over his neck, hoping to ease the pain. It had no effect.

The room was spinning and his vision was blurring again. He did not have much time. But how to counteract the bite? He struggled to lift the carafe. Held it in front of his face and tried to focus. With his free hand he described the sign of the cross. How did you make holy water?

'Our Father,' he murmured, 'Which art in Heaven, hallowed be thy name . . .'

He hurried through the prayer, then emptied the carafe over the burning pain at his neck.

The water turned to steam as it touched his broken skin. Scalded, he cried out in pain and collapsed to his knees. His hand scrabbled at the drawers of the desk.

In the middle drawer was a simple letter opener – a long, thin strip of shaped silver. It took all Sir William's remaining strength to bend it back and forth. He jammed it in the drawer and worked it until the metal gave and snapped in half. It would have to do. He was fading, he could feel it – even with the wound cleaned, he needed to cauterise it. To burn out the remaining infection.

He pressed the two strips of silver together in the rough shape of a cross, and clamped them to his neck.

The angry hiss of burning flesh.

A scream of violent agony.

A body falling.

As soon as George and Sir Harrison Judd were inside the Damnation Club, Judd excused himself.

'I have certain things to prepare,' he told George. 'Clarissa will look after you.'

'This way, Mr Archer.' Her voice was as soft and silky as ever. She was standing in a doorway, wrapped in her scarlet cloak. 'Bring your coat,' she told him. 'You will find it cold. For a while.'

Clarissa led him along a dimly lit oak-panelled passageway. It ended with a flight of wooden steps, the middle of each tread worn down by the passage of feet over the years.

The stairs led down into darkness. They seemed to descend for ever. But eventually George found himself in a small panelled room. There was no furniture, no windows – and he guessed they must be well below ground level. A single gas lamp sputtered unevenly on the wall.

'Where are we?' George asked nervously.

'Oh my poor George.' Clarissa stroked an ice-white gloved hand down his cheek. 'Do you want to know a secret?'

She did not wait for his reply, but pressed at the edge of one of the wooden panels in the wall. It sprang open with well-oiled ease.

'A hidden door,' George said.

'I told you it was a secret.' Clarissa beckoned for him to follow and stepped through.

It was like stepping into another world. George was indeed glad of his coat as the chill air clung to him. He was at the end of a long passageway. More than that, he realised – it was a tunnel. The ceiling was vaulted stone, supported by interwoven arches. Clarissa's cloak rippled in the breeze that George guessed was caused by whatever ventilation there was. Hot air escaping and drawing through cold air.

'We must be right under the building. Is this the cellar?' He looked around in astonishment and admiration. There were oil lamps burning at intervals along the wall, throwing pools of light, illuminating puddles of dark water on the tunnel floor and sending coils of smoke towards the roof.

'It is more than just a cellar,' Clarissa said.

'But it must be ancient. The design – the architecture . . .' George shook his head. 'Centuries old, at least.'

'At least,' she agreed. 'Come – this way.'

They walked slowly along the tunnel, George's feet splashing in a shallow puddle. The whole place looked and smelled damp, but even so it was a remarkable feat of engineering.

And that was before the tunnel was joined by two more, even larger tunnels.

'It's *massive*,' George realised. 'What is this place? It must extend under several streets.'

Clarissa smiled. 'It's a little bigger than that. I knew that as an engineer you would appreciate it.'

'You know of my training?'

'Kingsley,' she said simply.

George felt suddenly embarrassed and ashamed that he had forgotten the man – the reason he was here at all. 'Of course,' he said quietly.

'And it is for your engineering ability that we sought you out.'

'What? But I thought Kingsley . . .'

'Recommended you. He has great admiration for your expertise, as we have for his. And our enterprise has grown so big that Kingsley can no longer manage alone.' She walked on slowly. 'You know that several lines of the underground railway were diverted, the plans changed, so that they would not interfere with our caverns and chambers.'

'You mean – people know about them?'

'No. No one knows. No one outside the Damnation Club.'

'Then, how . . .?'

'Our influence is extensive.' She was striding more quickly ahead now. 'I am glad you are impressed. It will make things easier.'

'So where are we going?' George asked. 'I thought the ceremony would take place in the Club itself. I had no idea . . .' His voice tailed off and he hurried to catch up with Clarissa as she strode on ahead.

The occasional puddles were becoming more frequent. After a while – after what must have been half a mile – George and Clarissa were walking through an inch of water.

'It leaks in,' she explained. 'We are almost under the river here.'

'You mean the Thames? Here? Above us now?'

She paused and glanced up at the roof as if considering. 'Westminster. Or near enough.' She regarded him for a moment, then continued along the tunnel. 'We must hurry, or you will be late.'

The nearest lamp was flickering, throwing bizarre shadows across the dark, damp wall. The stonework glistened as if it was sweating. George ran his hand down the stone, feeling the viscous, wet surface. But it didn't feel like river water.

'Hurry, George,' Clarissa called back to him. 'We are almost there.'

Her laughter echoed round the tunnel. But George was standing beneath the flickering light, staring at the palm of his hand where he had pressed it to the wall. It had come away damp, smeared, dark, and as crimson as Clarissa's cloak.

'What's going on?' George demanded. But his voice was lost in her laughter, and in another sound. The whole tunnel seemed to throb with a low noise that reverberated through the tunnels. George could feel it under his feet, and pulsing inside his head. The sound was like a great heartbeat.

Clarissa seemed to sense how apprehensive he was growing. Seemed to know that if she gave him the chance, George would slip away. But they had come so far, so deep into the maze of tunnels that George doubted he would find his way back to the door into the basement of the Damnation Club.

Make a run for it now, and he might be condemned to wander round these damp, hellish tunnels for all eternity. George swallowed and determined to play along with whatever was happening. For now, at least.

There was a pipe running along the wall of the tunnel they were in. Another joined it, then a third. These connected to more pipes that disappeared into the walls, ran up to the roof, burrowed into the floor.

Clarissa waited while George examined them. The pipes were dark with corrosion and leaking at the joints, but they were obviously much newer than the tunnels themselves.

'That sound . . .'

Clarissa nodded. 'The pumps. We are getting closer to them. A great hall of steam-driven machinery that keeps the water moving through these pipes. They are not always visible, but they line the tunnels and interlink like the arteries of this domain.'

'To keep the water out?'

'Of course. Without the pumps, as you have seen the Thames slowly seeps in and would eventually flood these tunnels.'

There was something in the easy manner in which she answered, something in her smile, that made George sure that she was lying.

The chamber where they gathered was smaller than the great cavern beneath the cemetery. There was a stone table on a dais at one end, which looked to Eddie rather like an altar. Metal pipes were woven into the stonework, running round the walls and connecting together with heavy valves. Rows of stone benches ran lengthways along the chamber, and people were taking their places on them – two rows of benches, facing each other across a central aisle.

The other end of the chamber, opposite the dais and the table, was shrouded in darkness. There were lamps right the way along the walls, but they were dimmed at that end of the chamber – as if the light was afraid to show what might be lurking in the shadows.

The carriage had stopped between the rows of benches, before the stone table. Four men in black lifted down the stained, muddy coffin. They carried it reverently to the table – the altar.

The Coachman climbed down, and the carriage pulled gently away without him. It passed close to Eddie, and his eyes widened as he saw the horses properly for the first time. He had thought their ribs were showing through their sides. He was wrong.

The horses had no sides. The darkness between the bones was not emaciated, shrunken flesh but empty space. They were brittle, pale skeletons. The Coachman followed behind, and as he pushed back his hood, Eddie could see that his face was a skull with empty sockets for eyes, wizened skin drawn back from blackened teeth.

The Coachman stopped beside Eddie and Lord Ruthven. The stench was suddenly so powerful that Eddie almost fainted. The earthy, stale smell increased as the Coachman leaned forward.

'Yes,' he rasped. 'This one will do very well.' He turned in a full circle, arms outstretched as he addressed the gathered crowd. 'Soon we shall celebrate the arrival of a new member of our great family. Soon we shall pay homage to our Lord.'

He turned back to Ruthven. 'Despite your doubts and your attempted betrayal, our Lord has returned to us. No one can stop us now. Sir William has been dealt with.'

Eddie felt a jolt of shock, as if he had been thumped.

'Miss Oldfield is no longer a threat.'

He almost doubled over with sudden nausea.

'George Archer will be here directly.'

His head was in a spin. It seemed as if the whole place was thumping and contracting in time to his heart. The blood was rushing in his ears as the Coachman turned to Eddie.

'Which just leaves the boy to be dealt with,' he said. 'The boy, Eddie Hopkins.'

CHAPTER 14

It was all Eddie could do not to cry out in alarm. Even if he could get away from Lord Ruthven and the others he had no idea how to get out. He might be trapped down here for ever. But maybe it was time to take that chance.

He braced himself, ready to shove the Coachman and Ruthven aside and run for the nearest tunnel.

But the Coachman was already turning away. 'The boy was at the Damnation Club. He knows too much. Since we know that Archer is out of the way, the boy will be alone at Archer's house.'

Eddie almost laughed out loud. Of course – the Coachman didn't know who he was, how could he? He thought Eddie was just some kid that Pearce had given up to him. His legs were weak at the thought he'd nearly given himself away.

'I shall attend to it,' Ruthven was saying, with a deferential bow.

'Already done,' the Coachman rasped.

❧◆❧

It was a long time since John Remick had been inside a *home*. It amazed him how much softer everything was. How much more comfortable. Archer's house probably wasn't even that much of a home, but it was very different from the workhouse.

He felt as if he was waking from a long, deep sleep. He was confused and dazed, wondering what the Coachman had done to him. It was almost an hour before he was confident enough to explore the house a little. He felt he was intruding. Usually he didn't care what people thought. Apart from Pearce – and only then because the man would whip him as happily as he would any of the other kids. Remick was a survivor. He'd quickly learned that the only way to avoid being picked on was to be the most brutal of bullies himself.

But here in the easy comfort of Archer's home he began to wonder if he'd got it right. If he'd been able to stay with his mum, would he have lived somewhere like this? Or would they have been shunted from workhouse to poorhouse, to who knew where?

There was even a kitchen. Tiny, but a kitchen at the end of the narrow hallway. He was in the kitchen when he heard the knocking at the door.

The man at the door was a stranger. Tall and thin, wearing a top hat and a heavy cape against the cold of the night. His eyes were deep black.

'Eddie Hopkins, I presume,' the man said.

John Remick could tell – from the way he stood, the way he spoke, the way he slapped an ebony cane into the gloved palm of his hand . . . The man meant no good. Someone had it in for Eddie. Whatever Eddie had got caught up in, whatever Pearce and the Coachman were doing, it was a dangerous business.

Remick had never once asked what happened to the children the Coachman took away. Looking back at the man with the dark eyes, Remick was suddenly sure that Eddie had saved his life. The boy had taken his place – even after the beating Remick had promised him. Whatever Eddie was doing, it was for the good. If Remick could help Eddie, could somehow take the heat off him and let him get on with his business . . .

He thrust his hands into his pockets. He could feel the crumpled, ragged shape of his mother's letter and gripped it tight in his fist. What would she think of him? Eddie had asked. Would she be proud of her son?

'Yeah,' John Remick said defiantly. 'I'm Eddie Hopkins. What's it to you?'

Even as he said them, Remick knew they would be

the last words he ever spoke. But Eddie would be safe. And Mum would be proud.

'Some of this pipe work is new,' George realised.

'Our requirements change constantly. The river never rests,' Clarissa said.

There was a sound echoing the throb of the pumps. It reminded George of a church – the whole place with its high, stone roof, and the noise. It sounded like people chanting.

'You said you need an engineer. Is it for this? To keep the pumps working and the tunnels dry?' George wondered.

'The river is never silent, never quiet, never calm,' Clarissa said. 'The system needs constant attention. It is so complex now that only Christopher Kingsley understands it fully. But we also need to make use of the newer technologies. For all his expertise, Kingsley is such a traditionalist.'

The chanting was getting louder as they neared the end of the tunnel. 'So this is what Kingsley was working on when he died?' George said. His throat was dry at the memory of seeing his friend and mentor stretched out on the mortuary slab.

Clarissa turned to George. The flickering light was

red across her white face. 'Why, George,' she said quietly, 'whatever makes you think that he is dead?'

George stopped suddenly. 'I saw him,' he said, confused. 'I saw his body . . .'

But Clarissa had already moved on. She was standing beside a doorway in the tunnel wall, waiting for George to catch up. 'The Hall of Machines,' Clarissa said as he joined her. She stepped aside to allow George to enter the enormous cavern.

The sound of the pumps and engines increased as he stepped over the threshold. The air was heavy and damp with steam and he could taste the oil at the back of his throat. There were a dozen or more engines with their huge metal boilers arranged along the length of the cavern. A mass of pipes emerged from them, running down the walls and disappearing into the darkness.

In front of George thick ropes hung swaying, reaching up towards the high roof where they rattled against distant pulleys. The sound of chanting kept rhythm with the hiss and pulse of the pumps.

'You see why we need your help,' Clarissa said, her voice almost lost in the sound and the steam.

There was a hush as Marie came into the theatre. Henry Malvern was supporting her, helping her across to a seat in the front row. She sat down, gasping for breath.

Liz hurried to help. 'You shouldn't have come. You should be in bed.'

The woman looked even more pale and drawn, so frail and tired. It took her several moments to get her breath. She squeezed Liz's hand, and Liz could feel how very cold she was.

'I wanted to come. Just once more,' Marie said. Her voice was hesitant and faint – a shadow of how she had been just a few days ago. 'I want to see you play the role of Marguerite. Want to be sure it's in good hands.' She smiled to show it was a joke, but the smile was an obvious effort. Her face creased and wrinkled. Devoid of the usual layers of make-up, Marie Cuttler looked so very old.

Liz knew the lines already. She had a good memory, and was almost word perfect. She tried to lose herself in the world of the play, shutting out everything except the drama and Malvern's occasional suggestions and advice. Struggling to forget her father, and Marie's decline.

As soon as the rehearsal was over, Liz hurried to help Malvern get Marie to his carriage.

'You're treating me like a cripple,' Marie complained weakly.

'Nonsense,' Malvern told her. 'A week or two's rest and you'll be back on your feet. Just been overdoing it.' He glanced at Liz, and she could see in his expression that he did not believe this any more than she did.

'Sleep,' Marie murmured. 'Just need some sleep.'

'I'll come with you to her hotel,' Liz offered.

By the time they reached her room, Malvern was all but carrying Marie. She looked so slight and thin that she must weigh almost nothing, Liz thought. But Malvern seemed to appreciate having Liz there to open the door and to help Marie to her bed. He excused himself while Liz helped Marie into her nightdress.

'I'll get her a glass of water,' Liz said when Malvern returned. 'She needs to drink, and if she can eat something . . .'

'I'll talk to the hotel people. Have food sent in.'

Marie's eyelids fluttered as she drifted closer to sleep. It was difficult to know if she was even aware they were there.

Which made it all the more of a shock when Liz returned with the water. To find Marie wrapped in a tight embrace in Malvern's arms. Neither of them seemed to notice Liz as she crossed quickly to the door and let herself out. She could feel the blood burning in her cheeks as she hurried down the stairs.

The next opening in the tunnel, behind the Hall of Machines, led into another massive chamber. The light from the wall lamps was barely enough to illuminate the whole place, and one end was in total darkness. Rows of stone benches lined the chamber, filled with people sitting chanting. Between the benches stood a black carriage. George could make out one of the pale horses at the front of it tossing its head.

There must be a hundred people here, he thought. Perhaps two hundred. As Clarissa led George to the aisle between the two sets of benches, the people stood up. The chanting was replaced with scattered applause. George felt himself colour with embarrassment.

Clarissa was holding his hand, leading him up the aisle towards the carriage, and then past it. George frowned, suddenly anxious again. At the end of the aisle was a raised dais with what looked like a stone altar on it. And on top of the altar was a wooden coffin.

Four men stood round the coffin, one at each corner of the altar. As George approached, his heart thumping in his chest in time to the renewed chanting, the men stepped forward. They grasped the coffin lid and wrenched it free. George could hear the tearing of the wood, the squeal of nails.

Two of the men reached inside. A moment later, they straightened up and George saw to his surprise that each was holding a shoe. They set them down at the front of the altar and stepped away. The other two men now approached the coffin. Each of them scooped something out, then walked round the coffin to stand over the shoes.

'Soil from his final resting place,' Clarissa said quietly to George.

The men allowed the soil to trickle through their hands and into the shoes.

'What is all this?' George demanded.

'The Coachman will explain.' So saying, Clarissa stepped aside, standing in a space between two of the people in the front row of the ceremony.

George watched Clarissa as she started to chant with the others – a low, guttural sound that reverberated round the chamber. But he hardly heard it. He was standing open-mouthed, staring at the two people slightly apart from the ceremony. The lean, distinctive figure of Lord Ruthven. And beside him, unmistakable even in the dim, flickering light, was Eddie.

All other eyes were on the altar, and sensing that something else was about to happen, George turned back. What was Eddie doing here? How could they escape? It was obvious that whatever was happening, it wasn't good – for either of them.

The Coachman was standing behind the altar. He was looking down into the coffin, his face shadowed. But when he looked up – as he held aloft a plain, pewter goblet – his hood fell back and the crimson light shone across and over and *through* the skull that was his head. His eyes seemed to flicker with the light from behind them.

'Welcome, my brothers and sisters,' the Coachman rasped. His voice cut through the chanting. 'We are nearing the end of a long road. Soon, I will welcome my own sister back to us. Today is a step on that journey. But however much I feel her loss, however much I yearn for her awakening, there are more important matters at hand today.'

He held out the goblet, like a priest offering it to the congregation. 'Rebirth. Awakening. Death. I bring you all three. Our trinity of blood. For the first time in four thousand years we celebrate these three together. Out of death I bring you *undeath*. Out of sleep I bring awakening. Out of life I bring you death, and so the circle of mortality is closed.'

The Coachman held the goblet high above his head and the chanting broke off. 'I give you the blood of life.' Everyone was leaning forward, eager, waiting. Clarissa's tongue flicked over her lips.

The Coachman tipped the goblet, allowing the dark red liquid to splash down into the coffin. When it was all gone, the Coachman stepped back, spreading his arms in welcome.

George felt as if his whole life was draining away. With a wrenching crunch, the side of the coffin split apart – kicked away as the body inside shifted, turned. Sat up.

Christopher Kingsley, pale and dark-eyed swung his legs over the side of the altar, and into the waiting shoes. His eyes closed for a moment, and when they opened again they were fixed unerringly on George Archer – his former pupil, his erstwhile friend.

'George,' he said with obvious delight, his voice exactly as it always had been. 'As I lived and breathed, it's George Archer.' His mouth twisted into a sort of smile. 'How kind of you to come.'

CHAPTER 15

The low chanting had begun again, but to George it was
as if he and Kingsley were utterly alone.

'I saw you – in the mortuary . . .' George said, incredulous. 'But – you're alive!'

Kingsley was amused. 'Oh no, George. I am quite
dead, I assure you.'

'But how – what . . .?'

That made Kingsley laugh out loud. 'You are so naïve,
my friend.' He stepped down from the dais, standing
right in front of George now. 'We are vampires,' he said.
'All of us. That's what the Damnation Club is, who we
are.'

'Vampires?' George was shaking his head. 'But –
that's ridiculous.'

'Better keep your voice down,' Kingsley warned him.
'Not polite to call your fellows ridiculous.'

'They're not my fellows,' George protested. 'Look,

what's really going on here? I'm not a vampire!'

'I know,' Kingsley said quietly, with a hint of sadness. 'But you will be. Weren't you listening? Out of life comes death. Out of death – undeath. You are about to start your own journey. Here and now. As we watch, as part of the great ceremony.'

George stared, open-mouthed. There was something about Kingsley's eyes – a darkness that had not been there before. Not when Kingsley had been alive. Properly alive. Could it be true? At best they were all mad. At worst . . . He turned, ready to make a run for the tunnel. Maybe he could remember the way back.

But Clarissa was standing behind him. She grabbed his arm, her grip stronger than George would have thought possible.

'Do stay,' she breathed. 'We need you. *I* need you.'

'It's your choice,' Kingsley said. 'Join us. Or die.' He shrugged as if it was a simple decision. 'I made my choice a while ago, and so far I have no regrets. I had to wait years for this moment. Years of a twilight half-life waiting for death. Tending and maintaining and designing their pumps and machinery, but all the time waiting to welcome death's cold embrace. You're lucky to come to it so quickly.'

'What's going to happen?' George demanded, his voice shaking.

The Coachman was standing beside them now. 'Kingsley must drink his first blood. Then he will truly be one of us.'

'First blood?' George swallowed, his throat dry. 'You mean – *my* blood?'

'Oh no,' Clarissa said. But George's relief was short-lived. 'After he's drunk first blood – then he'll drink yours.'

'Bring you into the family,' Kingsley added.

'Initiate you into the Damnation Club,' the Coachman rasped. He raised his voice to address the silent crowd. 'We will continue with the ceremony,' he announced. 'Bring the boy.'

'Boy?' That could only mean Eddie.

'First blood,' Clarissa said. She let go of George's arm, and brushed the dust from his shoulders. 'Join us, George. Surrender your earthly mortality and live for ever. *Rule* for ever.' She stepped away, returning to her place with the others, watching.

Kingsley led George to the altar. He was in a daze, head throbbing with the heartbeat sound of the chanting, the pumping, the blood rushing in his ears. At the altar, Lord Ruthven was waiting. He avoided looking at George. Beside him was Eddie – pale and expressionless.

'Now is the time,' the Coachman cried, standing behind the altar to address the assembly. 'Here is the place.

I have given you rebirth. I now give you awakening.'

George was staring at Eddie, willing him to come out of his waking sleep. 'Eddie,' he mouthed. 'Eddie – we have to get out of here.'

Eddie's expression did not change. But he winked.

Ruthven had stepped away, leaving Eddie on one side of the altar, and Kingsley on the other. Making it look as though he knew what he was doing and was taking part in the ceremony George walked over to stand beside Eddie.

'You all right?' George hissed out of the side of his mouth.

'Oh yeah,' Eddie murmured back, still staring ahead. 'Going to have my blood sucked out and all, but I'm fine.'

'We have to get out of here.'

'You don't say?'

Further whispered discussion was curtailed as the Coachman continued with his speech. 'We are gathered here today to witness the Great Awakening. Our Lord walks among us once more. He watches over us and keeps us safe. And when we find the Fifth Casket, our Lord will once more be complete. And He will take his rightful place as our ruler. He will reign over us, as our supreme sovereign.'

The Coachman had spread his arms. As he finished,

he brought them together, pointing down the length of the chamber towards the far wall, drenched in darkness.

The lights sputtered and flared. The walls glowed red as the lamplight seemed to creep along them, into the darkness.

'Oh my cripes,' Eddie said out loud.

The whole assembly turned hungrily to watch as the light reached the back wall and illuminated the horror that hung there.

'Behold Orabis!' the Coachman cried. 'He is awake. Beyond the Lord of the Undead.'

The wall was a mass of criss-crossing pipes and cables and tubes. The sound of the pumps seemed to grow as the light increased – a great heartbeat of sound that emanated from the creature attached to the wall.

It was seated on a throne of wood and metalwork. Surrounded by valves and metal tubes. The thin pipes that lined the wall joined and connected before feeding into the creature's body.

Like a grotesque parody of sovereignty, Orabis stared out over the assembly. The wall ran red behind him. Viscous fluid dripped from the joints in the pipes and seeped from the wounds where they connected into his body. Dark eyes stared out from the emaciated face. The ragged remains of cloth wrappings hung decaying and rotting from the dark, dry, desiccated skin.

From the Hall of Machines behind him came the sound of the steam pumps as they hissed and spat and forced the blood round the system, through the body.

'Oh, my God!' George was unable to look away from the horrific sight.

'Your god indeed,' the Coachman said. 'That is why you are here. You will serve our Lord Orabis. You will help maintain and service the systems that keep him alive.'

'But – why?' George could hear the tremor in his own voice. 'What sort of existence is that?'

'He needs blood,' the Coachman said simply. 'Enough to awaken him at the Unwrapping ceremony. Just enough for him to get to the coach. Now he grows stronger with every moment, every drop, absorbing the life force, gaining in power.'

'You know more about the new technologies than I do,' Kingsley said. He sounded as if he was discussing a mundane engineering project. 'The newer steam pumps. The possibilities offered by electricity. Your help will be invaluable, George. I know how the system works and what is required. Together we will be such a team.'

The Coachman turned to face the assembly, to face his Lord. 'The time is now!' he said again. 'The place is here! Soon our Lord will again walk among us. The long years, centuries, millennia of waiting will be over. You know my sister and I have abstained from the blood of life since our Lord was so cruelly taken from us. But I tell you, my friends, soon my Lord and I will drink together.'

'My loyal, steadfast servant.' The voice was rich and soft. It seemed to emanate from the blood-soaked walls. The Lord of the Undead's eyes were black pools, staring across at George and Eddie. 'You have waited so long while I was lost and slept. But the waiting is almost over. Soon all my people, even Belamis your sister, will awaken to hear my will.'

'As soon as we have the Fifth Casket, my Lord, and you are whole once more.' The Coachman bowed. 'We do you reverence.'

The whole assembly slowly bowed their heads. Opposite George, Christopher Kingsley also bowed.

'What you waiting for?' Eddie whispered in the silence. 'This is our chance to get out of here.'

They wouldn't be bowing for long. But Eddie was right. If they waited any longer, it would be too late. Heads bowed, as if joining in the ceremony, George and Eddie backed away from the altar and stepped down from the dais.

The chanting had started again. The low murmurs of the crowd echoing the sound of the pumps, growing slowly louder and more enthusiastic. The Coachman was speaking over it, but George wasn't listening.

As soon as they were out of the main light and in shadow, Eddie and George hurried for the nearest tunnel. George had been afraid he might be lost down here for ever. Now that seemed the better option.

They were almost at the tunnel when the voice of Orabis cut through the chanting and the words of the Coachman.

'Stop them!'

George looked at Eddie. The boy's wide eyes probably mirrored his own.

'Run!' they both said together.

George's feet splashed in puddles of thick, dark liquid. The lights on the walls threw flickering crimson shadows across the tunnel. Their footsteps echoed another thump-thump-thump of sound.

'You know the way out?' Eddie yelled.

'No. Do you?'

'Not me. I came by coach.'

'Why? What are you doing here?' George demanded.

From behind them came the sound of more feet – running.

'Thought I was being clever,' Eddie said, a bit sheepishly. 'Wish I hadn't bothered.'

Their own shadows chased them along the tunnel

walls, distorted and grotesque parodies of the human form. They skidded to a halt as they reached a junction with two other tunnels.

'I don't remember this,' George said, hands on knees and bent double to catch his breath.

'Me neither. Want to guess?'

'That way.' George pointed to the tunnel off to the right.

Almost at once, they heard the rattle of wheels on stone, and saw the dark shape of the Coachman's black carriage hurtling down the tunnel towards them.

'Or maybe this way?' Eddie suggested.

George didn't waste breath agreeing. He grabbed Eddie's hand and they ran for all they were worth.

They could hear the carriage gaining on them. The sound of their ragged breathing might have been the snorting of the horses bearing down on them. George risked a backward glance as the tunnel curved slightly. He saw carriage and horses getting closer. The Coachman on the driver's seat, whip raised. The shadow of the carriage on the tunnel wall – a shadow that was *just* the carriage. No Coachman. No horses.

'In here!'

A deeper shadow in the wall ahead resolved itself into a side passage, too narrow for the carriage to follow. Eddie dragged George inside, and they stood panting in the blackness. Had the Coachman seen them?

The carriage rattled past, and George breathed a heavy sigh. 'Well done, Eddie.'

Eddie was grinning in the near blackness. 'Reckon we'll be safe here for a minute or two, till we get our breath back at least.'

Behind Eddie the passageway was dark and unlit. There was just a pale smudged shape in the gloom. The shape moved, came closer, resolved itself into a face. The mouth opened in a smile, to reveal the sharp teeth within.

'Safe?' The voice was deep and dark. 'Do you really think so?'

CHAPTER 16

The tall, dark figure stepped forward, allowing the erratic light from the tunnel beyond to fall across him. 'Nowhere is safe from Orabis and the Coachman.' It was Lord Ruthven.

'You going to turn us in, then?' Eddie asked defiantly.

Ruthven shook his head.

'Why not?' George wanted to know.

'Cos he's sick of it,' Eddie said. 'I saw his face during some of that. When I wasn't acting mesmerised.'

'There comes a point,' Lord Ruthven said quietly. 'Even vampires have morals. Well, some of us.'

'And what's with this vampire business?' Eddie asked. 'I thought they were monsters in penny dreadfuls that drank people's blood and turned into bats, or something.'

'Later,' George said. 'Let's get out of here first. Then we can find Sir William – he'll know.'

'He will indeed,' Ruthven said. 'But it may be too late for him.'

Eddie remembered what the Coachman had said. 'Been dealt with,' he echoed.

'What do you mean?' George demanded.

'I am afraid he may be dead already. Or undead.'

'Undead?'

'He means he's been turned into a vampire,' Eddie said. 'That's right, isn't it?'

'Sir William has been bitten. His blood is tainted.'

'So what do we do?' George's voice was trembling. 'First Kingsley, now Sir William.'

'Charlie too,' Eddie murmured. 'Friend of mine,' he explained. 'We got to get out of here, that's the first thing we do. We got to find Sir William. And Liz.'

'Liz?' George was aghast. 'What about Liz?'

'You mean Miss Oldfield?' Ruthven said.

'Of course. But how is she involved in all this?'

'She is to be –' There was a sound from the main tunnel close by, and Ruthven stopped abruptly. 'You must go,' he whispered. 'The Coachman's horses will smell you out if you stay down here.' He pushed past Eddie and George and looked out into the tunnel.

'How do we get out?' George asked.

'Go back that way,' Ruthven pointed back the way they had come. 'At the intersection, take the second tunnel on your left. That will bring you back to the Damnation Club.'

Eddie asked: 'But, aren't you coming too?'

Ruthven shook his head. 'The Coachman will soon be back. I shall delay him.'

'Is that dangerous?' George said.

'I am already dead,' Ruthven told him. 'The worst they can do is to kill me again.' But from the tremor in his voice, Eddie guessed that was not true.

The tunnel was empty, but it still resonated with the dull throb of the distant pumps. George and Eddie hurried back to the junction leaving Lord Ruthven hiding in the shadows. The low sound of the steam pumps was joined by a closer noise – the rattle of a carriage.

'Better get a move on,' Eddie said.

They started to run, the noise growing closer behind them. Looking back, Eddie could see the shadowy outline of the carriage approaching. The horses were galloping along the tunnel, their hoofs echoing off the walls and splashing through the viscous puddles.

'Not far now,' George assured Eddie as they ran.

Sure enough, they were soon at the junction. Second tunnel on the left, Ruthven had said.

But as they turned into it, both of them could see Clarissa standing at the head of a dozen figures. Her scarlet cloak glowed in the uncertain light.

'Not that way,' George decided, dragging Eddie back.

The carriage was almost on them. Their only option was to take the first tunnel and try to outrun the Coachman's horses. But Eddie knew it was a matter of moments before the carriage reached them and ran them down.

Flickering lights flashed past as they ran for their lives. The damp from the floor was seeping through Eddie's shoes. He skidded, almost fell, caught his balance and ran on.

'What's this?' George pulled up sharply as they emerged into an enormous area.

Eddie recognised it as the huge chamber where he had first arrived in the carriage. Where Kingsley's coffin had dropped down on to the carriage.

'Keep running,' he yelled.

But it was too late. The horses were charging straight at them, just yards away now. At the last moment, Eddie pushed George to one side of the tunnel opening and dived the other way himself. They both went sprawling as the carriage exploded out of the tunnel between them. The horses snorted and turned, bringing the carriage in a wide arc within the cavern.

'Where now?' George shouted.

'This way!' Eddie was sprinting towards the area where the roof was lower – the area below the graveyard.

'But there's no way out,' George yelled as he followed. 'All the tunnels are back this way.'

'Trust me!'

The engraved slabs of the roof rushed past as Eddie reached the lower section. Names of those above, sleeping, Eddie realised. Or those who had been removed and were perhaps now searching for him. So many names . . .

'Where are we going?' George demanded.

Behind them the horses had completed their turn and were charging again – right at Eddie and George.

'Up there.' Eddie pointed at the roof. At the dark rectangle where Kingsley's coffin had fallen through on to the carriage. The floor beneath was scattered with earth and stone.

George stared at it. 'You are joking.'

'You got a better plan? Give us a bunk up.'

'But where's it go? There's no light coming in – no way out.'

'We've got to dig.'

'What?'

There was no time for argument or explanation. George stooped down and made a cradle for Eddie's foot by lacing his fingers together. As soon as Eddie stepped into it, George hoisted him up.

Eddie managed to get his arms into the hole above. His head was in cloying, earthy darkness – inside the grave. He got his elbows over the edge, pulling himself up further.

A slab of stone broke away from the roof as Eddie put his weight of it. The stone crumbled and fell. It shattered on the ground ten feet below.

'Come on!' George yelled.

The carriage was almost on him. In a moment it would run down George, and crash into Eddie's flailing legs.

Finally, Eddie managed to get a good grip and hauled himself up into the hole in the roof, feeling the earth crumbling at the edges. The Coachman's whip cracked past Eddie's legs as he pulled them clear, thwacking into the side of the hole. Eddie could see George hurling himself to one side as the carriage almost caught him.

The horses were turning already, coming back.

George was on his feet, arms raised, leaping for the hole in the roof. But it was too high. Eddie braced himself and leaned out of the grave. George's fingers brushed against Eddie's hands.

'Higher!' he called.

The carriage was coming back.

George backed away – where was he going?

Then, with the carriage racing towards him once more, George ran towards Eddie. He took off, leaping high into the air. His hands smacked into Eddie's and like a trapeze artist George was swaying beneath the roof. Eddie struggled to take the weight, to pull him up. He could feel the ground – the roof – giving way under his knees.

Clods of earth showered down from the ceiling and scattered across the top of the carriage as it came to a halt beneath the hole. The Coachman was climbing back along the carriage roof towards George and Eddie.

But with the carriage there, George was able to brace his legs on its top and force himself upwards to join Eddie.

'What is this?'

'Your mate's grave,' Eddie told him. 'Get digging!'

They thrust their hands up into the soil above them, forcing a way through the hard-packed earth. Beneath them the cavern roof was giving way under their weight. The Coachman's bone hands reached into the grave, scrabbling round as he grabbed for them.

Eddie braced himself against the crumbling stone slabs and forced himself upright. His head sank into the ground above, but he kept pushing. Not yet shored up by an engraved slab of stone for Kingsley, the earth was held in place only by its own weight. It fell away as Eddie forced his way through. How far up did he need to go? How deep was the grave? Soil and dirt clogged his nostrils and worked into his mouth. He was choking, gasping, drowning in dust.

Then suddenly he could taste fresh air. He opened his eyes, and found his head was poking up into the night.

Mist swirled round the nearby gravestones. And a hand grabbed his leg.

With a yelp, Eddie forced his hands and arms upwards and heaved himself out. The hand was still tight on his ankle. An arm followed. And then – George.

'Oh, thank God it's you.'

'He's got me,' George gasped. 'Pull, for goodness' sake.' Even as he said it, he started to disappear into the ground, hauled back by the Coachman below.

Eddie heaved at George's arms, but it did no good. Slowly but surely George was being pulled into the collapsing earth.

Then suddenly there was a rasping, muffled cry from below the ground. The sound of a heavy stone shattering on the roof of the carriage as it fell. The earth round the grave collapsed, leaving a dark hole. George shot forward out of the ground and he and Eddie rolled across the damp grass.

'I think the whole area of roof gave way,' George said. 'There's just the turf keeping it together up here.'

'That won't stop him for long,' Eddie said.

Together they ran through the gathering fog, away from the empty grave.

Orabis, Lord of the Undead, looked down at the silent

assembly. Before him stood the Coachman and Christopher Kingsley, their heads bowed in penitence.

'They have escaped, my Lord.'

'Nothing will deter us from the great task,' Orabis declared. 'Soon we will rise and feed, and rule this Empire.' He raised his dark eyes towards the roof.

The whole assembly also looked upwards. All except one. The tall, gaunt man held by Clarissa and Sir Harrison Judd.

Lord Ruthven was pushed forwards. He stumbled in front of Orabis, standing between the Coachman and Kingsley.

'We have been betrayed,' the Coachman said. 'What should we do with those who do not share your vision, my Lord?'

'We shall release them from that vision. And from this earthly life.' Orabis twisted in the grotesque framework of pipes until he was staring down at Lord Ruthven. 'My powers have been sapped by the long sleep, and without the casket I can never be whole.' His face twisted into a mixture of snarl and smile. 'But taste what power I have. You betrayed us – you betrayed me. And you will pay for that.'

The Lord of the Undead's eyes seemed to shine, glittering in the lamplight. Lord Ruthven gasped and shuddered, held immobile in the gaze of Orabis. Clarissa and Harrison Judd let go of their captive and stepped away, watching in fascination.

Ruthven's whole body was shaking. His hair thinned and his cheeks sagged. He was crumpling up, collapsing to his knees as the life was drawn from him. His scream was a thin, pitiful sound as he finally fell forwards.

For a moment there was silence. Clarissa drew the toe of her shoe slowly through the pile of grey dust that had been Lord Ruthven, scattering it across the cavern floor as the chanting began again.

'Those pumps must feed blood into his body from storage tanks somewhere,' George said.

They were nearing the British Museum, both quickening their step as they approached.

'I can guess where they get the blood,' Eddie said. 'Lucky we didn't get ours added to the brew.'

'But why do they need so many engines, so many pumps?' George wondered. 'Perhaps they really do pump out river water if the tunnels flood.'

'Or perhaps they need blood for something else too,' Eddie suggested.

George grimaced. 'They're like great steam hearts, pumping the lifeblood round the system.' He shivered. 'Maybe they ventilate the tunnels. I guess even vampires need to breathe.'

'You reckon?'

'They don't need pumps like that though. You know,' George said as they started down the corridor towards the Department of Unclassified Artefacts, 'to ventilate the Houses of Parliament they just light a fire.'

'How's that help?'

'Hot air rises through the chimney in the middle and that draws in fresher colder air through the clock tower and the other towers. It's a terrific system. There are vents and shafts all through the Palace of Westminster to make it work. All planned in when it was rebuilt.'

Eddie stifled a yawn. 'Fancy.'

The door to Sir William's office was standing open. George and Eddie looked at each other, both suddenly anxious. George carefully, slowly, pushed the door fully open.

The body lay motionless behind the desk.

'Sir William?' George exclaimed. 'Get some water,' he told Eddie.

'Might be too late for that. Look at him.'

The old man's white shirt was a spattered red mess. Sir William's white hair was tangled and soaked in sweat. A dark scar was burned across the blood-slick wound in his neck – the shape of a cross.

As George watched, the pale old man's eyelids flickered. His lips parted slightly in a weak smile. Revealing his strong, white teeth.

CHAPTER 17

'He's all right,' Eddie said with relief. 'Isn't he?' he added anxiously as Sir William struggled to sit up.

'I hope so.' George was backing away warily.

'Of course I'm all right,' Sir William protested. He touched the wound at his neck gingerly and winced with the pain. 'Though I could do with a glass of water. And perhaps I could impose upon one or both of you to help me bathe this and examine the damage.'

'You were bitten,' George said.

'Yes.'

'By a vampire thing,' Eddie added.

'Indeed.'

'Is that . . . dangerous?' George asked.

'Extremely. But a good splash of holy water and a makeshift silver cross work wonders. Miracles even. Now stop fussing about, we have a lot to do.'

Sir William's strength quickly returned and he was soon back to his usual self. The wound seemed to have healed over, cauterised by the silver and holy water. By the time Eddie had finished recounting his adventures at the workhouse, the cross-shaped scar just above his collar was the only sign that Sir William had been attacked.

'They take the unfortunate children, and others, who will not be missed,' Sir William summarised. 'The police are discouraged from investigating when the bodies are found. *If* the bodies are found. But I imagine it doesn't take much to persuade them to focus their attentions on more worthy causes.' He shook his head sadly.

'This John Remick might be able to tell us more. If he's still at my house,' George said.

'Too risky. I imagine your house is being watched.'

'And Remick will have legged it off out of there if he knows what's good for him,' Eddie said. 'He won't go back to Pearce at the workhouse, neither.'

It was George's turn to tell them his story. He described his visit to the Damnation Club and the masked ball. 'I didn't realise you were there too, Eddie.'

'You'd have told me off for being out late.'

'Perhaps we could confine ourselves to the relevant narrative?' Sir William suggested. 'Time may be of the essence, but leave nothing out, any small thing may be a clue.'

'So,' George said as he finished his story, 'what are they planning and how do we stop them?'

'Why not let them get on with it and keep out of the way?' Eddie said.

'I doubt if that is an option,' Sir William said quietly. 'First, they know that for all their secrecy we three are aware of their existence. And second, I know from my own discussions with Lord Ruthven that matters are coming to a head. The status quo – even if it were acceptable – can no longer be maintained. The waking of this Orabis seems to be a pivotal moment.'

'It was horrific,' George recalled with a shudder. 'The way he was plumbed into the pipes. The way they seemed to be keeping him alive.'

'Undead,' Eddie remembered. '*Lord of the Undead* that Coachman called him.'

'Vampires are said to be undead,' Sir William explained. 'Our problem will be separating the real truth from the myths and stories that have grown up – that they have fostered and encouraged.'

'We can start with Orabis,' George said. 'Maybe Xavier Hemming knew the truth. Maybe that's why he had the mummy here in the first place.'

'An excellent notion, and a good theory. But we know

from the catalogue that Hemming did not commit himself to paper.'

'What do you mean?' Eddie asked.

'There's no notes of any use about the mummy,' George said.

'Doesn't mean he didn't write something down. Somewhere else,' Eddie said. 'What about those jars and stuff in the crate? Maybe he wrote about them.'

'No, he didn't.'

'But Eddie is right,' Sir William said thoughtfully. 'We may simply be looking in the wrong place. You say that Orabis was hailed by the others as Lord of the Undead? Lord Ruthven mentioned several possible sources of information, including the Book of the Undead.'

'And what's that when it's at home?'

Sir William rubbed absently at the scar on his neck. 'I have no idea. There is an Egyptian Book of the Dead. So perhaps it relates to Orabis in some way.'

'They've been around a long time, these vampires,' Eddie said.

'Indeed.'

'This fifth casket they're after,' George said. 'Is that connected too?'

'In what way?'

'You said Lord Ruthven was after a fifth jar, from the mummy.'

'But there isn't one,' Sir William pointed out.

'Unless it's hidden,' Eddie said. 'Like whatever this Hemming knew about the mummy.'

'He hid it all,' Sir William realised. His eyes were sparkling behind his glasses. 'Xavier Hemming *knew*. And he planned for this. He kept the mummy here, hidden.'

'Only somehow they found it,' George said.

'And he concealed the fifth jar or casket, whatever it is. He knew they needed that too.'

'But why? What's in it?'

'If we knew that, Eddie my friend, then we would be in a lot stronger position than we are now.'

'So, let's find out.'

'It isn't that easy,' George said sternly.

'Oh but it may be,' Sir William declared, standing up. 'If we find the Book of the Undead, that may be the clue we need to bring it all together. It's certainly important.'

'And where do we find that?' George asked.

'In Hemming's meticulous catalogues – where else?'

They found the entry in the catalogue of *Writings, Ancient*. Sir William led the way down into the archive beneath the Museum.

'Does either of you read ancient Egyptian hieroglyphics?' he asked as they made their way through the mass of crates and cabinets, shelves and cupboards.

'Er, not me,' George confessed. 'Eddie?' he asked with a wink.

'Haven't got to that yet in school.'

'Pity, pity. I have a smattering, but we may need more than that. I wonder if we can trust that fool Mason in Egyptology. Or our old friend Brinson, come to that.'

The cupboard was full of rolled parchment scrolls. There was a list of them glued on the inside of the wooden door, complete with the catalogue numbers.

'AS-931,' Sir William murmured as he traced his finger along the scrolls. Each had a small tag attached by string. 'AS-931 . . . Does not appear to be here,' he announced at last.

Eddie leaned past him, reaching into the cupboard. 'There's something jammed at the back here,' he said. He pulled out a dusty book bound in cracked leather.

'Hardly ancient Egyptian,' George said.

'No, no, let me see.' Sir William took it from Eddie.

The spine creaked as he opened the book. It was a notebook, the pages filled with the distinctive copperplate handwriting that George knew belonged to Xavier Hemming.

'Oh yes,' Sir William breathed. 'Well done, Eddie. We may not have the original – perhaps Lord Ruthven found that when he had the mummy itself removed. But this is Hemming's own translation of the scrolls stored in this section of the archive.'

'Does it include . . .?' George's voice tailed off. He could see his answer in Sir William's smile.

'Extracts from the Book of the Undead, translated by Xavier Hemming himself. And look – he has drawn a line down the margin of one passage in particular. I think, my friends, that this is the section he would want us to look at.'

Eddie's voice was little more than a whisper. 'Go on, then. Tell us what it says.'

Sir William adjusted his glasses, cleared his throat, and began to read.

And a third time they buried Orabis deep in the ground, covering his grave with sand of the desert and stones from the mountain. But again he rose, clawing his way through the earth with his bare hands. And this time the suffering was even greater and his vengeance was meted out on all of the people.

The vengeance of Orabis was so great that Pharaoh himself lost his first-born to the blood-sickness. And great was the lamentation of mighty Pharaoh who called on the gods of Egypt to rise against the usurper Orabis, so-called Lord of the Undead.

And so Anubis, it is said, gave power and wisdom to Pharaoh's daughter Heba who lured Orabis to the place of death. For even an Undead Lord can be killed here if his very heart be taken from him. Or else when Thoth weighed the heart of the Undead, the god would find him lacking and send him back to the World of Men, and Orabis would return.

The soldiers and priests fell upon Orabis and did bind him, like an embalmed mummy. They wrapped sand from his homeland between the bandages that he might sleep. They wrapped the herb that some call garlic round his limbs that he might not move. They hid from his sight behind polished silver to avoid his retribution should the Lord of the Undead rise again to visit the blood-sickness on them.

Anubis spake to Pharaoh's daughter. He told her that Thoth would receive the immortal soul of Orabis and would bind him for ever in sleep if his heart be cut out. For only when his heart no longer *beats and is destroyed or separated from his body can a creature such as Orabis truly die.*

They embalmed him according to ancient lore. They prepared Canopic Jars as is the custom. But as well as the lungs and the liver and the intestines and the stomach being placed in jars fashioned after the sons of Horus, a fifth jar was prepared. And this was in the form of Nehebkau the Scorpion, Guardian of the Gates to the Underworld. And into this jar was placed the heart of Orabis, removed from his chest by Heba daughter of Pharaoh even as it still beat and pumped the lifeblood.

The jar was sealed and buried. And Orabis was also sealed, in a sarcophagus lined with silver, and he was buried unmarked in the desert sand from which – as Pharaoh and his people prayed – he would never return unless his heart be restored and the blood once more flow through his wicked veins . . .

Eddie sat on one of the sealed crates, kicking his legs as he and George listened to Sir William.

'There the translation ends.'

'Good story,' Eddie said. 'Guess we know what's in

that fifth jar now.'

'The vampire's heart,' George said. 'Do we believe that? It sounds incredible.'

'But it would explain why he is plumbed into a system of pipes and pumps. To replace the heart he no longer has beating in his chest.'

'And they're after this jar so they can give him his heart back?' Eddie asked.

'It would seem so.'

Eddie grimaced. 'Maybe we should let them have it.'

'Absolutely not,' Sir William insisted. 'We can only begin to guess at the horrors Orabis would visit upon this city – possibly the world – if he were made whole again. For the moment he is weakened and ineffective. Which gives us time.'

'But time for what?' Eddie wondered.

'What indeed. Now, this Book of the Undead tells us several things. It was written by someone who had direct experience of dealing with Orabis, and whose motivation in writing must have been to warn others. So this isn't propaganda and lies. It is the truth, at least so far as the author understood it.'

'And that helps?' George wondered.

'It helps because it describes how Orabis was defeated. Now, we don't know where or what this place of death might be. But we do know that a vampire needs earth from his home close by when he sleeps. Possibly in actual contact. Ruthven told me that also.'

'And there's mention of the silver that lines the coffin,' George realised.

'More than that. It says they hid behind silver. Behind mirrors, perhaps?'

'And vampires have no reflection,' Eddie said. 'Charlie didn't show in the window, but my reflection was there. Right creepy, it was.'

'They have a special relationship with silver, and with light. Again, Ruthven mentioned this and the translation seems to confirm it. No reflection, an aversion to silver and to bright light – especially sunlight.'

George snapped his fingers as something else occurred to him. 'And they don't appear in photographs!'

Sir William smiled and nodded. 'Yes, well done.'

'So, we've got the evidence,' Eddie said. 'Let's go to the coppers. Let the police handle it.'

'A possible course of action,' Sir William admitted. 'But one which I fear is doomed to failure.'

'And why's that, then?'

'Because we know from George here, that the Commissioner of the Metropolitan Police, Sir Harrison Judd, is a member of the Damnation Club. And Sir Harrison was at the Unwrapping, remember. It was he who nudged Brinson so he cut himself and the blood fell on the mummy.'

'But then, who can we trust?' George asked. 'We know some of the people. We saw some at the ceremony in the catacombs. But the Damnation Club has members from the highest ranks of society. There are rumours that the Home Secretary . . .' He broke off, shaking his head. 'We can't do anything, can we? They have people everywhere.'

'Even in the Museum and the Royal Society,' Sir William said quietly. 'Like Lord Ruthven. I am afraid we have no way of even knowing who is our enemy.'

'Course we do,' Eddie said. 'We take photographs and see who shows up in them.'

'Yes, that might work,' Sir William agreed. 'A good idea, young man. Don't you think so, George?'

But George was looking anxious. 'I just thought – Eddie said the Coachman mentioned that Liz was not a threat to them. And when I was at the ball at the Damnation Club – I thought I saw her there. You don't think . . .?'

Eddie almost laughed at the suggestion. 'Nah – course not. Liz? She couldn't be.'

'Unlikely, I agree. But we should make certain immediately that she is all right,' Sir William said. 'And we'll take a mirror.'

CHAPTER 18

As soon as Liz opened the door, George could see there was something wrong. The early morning sun had struggled through the London smog and Liz blinked as she stood in its full glare.

Sir William had a small mirror concealed in his hand, and angled it to look briefly at Liz's reflection. He nodded with relief at George and Eddie, and pocketed the mirror.

'I'm sorry,' George said. 'It's very early. We should come back later. Your father will . . .' He broke off as Liz turned away. 'What is it? What's wrong?'

It was not until they were inside, sitting in the small front room, that Liz told them of her father's sudden decline and death. George immediately moved to sit beside her, holding her hands in his. Sir William excused himself to make tea, and Eddie fidgeted with embarrassment.

'Perhaps we should not have come,' George said. 'If you'd like us to leave you in peace . . .?'

Liz shook her head. 'No. No, I am glad you are here. It seems a long time since I last saw you. So much has happened since, with Father and Marie and everything.'

'Lots been happening to us too,' Eddie put in.

'Later,' George mouthed at him.

'Suit yourself,' Eddie said. 'He *was* very old,' he told Liz.

'Eddie!' George snapped back. He felt awful that he had not been there for Liz when she needed him.

But Liz smiled thinly. 'Thank you, Eddie. He did seem it, though he wasn't so old really. Just frail. And I suppose I always expected . . .' She turned away, biting her lip. 'He seems so much better now. So relaxed. At peace.'

Eddie looked alarmed. 'You ain't still got him here, have you?'

'No. He is laid out in the family crypt. At St Bardolph's. Just until the funeral.'

'I am so sorry,' George said. 'You should have let me know. I could have . . .'

But Liz was shaking her head. 'I've been all right. Really I have. I am in a play at the Parthenon Theatre.'

'With Henry Malvern?' George asked. Liz nodded, and he felt his heart sink.

'He has been so very understanding,' she said. 'Such a comfort.'

'So, you didn't need me then,' George murmured.

If Liz heard him, she said nothing. Her voice had taken on a new strength as she described the play. Sir William returned with a pot of tea and poured a cup for each of them.

'And with Marie Cuttler taken ill, it seems I am to play the lead role of Marguerite,' Liz finished.

'That is excellent news,' Sir William enthused. 'And despite your recent loss – for which I offer sincere condolences and sympathy – I am delighted to find you so well.'

'I wish Marie was well,' Liz told him. 'It's so strange. So like father. And so like the play.'

'The play?' Eddie said. 'What play?'

'*The Lady of the Camellias*.'

Sir William set down his tea cup and leaned forward in his chair. 'But *The Lady of the Camellias*, surely, is about a woman who dies from consumption. She weakens, grows pale, fades away. The white plague.'

'That's right,' Liz said. 'I think perhaps that is what Marie has. A wasting disease.'

George caught Sir William's eye and could tell they were both thinking the same thing. 'Could be coincidence,' he said.

'This play is occupying a lot of your time,' Sir William said.

'Of course.'

'Which would not be the case if Marie Cuttler were well enough to play the leading role.'

'True.'

Eddie leaped to his feet. 'Here – you don't think . . .?'

Sir William waved him to silence. 'I think nothing. But I would like to meet Marie Cuttler. Possibly I can help.'

'Do you think so?' Liz asked. 'Of course, I shall take you to her hotel. Though it is early.'

'Straight away, please,' Sir William said, in a tone that left none of them any illusions about the urgency. 'Oh, and if you have any, bring some garlic.'

Liz frowned. 'I can look in the pantry. I think we have some.'

'Why garlic?' Eddie asked.

'A traditional defence. And they used it to bind Orabis in his coffin, remember.'

'I can nick some from the market,' Eddie offered. George glared at him. 'What?' Eddie demanded. 'Important, isn't it?'

'No, no, no,' Sir William shook his head. 'Miss Oldfield – on the way I shall explain what is happening. But for now please find any garlic you can. And if your father had a silver crucifix, that would also help.'

The hotel room was in near darkness although the sun was shining brightly outside. The curtains were drawn, and the lamps were turned down low.

After Liz had quickly introduced them all to Marie, Sir William sent Eddie and George to the hotel kitchens to ask for more garlic. 'How long have you been ill?' he asked as he felt for Marie's pulse.

'Who can say?' she replied weakly. 'When does tiredness become an illness? I'm just exhausted. I'm not as young as I used to be.'

Sir William reached up to tilt Marie's head gently to one side. The high collar of her nightgown reached up to her chin, and he regarded it suspiciously for a moment.

'Something wrong?' Marie asked. 'Are you a doctor?'

'Oh no. No to both questions.' He stepped back, and gave her a reassuring smile. 'As you say, tired and under the weather. Would you like me to open the curtains? It's such a lovely day and I'm sure the sunshine will do you good.'

'No,' Marie said quickly. 'Thank you, but the bright light gives me a headache.'

'You do look very pale,' Liz said.

'Oh I agree,' Sir William said quickly. 'Do you have a mirror? I think you should see just how pale you look.'

Sir William watched carefully as Marie looked at

herself in a small hand mirror from the dressing table. 'I do look so tired,' she said. 'So old.'

'Perhaps some fresh air would help . . .?' Liz suggested.

Marie shook her head, passing the mirror back to Sir William. 'Please. It's kind of you to come, but I am tired. Always so tired.'

'You get some sleep,' Sir William told her. 'I'm sure it's the best thing. And I'm sure you will recover soon. But if you will allow, I'd like to put some garlic out in the room.'

'Garlic? What on earth for?'

'The aroma clears the nasal passages and aids the breathing. I think you will find it most efficacious.'

'I'm sure it will help,' Liz said.

'Very well then.'

George and Eddie were back with several garlic bulbs. Together they separated the cloves and Sir William cut them in half with a pocket knife. He held one half clove to the outside of the door, squeezing it and smearing a cross with the oil. They arranged the other pieces inside the door and along the window sill.

By the time they finished, Marie had lapsed into sleep.

'Place your father's crucifix on the pillow, close to her,' Sir William told Liz. 'Let's hope she will sleep peacefully now.'

'Do you really think this is necessary?' Liz asked. Sir William had given a brief account of their various adventures and experiences in the cab on the way over to the hotel.

'I do,' he said. 'And let us hope it is enough.'

The woman in the bed stirred. She cried out in her sleep, and was suddenly awake. She sat up, looking round.

'Are you there?'

The effort of talking made her cough, and she collapsed back on to the pillow. As she caught her breath, she reached for the cord hanging by the side of the bed.

'Have my friends gone?' Marie asked the man who answered the bell.

'They have, ma'am. I believe you were asleep and they did not wish to disturb you.'

'They mean well.'

'I'm sure they do. Is there anything else?'

'Yes, please. As I say – they mean well. But the smell of this garlic is making me cough so much. Please have it removed. All of it. Every bit. And wash down the front of the door.'

Only when all the garlic had been cleared away did Marie turn her attention to the crucifix on the pillow beside her. She reached for it hesitantly. Touched it. Felt the burning heat and pulled her hand back. Then she folded the pillow in half, smothering the crucifix. She picked up the folded pillow and hurled it into the corner of the room.

Exhausted by the effort, she fell back.

'Well done, my darling,' the figure standing close beside her said. 'You will soon be well again, I promise.' He leaned over the bed. 'You have my word.' She pulled down the collar of the nightgown as his lips brushed gently against it.

'My word,' he whispered. 'Written in blood.'

CHAPTER 19

The archive beneath the Museum was enormous. Liz had never been down here before and she looked round in fascination. The fact that both George and Eddie seemed to take it for granted brought home to her how much she had missed them both. If only she had discovered this amazing place with them. But now there wasn't time to marvel at it, and the initial excitement was tinged with concern for Marie and sadness for her father.

'So why didn't we look in this notebook before?' Eddie asked.

Sir William took down a large volume from a high shelf. The books were so tightly packed he had to tease it out gently. 'We checked the catalogues, which describe the objects that Hemming kept in his collection.' He snapped the book shut and replaced it on the shelf, reaching for the next volume. 'But Hemming *might* have included more information in his original notes. Now the notebooks, unlike the catalogues, are in date order. He listed things as he acquired them. So, knowing from the catalogue the date he got hold of the other jars . . .'

He was already looking through the next volume of Hemming's notebooks. 'Ah, yes. Here we are.' The smile froze on Sir William's face.

'What is it?' Liz asked.

'I think we can safely say that Hemming did indeed possess all five jars.'

'So what's it say?' Eddie asked.

By way of answer, Sir William tilted the book so they could all see. 'Nothing.'

The page was torn across, the bottom half missing.

'Another dead end,' George said.

'May I look?' Liz asked. It was probably no help, but she had noticed that the writing was smudged. As if Hemming had written his entry hurriedly and then closed the book without first blotting the ink. The notes about the mummy were smeared and had left several small inky stains on the opposite page.

Further down the page were more small blots of ink. Faint, but visible. On the opposite side to where the page had been torn out.

'Look,' Liz said, putting the book down on a crate

and pointing to the ink stains. 'We should have borrowed Marie's mirror.'

Sir William coughed, looking slightly embarrassed. 'Actually, I have one with me. I brought it along in case Marie did not possess a mirror, so as to, er . . . Well, never mind.' He produced a small mirror, just a few inches across, from his pocket and held it edge-on across the page.

'Can you read it?' Eddie wanted to know. 'What's it say? Give us a look!'

Liz struggled to make anything out from the smudged ink stains. 'That might be "jar" I suppose. This smudged line – it looks like he crossed something out. But there's no way of knowing what.'

'What about this?' George wondered, pointing to a cluster of stains in the margin.

'That says "secret", I think. And that might be "grave".'

Sir William had taken off his glasses and was peering closely into the mirror. 'I think you are right. I think this is a note Hemming scrawled after he crossed out the entry. He was saying he would take the secret – the secret of the fifth jar, I imagine – to the grave.'

'And then he decided that wasn't enough,' George said. 'Just crossing out the information. So he tore out the page.'

'Probably burned it,' Eddie said with a sniff of disappointment. 'At least the ink shows up in the mirror,' he added with a sudden grin.

Liz handed the mirror back to Sir William. 'You know I was in need of a small mirror the other day,' she said, remembering. 'When I found Father. I knew at once – I think you do. But I had to be sure.' She could feel the tears welling up in her eyes again. 'Oh dear.'

George put his arm round her shoulder. 'It's all right.'

'I had to be sure,' she said again, dabbing at her eyes with her handkerchief. 'I found a mirror, and I held it close to his mouth. And I hoped, prayed, that the mirror would mist over. That he was still breathing. But he just faded away.' She trembled suddenly as she remembered. 'It was like his soul had gone.'

'The memories won't always be sad ones,' Sir William said gently.

'It was as if he didn't exist,' Liz went on quietly. 'No breath on the mirror. He was so faint. I could see the pillow and the bed sheets through him. It was as though he was being taken from me as I watched. His reflection fading almost to nothing.'

George pulled away his arm so suddenly that Liz looked up.

Sir William was standing open-mouthed.

'Bloody hell!' said Eddie.

The smog had returned, making the world hazy and indistinct. Everything had a yellowish tinge to it as Sir William shouted to the cab driver to hurry.

Eddie was not in a rush. He reckoned he'd had enough of graveyards for one day. He didn't fancy going back. And neither did Liz, by the look of her. She was silent and pale, her hands clenched tight together. George was watching her anxiously. No one spoke.

The cab dropped them at the cemetery gates and was soon swallowed again by the fog. The muffled sound of its wheels on the cobbles persisted for a while, then even that was gone.

'What do you think we shall find?' Liz asked nervously.

'I really don't know,' Sir William confessed. 'I hope we shall find your father's body exactly as it was left in the family mausoleum.'

'Comes to something when you hope people are still dead,' Eddie muttered.

'You know the way?' George asked Liz as he opened the gate to let her through.

'I think so. I've only been here once and it wasn't so foggy.' She forced a feeble smile. 'It's not somewhere I frequent.'

Gravestones and monuments loomed out of the fog and were then lost again. An angel with chipped wings watched as Eddie walked past. The pale brittle bones of a skeleton reached for him out of the murk – and turned out to be the branch of a silver birch tree.

The swirling fog was so thick on the ground that Eddie only knew they had left the path because he could feel the give in the turf under his feet. George and Sir William were grey ghosts. Liz was all but lost as she led the way. Bleached of colour she looked like one of the angels that stood guard over so many monuments and tombs.

Finally, a large silhouette darkened out of the fog. The stone was glistening as moisture coalesced on it. The low, arched door was pitted and the bottom had rotted away. The grass was longer round the edge, making it look as if the whole structure had been forced up out of the ground in preparation for the Day of Judgement.

'Is this it?' George asked.

'What do you think?' Eddie said. He was cold and tired and the graveyard dirt on his clothes was turning to mud in the damp air.

'This is it,' Liz said quietly. 'I'm sorry. The door is locked. I should have thought.' She pushed at it tentatively, just in case. 'We'll need to get the key.'

'Who has it?' George asked. 'I'll go.'

'Oh, I don't think there's any need,' Sir William said. He pushed carefully at the rotting wood. 'Time is rather of the essence. Would you – George – please be good enough to place your boot just here.' He tapped at a point close to the keyhole.

'I beg your pardon?'

Eddie sighed. 'He wants you to kick the door in. Unless you want a lady or an old man or a kid to do it?'

'Do you think I should?' Still George hesitated. 'Liz?'

She nodded and turned away.

'Go on,' Eddie urged.

George stepped up to the door, examining it. 'Just here? Right then.' He took a step back, gathered himself, then kicked hard.

The wood splintered and gave. The door crashed open, tilting to one side as a hinge gave way. Several planks came off the frame and clattered on to the stone floor of the mausoleum.

Eddie followed Sir William inside, George and Liz close behind him. The fog rolled in across the floor. It was not a large building – a single room. Stone arches on each wall framed alcoves which housed pale caskets. In the centre of the room was a low stone table. The remains of crushed, dead flowers were strewn across the top of it. Anaemic lilies and blood-red rose petals.

Sir William walked slowly round the table. 'Was he here?' he whispered.

There was something about the place which made them all talk in whispers.

'Yes.' Liz reached out, running her fingers through the dead flowers.

'But the door was locked,' George said. 'He can't have gone.'

Eddie was looking round, his eyes adjusting to the murky gloom. He could see the caskets on shelves in alcoves. Several low stone tombs. There was a narrow alcove that looked like another doorway at the back of the mausoleum where a figure stood silent and still as a statue.

But it was not a statue.

'Actually, I don't think he's gone at all,' Eddie hissed. His hand was trembling as he pointed towards the figure stepping out of the alcove.

The man's face was as white as the lilies, his eyes dark. He walked with a slight stoop. His voice was as cracked and fragile as the flaking stone around them. 'My friends – how good of you to come. I was expecting you.'

Reverend Oldfield spread his arms, as if about to bestow a blessing. He turned to face Liz. She took a step backwards, hands to her mouth in horror.

'My daughter. My beautiful Elizabeth. I am so very pleased to see you.'

CHAPTER 20

'Father?' Liz felt numb. Despite everything Sir William and the others had told her, she realised she had not expected to find it was true. Now here was her father – back from the dead. Should she be elated, or terrified?

Horace Oldfield nodded. 'Yes, I'm your father.' There was a sadness in his voice as he went on. 'And yet I am not your father. I am not the man I once was.' He closed his eyes for a moment. 'I had hoped to spare you this. To spare you any knowledge of such things. I struggled so hard to protect you, after I lost . . .' He opened his eyes again and stared at Liz. 'Too hard, perhaps. I thought I was doing the right thing.'

'But, what's happened to you?'

'I am resurrected. I am cursed.'

'Can you help us?' Sir William asked. He stepped forward, facing Oldfield. 'Can you help destroy this evil?'

'Evil? Yes, evil,' Oldfield said. 'Yet, now, feeling it

inside me. Was I wrong?' He turned to Liz again. 'Tell me I was right,' he implored her. 'All those years ago.' There was anguish behind his words. 'Tell me I did the right thing.'

'You always did the right thing, Father. How can you doubt that?'

'So, what's going on then?' Eddie demanded. 'Is he a vampire or what?'

'Eddie!' George reprimanded.

But Oldfield's pale lips curled into a slight smile. 'Yes, I am one of the undead. Demonstrably so. For my sins – literally, perhaps.' He let out a great sigh, his stooped shoulders heaving. 'I tried so very hard. I did my best to keep from you how awful and evil a place our world can be. I hid the events of the past to protect you. Forgive me that now.'

Liz was shaking her head. She could feel the cold trails of silent tears down her cheeks. 'Anything.'

'I tried to keep you from the theatre, even. To protect you.'

'Father – it's all right.' Her voice cracked as she suppressed a sob. 'I love you.' She took a step forward.

But he raised his hand, warning her to stay back. 'No, my child. I can feel it inside me – the power, the ambition, the craving for life at any cost. Before it overwhelms me . . .' He paused, breathing heavily. 'There are things you must know. Then there are things you must do. Promise me that.'

'What things?' Liz asked.

'Promise me!' Oldfield shouted, his voice echoing off the cold walls.

'Yes, yes – I promise.'

'What can you tell us, sir?' Sir William prompted. 'Do you know the truths among the lies?'

'I know everything. Even the Great Lie, I know that.'

'The Great Lie?'

'No time now.' Oldfield wiped his hand across his brow. 'Immortality,' he murmured, 'and yet so little time.' He gathered himself, straightened up – suddenly a figure commanding authority. More alive than Liz could remember him. 'I kept a journal. It is all in there. You must find it and read it. Then you must decide what you can do. Though it may be too late to do anything more than save yourselves.'

Liz remembered her father mentioning a journal before, but she had never seen it. 'Where is this journal, Father?'

'The year 1858. That was the year it happened. The year I discovered the evil that walks this earth and determined to end it for ever.' He laughed, a cold chilling sound. 'How young and naïve I was. How proud. How ignorant of what it would cost me.'

'What did you learn?' Sir William asked. 'What did you do?'

'Oh, they never forgot. I hurt them. Especially the Coachman. I took from him the one thing he was afraid to lose. And I delayed them and they never forgave me for that either. Or my family,' he added, his dark eyes fixed on Liz. 'The journal is hidden where they could never find it, even if they knew it existed. In the outhouse, the old shed at the back of the garden.'

Liz frowned. 'But, Father, it's empty. There's nothing in there.'

'There are other things you must know,' he went on quickly, as if he had not heard. 'I hope and pray I have time to tell you. But if not – then you must end it.'

Liz again stepped forward, and again he waved her away. 'What do you mean?'

'End it. For me. I can't . . . I can't let them take me. Already it's coursing through my veins, clouding my judgement. I have seen it happen. Seen what it can do to those I love, to my own flesh and blood. Before I lose my soul completely, you must – you have to. Kill me.'

Liz gasped and turned away.

'You promised me, Elizabeth. If you love me, then do it.'

'I can't,' she sobbed.

Cold hands clasped her shoulders, turning her slowly

round. She caught sight of George's horrified expression as she turned. Sir William, grim and determined. Eddie staring at the old man who had his hands on her shoulders. Her father. His eyes were deep and dark. His voice seemed to reverberate inside her head.

'You must. Do it for me.'

'But – how?'

'The heart. The vampire's heart is the key. Destroy the heart and you destroy the vampire. A wooden stake will rupture the heart. Or else you can starve it of the air it needs.'

'Suffocation?' Sir William asked quietly.

Oldfield let go of Liz and stepped away from her. 'Not advisable. The vampire's strength is far greater than that of a mortal man. The blood is so much richer and more powerful. But that too can be their downfall. In some countries the people know they are safe from vampires where the air is thin. They flee to the mountains when the blood harvest begins.'

'Lord Ruthven mentioned they can drown.'

Oldfield nodded. 'Hence the stories that they fear running water. But the truths about them are shrouded in lies.' He staggered back suddenly, hands to his head. 'I don't have long. It's all in the journal. Everything. Know a vampire by the soil in his shoes. See how they shun the brightness of the sun. Most of all, the wolf bat . . .' His words were lost as they became a cry of pain.

'Father!' Liz ran to him.

The old man was bent almost double. He pushed her gently away. 'It is almost time, my child. She will come for me, unless you hurry.' He held her arms for a moment. 'Save me,' he urged. 'The wood from the door. Be strong.'

'George,' Sir William said quietly.

Liz could see George move slowly towards the doorway. The fog was rising like steam around them.

'Everything is in my journal,' Oldfield said. He sounded weaker now and was swaying on his feet as he struggled to stay upright. 'The journal in the box. Everything except the Great Lie. Couldn't write that down. Couldn't risk them discovering that I knew.' He leaned back, bracing himself against the stonework. 'Left them a trap. Turned their lie against them.' He blinked, his forehead creasing in confusion. 'So hungry,' he gasped. 'So very hungry.'

George was giving something to Sir William. He walked over to Liz and pressed it into her hand. A broken shaft of wood from the door, its end a sharp point.

'He wants you to do it.' Sir William's face was a mask of sympathy and sadness. 'He loves you so very much. You have to do this for him. You have to let him know that you are strong enough. Brave enough. Loving enough.'

'Hungry!' Oldfield roared.

Liz turned quickly, the wooden stake in her hand.

The man opposite was not her father. She tried to tell herself that. 'My father is dead,' she murmured.

He didn't even look like her father now. He straightened up, so much taller. The weakness of old age dropped from him. His dark eyes glistened, and his pale lips parted to reveal long, sharp teeth.

Eddie swore.

'Quickly,' Sir William urged.

'I'll do it,' George said.

'No,' Liz told him. '*I* have to.'

The creature that had been her father rushed towards Liz, grabbing her roughly. His face pressed down towards her neck. She jammed the stake against his chest, felt the rotting wood splintering in her hands.

'Now!' Sir William shouted.

The vampire was pushing her, forcing her back against the wall. Bearing down on her. Liz shut her eyes and turned away.

'Look at me!' her father yelled in a voice that was barely his own – a ghastly, throaty rasp of sound.

Liz opened her eyes. Her hands were numb as her father pulled the stake from them. And rammed it back at her.

Liz gasped. The blunt end of wood ripped through

her dress below the shoulder, under her arm. It scraped against her inner arm before it embedded itself in the crumbling stone wall behind her.

For a moment, no more, the vampire's face was once again her father's. He nodded, staring down at the sharp wood pointing back at him. Then he looked deep into his daughter's eyes, and he smiled.

'Be brave,' he said quietly, his voice once again as she remembered. 'I love you.'

Then his eyes darkened, and his lips parted, and he hurled himself at her. At the sharp wood. There was a crunch as it penetrated. Then he fell back, the wood stuck firmly in his chest. His eyes glazed, and his blood mixed with the fog as it soaked the stone floor.

CHAPTER 21

The door to the shed opened outwards, and George had to trample down the long grass before he could wrench it open. A shower of dust fell from the frame as the lock tore through it, and the timber creaked in protest. But he managed to make a big enough gap to squeeze inside, followed by Eddie, Liz and Sir William.

'Nothing but dust and cobwebs,' Eddie said.

The dust was everywhere. It hung in the air like the smog outside. Cobwebs criss-crossed the narrow rafters. Several dark shapes hung from a cross beam – sleeping bats. George drew in a deep, dusty breath.

'Bats,' Liz said. 'He mentioned bats. And there was something on father's pillow. I thought it was a bird, but – it was a bat, I'm sure. It flew out of the window.'

'You think they're going to wake up and turn into vampires?' Eddie asked.

'I think speed is of the essence,' Sir William told him.

'Let's find this journal and leave the bats and the spiders in peace.'

George was looking round. A garden spade and fork were rusting against the back wall, together with a pile of broken and chipped flower pots. One wall had a narrow shelf running along its length. But the shelf was empty, apart from dust and dirt and several dead flies. Their bodies were dried-up husks.

'Funny place to keep biscuits,' Eddie said.

'Keep what?' Liz said.

'There's a biscuit tin over here, look.' Eddie moved aside the spade and some of the flower pots to revel a metal box behind them. It was layered with dust and wreathed in cobwebs. Strands pulled away and broke as he lifted the box, suddenly sounding apprehensive. 'You don't think they'll be stale, do you?' he asked as Liz picked up the tin.

'I don't think it's biscuits, Eddie,' George told him.

They crowded round as Liz slowly opened the box.

Eddie gave a shriek and leaped backwards.

'It's all right,' Sir William said. 'I think it's dead.' He produced a pencil from his pocket and eased it under the dark shape inside, lifting it out of the box and tipping it on to the open lid. 'Sleeping anyway,' he decided. The bat lay twitching on the box. 'There's another one in there. Both apparently dormant.' He prodded the second bat out on to the lid beside the first.

'How did they get in there?' Eddie asked. 'Frightened the life out of me, that did.'

'We noticed,' Liz told him. She held the box in one hand and reached inside with the other, feeling through a mass of cobwebs.

'Be careful,' George warned. 'It could be anything.'

'Books,' she declared. 'There are several of them.' Liz closed the box, the two bats falling back inside. She handed the box to George and showed them the small, leather-bound notebooks she had removed.

Sir William sat with a plate of bread and cheese balanced on one arm of his chair. Between eating, he leafed through the notebooks.

'It appears that the incident to which your father wished to draw our attention occupies the last of these volumes. Perhaps he stopped keeping a journal after that. Or perhaps he felt the later journals did not need hiding.'

'So what happened?' Eddie asked.

'In a moment. Let me explain the context, what Oldfield was up to and who he was. Then we shall better understand what happened to him.'

'He was ordained not long before that,' Liz said. 'I remember him telling me. And for all his frailty, he was not so old as he appeared.'

'Events took their toll,' Sir William said.

'The events in the journal?' George asked.

Sir William nodded. 'I fear so.' He paused to pop a piece of cheese in his mouth. 'Horace Oldfield, according to a reference in his journal, was ordained to the priesthood in 1856, at the age of thirty.'

'I'm not sure what he did before that,' Liz said.

'It is not clear,' Sir William told them. 'He lectured at Cambridge University for a while, where he had studied for his degree. He travelled extensively as well. And in the fifties he felt drawn to the priesthood. He was offered a curacy in South London in 1857.'

'St Agnes Martyr,' Liz put in.

'He was, it seems, diligent and well liked. The incumbent was elderly and more and more of the parish duties fell to Horace Oldfield. Then, we come to April 1858.' He picked up the journal and opened it.

Eddie, Liz and George leaned forward, listening with rapt attention as Sir William began to read.

I have never written of my travels before I was called to God. But for several months I spent time in the mountainous regions of Eastern Europe. Perhaps what I learned there began the process of my decision to be ordained. Perhaps I decided then that if creatures of such evil malevolence existed, then God would need all our help to stand against them.

I spent a week once in the company of the elder of a small village in the Carpathians. His name was Klaus, and by day I read in his small library. In the evenings we sat in the local hostelry and he translated for me the stories of the other customers. By night we remained locked in the house, like the other villagers in their homes. Listening to the sounds of the wind and the baying of the wolves. And in the morning we woke and prayed that none of the village children was missing.

He had made the study of local legends his life's work, having lost his only son and his young wife many years before. He had succeeded in separating the truth from the myth, he told me. And from him I learned such terrible things.

Of course, once I returned to England, my experiences and discoveries seemed at best exaggerated, at worst ridiculous. How much had I imagined, how much had the local people invented and embellished? Certainly the parish of St Agnes was not the place I ever expected to put my reluctant learning to the test.

I have not written for over a week. Not since I received my dear sister's letter and was so overjoyed at the news of her imminent visit. How quickly things change. I was then so full of hope and anticipation and life. But now I can feel that life ebbing away. I know I must commit the horrific events of the past days to these pages.

Though it seems a lifetime ago, it is only ten days since Reginald Carr came to see me. He had been to the rector already and told his story, only to be met with platitudes and a distinct lack of sympathy. When he said he wished me to perform an exorcism on a haunted house, I began to feel the same scepticism. Surely in the middle of the nineteenth century no one can still believe in such things?

But then I recalled my experiences in the Carpathians, and I agreed to hear the man's story. He had purchased, he told me, a property at the end of Mortill Street. It was an old house, in dilapidated condition, which he was planning to renovate. He is, he explained to me, a builder by trade and having saved an amount of money over the years wished to reinvest it in bricks and mortar. I asked what was the nature of the haunting that he perceived. He grew very uncomfortable and I could tell that he was far from happy even to discuss the matter. But I pressed him nevertheless. Was it that the house made noises? It was. But surely, as a builder he knew that every house has sounds and settles or decays in a different way? He did. And these sounds were not the noises of an old house slipping further into disrepair.

And then there were the figures. Dark, lean, hungry creatures that came and went during the darkness. They entered the house, but they did not come out. Had he seen them himself? He confessed that he had, but only once. For the most part he relied on the testimony of an elderly lady, a spinster, who lived nearby.

'There are no houses adjoined to the property,' he explained. 'No one in their right mind would build close to it. But further down the street, that is where Miss Radnor lived.'

'And she tells you that the house is haunted?' I could not resist a smile as I said it.

'This is no laughing matter,' he rebuked me. I apologised, and he told me that he too had been a cynic. He had no more believed the old lady's assertions than I had been inclined to believe him.

'But the sounds I have heard, the things I have seen.' He shuddered, and immediately accepted my offer of a small glass of brandy, which he drank in a single desperate gulp.

'You must see the house for yourself,' he said. 'I would sell it, but I would find no buyer. And how can I knowingly pass on such a thing? What would my conscience or my God have to say about that?'

'Perhaps,' I said, thinking I perceived the real source of his discomfort, 'I should speak with this Miss Radnor.'

'Then I hope you are still on good terms with the Almighty,' Carr told me. 'For her soul is no longer on this earth. And her body . . .' He held out a trembling hand, and I refilled his glass without comment. 'Her body was found in the street three days ago. They say her heart gave out, but I know the surgeon who examined her.'

'And what does he say?' I asked. Though somewhere deep inside, I think I already knew his answer.

'He says that if her heart gave out it was through a lack of work. A lack of anything to pump round her body. He said that the poor woman was completely drained of blood.'

In spite of my rising trepidation, I assured Carr that I would visit the house. He apologised for not coming with me, but asserted he would no more set foot in that house before it was exorcised than he would drink the ocean. Though the way he was now going at the brandy, I wondered if he might not be preparing to give it a try.

My fears growing with every moment, I resolved to visit the house the next day. I dared not venture out there at night, and I prayed that tomorrow would be sunny and bright.

In fact it was dull, with a miasma of smog hanging in the air. But I determined not to wait. With my Book of Common Prayer, a Bible, a flask of holy water from the church font, a silver crucifix and several other items I felt might be of value, I set out for Mortill Street.

If ever a house had been designed to look haunted, this was it. The place was in a sorry state. The windows were broken and boarded, the front door rotting away. The steps to the porch had collapsed and the garden was overgrown with nettles and brambles.

I could tell as soon as I was inside that this was a house of evil. I do not use the word lightly, but the whole place resonated with the fear and oppression that I had come to know so well while staying with Klaus the village elder.

It is hard to describe the events that took place that afternoon and evening. But suffice it to say I soon discovered that the whole house was infested with the creatures of the night. They rest, sleeping like dormant animals, for much of the time and had made this place their own. It was as if the very walls breathed with their foul presence.

I stood in a circle of chalk and holy water in the hall of the house, holding my crucifix and my Bible as I recited the words of power. I said the Lord's Prayer and took communion. I repeated the words I had learned from Klaus in his library and I listened to their shrieks and screams as I bound them to that place. Their hands clutched and tore at me, but in my circle and my faith I remained secure.

Klaus had told me he believed the words of power worked because they believed them to be a powerful restraint. But that belief would soon wear off. If I was to entomb them, I would need more. I would need a more physical restraint to make this house a prison for ever.

Carr was happy to be rid of it. He accepted the small amount I could afford, and I had Mr Jenkins of Jenkins and Mallerby draw up a covenant so that the house would stand for as long as there is a legal process and justice in the world.

All the time, all that week, I worked. I had brought back what I needed from my travels – as a curiosity as much as insurance. I had barely sufficient for the task, but as the years passed, there would be more. I knew from Klaus of the Great Lie. I dare not speak it here. But now I turned that Lie against them as I set my trap.

If ever they woke, that would be their destruction. They were safe only while they slept. They could survive for all eternity, but only if they lay dormant, entombed with their evil.

All but one. All but the one who broke the circle. That last night, as I laid the traps and performed the rites again, he came at me out of the gathering night, stronger than the rest. Perhaps he had not slept. Perhaps he was a guardian of some sort. That might explain his rage, if he knew he had failed his fellows and allowed a mere mortal to defeat them. And if he must account for that failure. He railed at me like a man possessed – which in a sense he was. When that failed, he pleaded. He said when the Coachman found what I had done, how I had imprisoned his sister, we would all pay a heavy price. A life for a life. Undeath for undeath.

Time and again he came at me. Time and again I beat him back. Until, at last, he fled into the darkness. And as he went, his coat spread behind him like the wings of a bat, I knew that of all of them he was the absolute worst, most pernicious and evil. I had let him escape, and for as long as I lived he would be forever in my mind, colouring my thoughts and judgements. Waiting for his revenge. Only vaguely remembering how he had mentioned a sister . . .

It was gone midnight by the time I stumbled home, exhausted and terrified. But the work was done. I washed the dust of that house from my body, and I stared into the mirror hoping to find some glimmer of satisfaction at what I had achieved. Or at least, to reassure myself I still reflected in its surface.

An old man stared back. Sapped of his life energy,

with sunken eyes and greying hair. I knew I had paid a price. And I knew also that for what I had bought, whether it be an end to the evil or merely a little time for the world, it was a small price to pay.

I had no idea of the price that would be exacted so soon after. I had dismissed from my mind the threats and entreaties made that night, and forgotten all mention of the mysterious Coachman and his sister – trapped within that house.

Until the following week. Until I met the train that was bringing my own sister to me. And found that she was not on it.

A life for a life. Undeath for undeath.

Oh what have I done?

Her cloak was like a bloodstain in the swirling colourless mist. Clarissa made her way eagerly through the grave-yard, her anticipation increasing with every step. Soon, so soon, he would be waking – he might even be awake already. If she could have come here earlier she would, but the Coachman had delayed her. He of all people should have recognised her hunger.

Hunger that turned to trepidation as she found the

splintered door. Turned to anger as she saw the broken body lying on the ground. Turned to heartbreak as she knelt beside the lifeless corpse and tore the stake from his chest.

Clarissa buried her head in the cold flesh, her cloak pooling round them both. She had felt no sadness, no fear, no grief for almost thirty years. Now she felt them all, as she wept for her dead brother.

CHAPTER 22

A few stray wisps of fog lingered like cobwebs. But the afternoon sun had burned off most of it and the day was clear and bright. Despite this, it was very cold, and Eddie's breath hung in the air with the remnants of the fog.

'You don't think this place will still be there, do you?' he asked.

'Why not?' George said.

'Well it was back in 1858. That's . . .' He gave up trying to work it out. 'That's years ago.'

'Nearly thirty years ago,' Liz said gently.

'Houses are built to last for a long time,' Sir William pointed out.

'Except it was already falling down. Said so in that diary.'

'True,' Sir William accepted. 'But Liz's father also said he hoped his trap would last for a very long time.

Perhaps for ever. It is imperative that we discover what this trap was, and as soon as possible. If we are to hold out any hope of defeating this evil – and I do not use that word lightly   then we must arm ourselves. And the only weapon we have,' he said, turning to Liz, 'is your father's knowledge and his trap.'

'But we don't know anything about the nature of this trap,' George pointed out. 'It may be nothing at all to do with the house.'

'We'll soon find out,' Liz said. They had just turned into another street. She pointed to a cracked and stained sign attached to a broken fence. 'This is Mortill Street.'

'How will we know which house it is?' Eddie wondered.

Ahead of him, Sir William, Liz and George had all stopped.

'I don't think that will be a problem,' Sir William said.

He stepped aside, and Eddie could see past him up the road. The houses on either side were typical terraced houses. A little run-down and neglected, but otherwise very ordinary. Distinctly out of the ordinary was the house facing them at the other end of the short street. Its windows were boarded over, and the steps up to the porch had rotted almost completely away. A section of the roof had collapsed, the brickwork was chipped and scarred.

Just looking at the house made Eddie feel nervous and afraid. They all walked slowly along the street, and he sensed that none of them wanted to be there.

'Can we just walk in?' Liz wondered.

'It's your house,' Sir William pointed out. 'Held in some sort of trust I imagine, but your father bought it.'

'I'm not at all sure that I want it.'

'It looks about ready to fall down,' George said. 'Eddie was right. It may not be safe.'

'Oh, I'm sure it isn't safe,' Sir William said. 'That, if you recall, is why we are here.'

The garden was so overgrown with grass and nettles that it was impossible to see where the path to the front door might have been. The fence had given way under the assault of the brambles that were entwined through it, and lay in a tangled line across the edge of the pavement.

'Shall we?' Sir William asked. Even he was unable to keep the edge of trepidation out of his voice.

From behind them came the sound of a door slamming. Eddie turned to see a man coming out of the front gate of the nearest house. He was old and stooped, with a hooked nose and wispy grey hair. He hurried up the road towards them.

'Come to complain to the owner,' George said quietly to Liz. 'Thinks you might have let the place go a bit.'

'Oh sirs, madam,' the man called out as he approached them. 'Is it time already? I wasn't expecting you until this evening.'

'I think you're making a mistake,' George said, confused.

But Sir William stepped in front of him. 'A mistake,' he quickly clarified, 'in your timing. We are here *now*.'

'And I am honoured to meet you,' the man said. 'Honoured. Truly honoured. The, er, other gentleman – is he not with you?'

'Alas no,' Sir William said. 'He has other matters to attend to. I'm sure you understand.'

'Oh completely. Absolutely. Yes, indeed. A busy man. But I thought he'd be here. And . . .' The man hesitated, suddenly nervous, 'the promise he made me, all those years ago. That's today too, yes? He hasn't forgotten?'

'Nothing is forgotten,' Sir William assured him.

The man gave a sudden nervous laugh and grabbed Sir William's hand, pressing it to his cheek. 'Oh sir, thank you sir. He did promise me. "Bradby," he said, "I'll see you all right. When the time comes you'll join us in . . ."' His voice tailed off. 'I'm sorry, sir, you know all about that I'm sure.'

'Of course.'

'But I wasn't expecting you until after dark. Despite the fog.' Bradby was rubbing his hands together. 'No one's been here, not for years. Not since. Well, since I was young and I was promised. Except the Coachman. He comes to visit her. Not often, maybe once a year. Never goes inside, of course. He kind of watches. Sits there on his coach for hours sometimes. If it weren't for the fact he's been told to wait, and not take any risks before the right time, well he'd have had me clear the place years ago. Make her safe, and all.'

Bradby led them up the road towards the house. 'I've touched nothing,' he assured them. 'Just made sure everything's as it was left. I haven't, you know . . .'

'What?' George prompted. 'What haven't you done?'

'Well, sir, I've not removed them. I can go in and do it now. Make a start, anyway. I know exactly where they all are. Taken careful note, you see.' He tapped the side of his beaked nose with his index finger. 'Won't take long, once I get started.'

'We'll come with you,' Sir William said.

Bradby took a step backwards. 'You can't go in there, sir. Not with the traps laid and . . . and everything.'

Sir William smiled. 'We have protection.'

'Protection? I thought sleeping was the only protection.'

'Ask no more.'

'Very good, sir. Madam.' He nodded at Liz. 'One thing, sir.'

'Yes?'

'When he summons you, when the Lord of the Undead calls all his subjects to the assembly. Tonight . . .' He seemed to think they would know what he was asking.

'Tonight,' Sir William echoed. 'Yes?'

'Well, I will be there, sir? Won't I? I mean as one of you? After I clear the traps and give my blood – for the awakening. I will be there?'

'That depends on how events turn out in the next few hours. Now, show us the house. Tell us everything.'

Encouraged, Bradby led the way through the grass and nettles to the front door. Eddie could see now that the house was more secure than it seemed from a distance. The boards on the windows were fixed solidly in place, and the front door was in good condition. Bradby produced a key and unlocked it.

'I'd best go first,' he said. 'And watch out for the circle, inside the door. You don't want to go treading in that.'

Eddie pushed eagerly past George, only to find Sir William had turned and was blocking his way.

'I think perhaps Eddie and Miss Oldfield had best wait outside,' Sir William said.

'What? You're joking!'

Liz also started to protest, but Sir William held up his hand. He glanced over his shoulder, making sure that

Bradby was not within earshot. 'I think it would be safest. We have no idea what we shall find in there, and our guide is likely to realise at any moment that we are not who he supposes us to be.'

'All the more reason for us all to be there, in case there's trouble,' Liz pointed out.

'All the same, I would rather that you two were out here. Safe. If anything happens to me and George, then you at least can escape and spread the word.'

'I agree with Sir William,' George said.

'Yeah, well you would,' Eddie told him. 'You ain't got to freeze to death out here and miss all the fun.'

'Our friend was expecting someone,' Sir William pointed out. 'As well as being safe, I'd like to think we will have sufficient warning if any more visitors arrive.'

'All right,' Liz agreed, though she looked disappointed.

'Well done,' George said quietly. 'We won't be long.'

Eddie could see this was not an argument he was going to win. 'You need us, you shout.'

'You can count on that,' Sir William said.

Bradby was waiting in the hallway. The bare boards were cracked and rotted, and the paint on the walls was peeling away like thin paper. The faint trace of a chalk circle was just visible on the floor, close to where the stairs rose to the upper floor.

The air was heavy with damp, decay and dust. What light there was edged past the boards over the windows so that the whole place was in twilight. Bradby took an oil lamp from a window sill and busied himself lighting it. It was clear he knew his way around.

'What do you want to see?' he asked. 'Even with protection, I assume you'd rather keep clear of the traps.' His lips parted in a broken-toothed smile.

'Where would you suggest we start?' Sir William asked. 'We want to see everything. Given,' he added quickly, 'that the time is nearly upon us.'

'The awakening,' Bradby said. 'He'll be here for that. He'll want to see her rise, mark my words. Tonight.'

'As you say.'

'Most of them are in the cellar. You want to start there?'

'That would seem sensible.'

There was a door under the stairs. It creaked open, showering dust. Stone steps led down into darkness. Bradby raised the oil lamp to cast as much light as possible and started slowly down the steps.

'I don't come here much,' he confessed.

The whitewashed walls were stained and damp. By the time they reached the bottom of the steps, George could see that the lower parts of the walls were crumbling.

'Well hidden, aren't they?' Bradby said. He held the lamp as high as he could, turning to show off the whole cellar. 'I know there are so many houses now, but I reckon this one is one of the best. Most secret. Because of her, I've no doubt. The Coachman wouldn't take any chances.'

They were in a large area, split by several thick walls. Some were structural, rising up through the house above. But there were others that seemed to serve no purpose. Bradby was walking slowly round, between the walls, as if he was browsing past library bookcases.

'If you didn't know they were here . . .' Bradby said quietly as Sir William and George hurried after him.

'Didn't know what were here?' George asked.

Bradby hesitated, and Sir William tensed. George sensed he had asked the wrong question.

'Of course,' he said quickly. 'Forgive me.'

Bradby regarded him with a moment's suspicion. Then he shrugged. He reached between George and Sir William to pat the nearest wall gently. 'Such workmanship.' He was grinning again, and George gave a silent sigh of relief. 'No one would ever . . .'

The grin was gone. He moved the lamp slowly back and forth.

'Is there a problem?' Sir William asked.

Bradby was still moving the lamp, but George couldn't see anything of interest he might be trying to illuminate. Until the man said quietly, nervously:

'You have shadows.'

'I beg your pardon?'

Sir William's hand was on George's arm. 'Vampires,' he said, 'do not cast shadows. Therefore . . .' He shrugged, leaving the conclusion unspoken.

'You're not . . .' Bradby stammered. 'I shouldn't have . . . Oh my Lord, if he thinks I've betrayed him, betrayed his sister – the Coachman will kill me.'

With a sudden movement, he pushed past Sir William, and made for the stairs.

Instinctively George ran after him. 'Come back!' he yelled. 'You have to tell us what's going on here.'

Bradby started up the steps, George close behind. The man was old, and George would soon catch him. Realising this, Bradby turned, and flung the oil lamp back down the steps.

George ducked, and the lamp crashed past him, smashing on the floor close by. Darkness. Then a roar of flame as the oil spilling from the broken lamp caught fire. In the flickering light, George lunged forward and grabbed hold of Bradby's sleeve, pulling him back.

The cellar was lit in orange and red as Bradby cried out and fell backwards.

George tried to catch him, but the man continued falling, past George, down the steps. Bradby's cry of fear echoed round the enclosed space as he tumbled. Then his head cracked into the base of one of the walls. His cry stopped abruptly. A dark trickle became a thin stream, running out from under the man's body, glowing scarlet in the firelight.

Sir William was coughing from the black smoke rising from the burning oil as he joined George on the steps.

'I doubt we'll learn much from the poor fellow now,' he said.

'I was trying to stop him,' George said, numb with shock. 'I never meant . . .'

'I know, I know.' Sir William nodded sympathetically. He glanced back down the stairs to where Bradby's body lay. And froze.

George too turned to look. The blood from Bradby's split head was pooling round his body. But where it touched the nearest wall, the blood was running *upwards*. A tracery of red, spreading like filaments across the whitewash.

They hurried back down into the cellar to examine the wall. As George approached, he saw that the wall was glowing red. Pulsing. The pool of blood shimmered, then it too split into rivers, running swiftly across the uneven floor towards other walls. Soon spiders' webs of red criss-crossed the walls like veins.

'How fascinating,' Sir William said.

'What is it?' George wondered.

'Blood that defies gravity. Drawn, somehow, to these walls. A capillary action?'

'But they're just walls. Aren't they?' George leaned close to examine the plaster in front of him. Behind the glow there was something, a shape, a shadow on the whitewash. Like a silhouette, light shining through from behind the shape.

'I think perhaps we shouldn't linger,' Sir William said.

But George was intent on the shape on the wall. Or *in* the wall. 'My God,' he realised. 'I think there's something *inside*.'

The sun was dipping out of sight behind the houses, and the smog was thickening. Eddie stamped his feet and blew on his hands in an effort to keep warm. Liz had her jacket pulled tight and her arms folded.

'They won't be long,' she promised Eddie.

'Course they won't. Probably not much to see.'

'I wonder what Father did in there,' Liz said. She was staring back at the old house.

'I think all these houses are empty,' Eddie said, looking back down the street. 'I've been watching and there's no sign of life at all. Just creepy old Bradby left. Everyone else has probably moved away.' He pointed along the street. 'Look, there's grass growing between the cobbles. Shows no one ever comes here. Not a living soul.'

'In which case,' Liz said, 'I wonder who this can be.'

A dark carriage had turned into the street. Pale, skeletal horses were heading towards Liz and Eddie, gathering speed as the carriage rattled along the cobbles. The driver raised his whip. He wore a dark, hooded cloak that shadowed his face.

'Like I said,' Eddie told Liz, 'not a *living* soul. I think it's time to give them that warning.'

The carriage hurtled towards them, not slowing at all as it neared the end of the street.

'I think it's time to run,' Liz said.

A pale, emaciated arm smashed through the wall and grabbed George by the neck. Plaster dust showered down as a second arm punched through close by.

George yelled in fright and surprise, leaping back and breaking the grip. He rubbed his sore neck, looking round. Sir William too had backed away from the wall. A forest of arms erupted. White dust fell like snow.

Fingers clutching. Then feet kicking through – boots, shoes, even bare toes. Followed by the first head.

Dark eyes glinted in the failing firelight, turning towards George.

'Is it time already?' a voice croaked, dry and ancient.

A figure forced its way through the surface of the wall and stepped into the cellar. Then another. And another.

George was running for the stairs, Sir William beside him. Halfway up, a hand exploded from the stonework beside them. A head burst out of the next step, and George had to leap over it.

Top of the stairs, and out into the hallway. Wooden floorboards were heaving and rattling as they were forced up from beneath. Chunks of plaster fell from the ceiling.

'The whole house,' George gasped.

'It's infested!' Sir William cried. 'The blood woke them!'

There was a sound like a distant train – a rumbling drumbeat of sound. George covered his ears, struggling across the lurching boards. Hands, arms reaching up at him. Thrusting through the walls. And a black cloud descending in a rush from the ceiling, down the stairs. The sound – the steady, insistent beat of their wings.

Leathery shapes slapped at George as they swirled in a blizzard through the house.

'Bats,' he realised. 'Vampire bats. Hundreds of them!'

'*Thousands.*' Sir William's voice was almost lost in the maelstrom of sound.

George battled towards the front door. How far could it be now? He felt a hand clutch at him, tried to throw it off, and realised it was Sir William.

A bat tangled in George's hair, scratching and biting in a fury. A hand gripped his leg and dragged him over. He fell headlong, the floor bucking under him like a wave crashing on the beach. More hands clutched, dragging him down, and George's world went black.

CHAPTER 23

'Into the garden!' Eddie yelled. It was so overgrown he hoped the carriage would not be able to follow. Liz needed no extra encouragement. She and Eddie ran for the gap in the broken fence. The carriage thundered after them.

Above the sound of the carriage, the snarls of the Coachman, and the snorting of the horses, there was another noise. It was coming from inside the house. A high-pitched shrieking mixed with a rumble like thunder. The sky above Eddie had turned black, a mass of dark creatures squeezing out between the boards that covered the upper windows and rising from the broken roof. Bats – reinforcements for the Coachman, Eddie realised – they were doomed now, surely.

The carriage skidded to a halt as the horses drew up. One of them reared on its hind legs before crashing down again, its hoofs slamming into the cobbles with a noise like gunshots.

The Coachman was standing, whip in hand, shouting at the horses: 'They have woken too soon!' The deep pits of his eyes locked on Eddie for a moment, but he sensed that they were seeing something quite different. 'Belamis!' the Coachman roared in anguish. 'You will be avenged!' Then the whip cracked down on the horses.

The carriage turned in a tight circle. Above Eddie, the bats were diving once more, surging through the open front door like a black ribbon.

'We have to get them out of there,' Liz shouted. 'The bats are protecting whatever's in there.'

Eddie grabbed her hand and they ran for the door, their free arms in front of their faces to ward off the dark creatures.

Sir William was almost at the door. His face was scratched and his clothes torn. He looked flustered and exhausted. 'I've lost George,' he shouted above the shriek of the bats.

Eddie dived in, keeping low in an attempt to avoid the flying danger. But if anything there were more of the creatures lower down. He got a confused view of arms thrusting up through the floor, the dark shapes of the bats, and – at last – George. He was swatting at the bats for all he was worth.

A hand had hold of George's leg, and Eddie managed to prise it away. He pulled his friend to his feet and together they stumbled back towards the door. They tumbled down the broken steps and rolled painfully through a patch of grass and nettles.

'Thank you,' George gasped. 'I thought I'd had it.'

'I thought we both had,' Eddie said. 'The Coachman was here. He saw it all.'

George leaped to his feet, looking round urgently. 'Where is he now?'

'Oh he hoofed it. Drove off. He was shouting about how it was too soon or something.'

'Interesting,' Sir William said. He helped Eddie up. 'Perhaps he feared your father's traps,' he told Liz.

'For all the good they did,' George said bitterly. 'We nearly died in there.'

'The unfortunate Mr Bradby did die,' Sir William pointed out.

It was quiet again, and Eddie turned in a full circle trying to work out why it was suddenly so quiet. 'Where did the bats go?'

'And why aren't the vampires coming after us?' George added. 'The sun's gone down now. There were hundreds of them in there. Thousands if those bats turned back into . . .' He shuddered and left the thought unfinished.

'I wonder,' Sir William said thoughtfully. He clicked his tongue as he considered, then decided: 'I think I'll just nip back inside and see what's going on.'

'Rather you than me,' George muttered.

'It's all right, George,' Liz told him. 'You can stay out here with Eddie.'

'No way,' Eddie retorted. 'I'm coming inside this time. Just try and stop me.'

George sighed and turned towards the house. 'All right. But be ready to run.'

They did not have to go very far to see what had happened. The boards had been ripped off several of the downstairs windows and the evening light spilled into the dusty house.

A figure was stretched out across a window sill at the back of the hall, as if trying to escape. Other figures lay silent and still on the floor. Some were halfway out of the walls, others were frozen as they clawed their way through the floor.

Eddie stood looking round in astonishment. Sir William hurried to the door under the stairs. He returned a few moments later, ashen-faced.

'It's the same down there. Exactly the same.'

'What's happened to them?' George said.

Sir William was examining a woman – she looked young but pale and emaciated. From the waist down she was walled up in the hallway, but her upper body had thrust through as she tried to escape. Now she hung limp and lifeless, long dark hair falling from her lowered head. Sir William pushed the hair aside, feeling for a pulse in her neck. Where his fingers reached, Eddie could see the raised, reddened pin-prick marks in the skin. As he watched, the skin was cracking and flaking as if ageing before his eyes, turning to dust . . .

'They're dead. Quite dead,' Sir William said. 'All of them. Even the bats have gone, crumbled to dust.'

'Father's trap worked,' Liz said in awe.

'So it would seem.'

'But what *was* this trap?' Eddie demanded. '*How* did it work?'

Sir William shook his head, sending dust and bits of plaster flying from his mass of white hair. 'I don't know. I really don't know. All I can tell you is that these blood-less creatures are dead. Every last one of them.'

It was a relatively short walk back to Liz's house. George wondered if Oldfield had deliberately stayed close to the house so as to keep an eye on it. He kept expecting the Coachman to return, but there was no sign of the ghostly carriage. Whatever traps Oldfield had laid all those years ago had certainly been effective.

Liz was soon due for a rehearsal at the Parthenon Theatre and insisted she was going. 'I can't let them down, not with Marie so ill.'

'Can't let Henry Malvern down, you mean,' George muttered. More loudly he said: 'But it isn't safe. We need to stick together.'

'Oh, I think it may be all right,' Sir William said. 'Eddie tells us that down in the catacombs the Coachman was of the opinion that Liz was no threat. They seem to assume you are too stricken with grief for your father,' he said to Liz, 'and possibly keeping busy with the theatre to take your mind off things.'

'But we don't know that for sure,' George protested.

'We know very little for sure. Which is why I am keen to examine these journals for any further clues.' Sir William brandished the metal box that Eddie had mistaken for a biscuit tin. 'And the best place for that is back at the Museum. Where I would welcome your help, and young Eddie's.'

'Righty-o, guv,' Eddie agreed enthusiastically.

George was still unhappy as the cab drew up close to the British Museum.

'I still say we should have insisted on Liz staying with us,' George grumbled.

The fog was thickening, swirling round them like smoke as they approached the main gates.

'Oh George, George, George,' Sir William said. 'I thought you understood.'

'Understood what?'

'We are all of us, including Miss Oldfield, in the most terrible danger. That man Bradby told us, remember, that whatever is going to happen will happen tonight. Either because that is their plan, or because we have galvanised them into action.'

'Then why did you send Liz to the theatre?'

Sir William sighed. 'Tell him, Eddie.'

'Cos the vampires know that Sir William and you are the greatest threat. They think I'm dead or missing, and Liz is grieving or whatever. If she sticks with us she's in *more* danger. At the theatre, she's well out of it and as safe as she can be. Right?' he checked with Sir William.

'Right.'

'Oh,' George said, feeling a little embarrassed. 'Right. I see. Sorry.'

Sir William put his hand on George's shoulder. 'That's quite all right. It's only natural that you should be worried about her. After all . . .'

'After all? After all – what?'

'Nothing,' Sir William said hurriedly. 'Just something else that Eddie and I have worked out and which you'll come to all in good time.'

George had no idea what he was talking about, and was not at all reassured by the smirk plastered across Eddie's face. But there was no opportunity to pursue the matter as Sir William suddenly turned, and led them on past the Museum gates.

'What is it?' George asked.

'Peelers,' Eddie hissed. 'Waiting at the Museum door.'

'But that's good. Isn't it?'

Sir William shook his head. 'Ordinarily, yes. But let us consider why they are here, and who they might be waiting for.'

George felt suddenly cold. 'You think they're looking for us?'

'I do.'

'But – even Sir Harrison Judd can't just have us locked up, can he?'

'Bet he could,' Eddie said. 'Throw away the key too.'

'But Sir William – you're well known. There would be a scandal, an inquiry.'

'Perhaps. But it would all take time. And from what we know, he only has to keep us out of the way for tonight. By the morning, it may no longer matter.'

'So what do we do?'

'Somehow we find out if they really are after us, or whether their presence is merely a coincidence.'

Sir William and George both turned slowly to look at Eddie.

'Oh no. Why me?'

The two uniformed policemen standing outside the door seemed hardly to notice Eddie as he approached. He got right to the door without being challenged. Which was no help at all – he needed to know why they were there.

'Let me through, please,' Eddie announced loudly. 'Important message for Sir William Protheroe.'

The policeman did not react, and Eddie was beginning to think they were just pausing on their regular beat. He put his shoulder to the door.

'Hang on there, son.'

Or maybe not. 'What is it?' Eddie demanded, still leaning on the door. 'This is urgent.'

'I think you'd better give us this message,' the second policeman said. 'We'll see it gets passed on.'

'Oh, no – can't do that. It's personal and confidential for Sir William. From a Mr George Archer. I've come all the way from Shoreditch on a promise of tuppence if I deliver it straight away and in person.'

A heavy hand turned Eddie round and he found himself staring into the faces of the two policemen as they leaned towards him.

'Listen, sonny, Sir William Protheroe isn't here. We know because we're waiting for him.'

'And Mr George Archer,' the second policeman said, 'is another gentleman we'd like to talk to. So you'd better tell us where he is.'

'He was in Shoreditch,' Eddie confessed. 'But that was half an hour ago or more. What d'you want him for?'

The police straightened up and looked at each other. 'We want him,' the first policeman said, 'to ask about the body of a young boy of about your age that was found in his house.'

Eddie blinked, and felt the colour drain from his face. John Remick – he'd sent the boy to his death. He might have been a bully and a thug but no one deserved that.

The policemen had noted Eddie's shock. 'So if you've got a message from this child-murdering swine, you'd best tell us right now so we can catch him before he and his accomplice Protheroe come looking for you.'

Eddie nodded. 'He said to tell Sir William he'd meet him in the Bear and Ragged Staff at nine o'clock.'

'Where's that?'

'Eddie shrugged. 'Shoreditch, I guess. Now,' he added squaring his shoulders and adopting an air of righteous indignation, 'where's me tuppence?'

The safest place, Sir William decided, was the Atlantian Club.

'The chief steward, Vespers, can accommodate us in

a private room,' he said. 'There we can examine these journals again in detail.'

'What do you think they will tell us?' George asked.

'I really don't know,' Sir William admitted. 'Perhaps very little. From a brief look I am afraid nothing stood out beyond what we have already seen.'

'Except the dead bats,' Eddie said. 'What you keeping them for, anyway? they might turn into vampires. That happened in a penny dreadful that someone told me about.'

'Improbable,' Sir William said. 'But as we know only too well, the improbable has a habit of becoming not only possible but fact. Ah, here we are.'

Sir William led them up the steps to the imposing door of the Atlantian Club. A uniformed doorman stepped out of the fog to greet them.

'Stephen, would you please let Mr Vespers know that I require a private room for a discussion with my friends and colleagues?'

'Of course, sir.'

'And if anyone asks, we were never here.'

The stage door was standing open, but inside the theatre was in near darkness. Liz could make out a glimmer of light coming from the stage, but there was no sign or sound of anyone else.

She was late. The rehearsal should be well under way by now. 'Hello?' she called. 'Anyone there?'

No answer.

The lights at the front of the auditorium were turned down low. Liz walked to the front of the stage and peered out into the gloom. She gave a startled cry and spun round as somewhere behind her a door slammed shut.

'Who is it?'

Someone was watching her from the wings. A dark shape, a vague figure.

'Henry – is that you? Where is everyone?'

The figure stepped out on to the stage. It was not Malvern, it was a woman. Liz gave a short laugh of relief. 'Marie. How are you feeling? Where is everyone?'

Marie Cuttler walked slowly towards Liz. She looked in better health than Liz had seen her for a while.

'I knew you'd come,' Marie said.

'There is a rehearsal. At least, I thought there was.' Liz took a step backwards. There was something about Marie's tone, her voice. Her feet were bare. And why was she wearing her nightgown? She seemed to be fully recovered, but even in the low light she still looked so very pale.

'The rehearsal was cancelled. Henry sent everyone home.'

'Why? What's happened?'

Marie stopped a pace in front of Liz. 'It was a mark of respect. The show will be postponed.' She reached out and stroked her fingers down Liz's cheek.

'A mark of respect? For what? I don't understand.'

Marie's fingers were ice cold. Her skin was ice pale, almost translucent. 'Why, a mark of respect for *me*, of course. Don't you think that was sweet of him?'

'For you? But you look so well. So much better.'

'Much, much better.'

'Then – why?'

Marie's fingers had reached Liz's neck. They tightened into a firm grip, so cold they burned into her.

'Because I died, of course.'

CHAPTER 24

With a gasp, Liz leaped back. Her feet caught in her skirts, and she fell – breaking free of the icy grip on her throat. Above her, Marie's face contorted into a snarl of rage.

'Understudy! You thought you could assume my role, didn't you? How can you do that when you're drained of blood?'

She reached down for Liz again. Tangled in her dress, Liz struggled to push herself backwards, out of the way.

'I never asked for the part,' she said. 'If you're up to it, you can play Marguerite. I really don't care.'

She managed to get to her feet at last, backing away as Marie circled round her.

'Not the play,' Marie hissed. 'My role, my position, my right. With *him*!'

'Henry?' Liz wondered.

'You know so little.' Marie lunged suddenly. Long,

sharp nails whipped past Liz's cheek. 'I was to serve my Lord. But not any more, thanks to you.' She leaped at Liz.

Liz threw herself aside, and Marie landed close by. She had dropped to all fours, lips drawn back over her teeth like a hungry dog. She came at Liz again, moving slowly, in a crouch. Like partners in a grotesque dance, the two women circled each other.

Hampered by her skirts, Liz knew if she tried to run Marie would catch her easily. Instead she backed away as fast as she dared, ready to dodge aside if Marie came at her again.

Liz was almost at the edge of the stage, shadowed by the side curtain, when Marie pounced. The force and speed of her attack drove Liz back. Strong arms wrapped round Liz's shoulders as Marie tried to force Liz to the ground. Liz scrabbled behind her, grabbing for anything that would help her keep her balance and stay on her feet. If she fell, she would be lost.

Her hand closed on a lever. But her weight forced the lever back, and Liz fell. Somewhere out on the stage she could hear the snap of a mechanism as the lever moved. Then Marie was on top of her, hands scrabbling for Liz's neck as Liz struggled to throw her off.

With an almighty effort, Liz rolled to one side, sending Marie flying. Liz got to her feet, gathered her skirts and ran back on to the stage.

'Is anyone there?' she yelled. 'Help – someone, any-one!'

'There's nobody,' Marie told her, emerging from the shadows and advancing again on Liz. 'The doors are locked. You really can't escape me.'

Liz was taking ever shorter steps, almost shuffling across the dark stage. Marie was close now, getting closer. Her long, thin fingers slashed within an inch of Liz's face.

All the time, Liz was looking round, peering desperately at the floor. Then her foot disappeared into nothing. She stopped quickly, swaying as she caught her balance. Could she escape? Would she be quick enough?

'Whatever this role is, whatever you were talking about, I know one thing,' Liz said. She hoped her words would enrage Marie further, cloud her reason, and give Liz the time she needed.

'What's that?'

'I'll be so much better at it than you.' Liz stepped back.

Marie gave a shout of anger and leaped at Liz. Her nails ripped through empty space. Her teeth closed on nothing. She landed and turned in one fluid movement. But the stage was empty. Liz had vanished.

The volumes of Oldfield's journal were spread out on a large table. Sir William was busily arranging and re-arranging them. The metal box in which they had been stored was open at the end of the table.

'The late Reverend Oldfield's journals cover a lot of ground,' Sir William said. He moved to the end of the table and, as if describing a picture, explained: 'We have a history, an account of an event. If we had brought Hemming's translation of the Book of the Undead with us, that would precede these journals as an account of far older events. Older, but connected.'

'And what else?' George asked. 'We know about photographs and shadows and light.'

'Which Oldfield's journals also touch on.' Sir William sighed and shook his head. 'All of this we know, like the craving for contact with home soil and the need for rich oxygen. There must be more.' He slammed the flat of his hand down on the top of the table in sudden frustration. 'Somewhere here, there must be more.'

Eddie was disappointed. 'So, we've learned nothing new?'

'Oh, I didn't say that,' Sir William admitted. 'In fact, we have learned a great deal. None of it, however, good.'

'Like what?'

'We knew that there was a danger that a new invention – the development of photography – might force the vampires into the open, into taking action. I suspect that there is another reason why they have become more active now. A reason hinted at in Oldfield's later writings.'

'And what's that?' George asked.

'Their own history. This is a time predicted by vampire lore. It is when, apparently, the ancient Lord of the Undead – known to the Egyptians as Orabis – will come again to lead his people. In this time of crisis, the greatest and most dangerous vampire of all is about to rise and claim his inheritance.'

'But they didn't know it would be a time of crisis, surely?' George said.

'Probably not. But it does coincide with the time when sleeping vampires will awaken, and trade places with those now awake. Some of those in positions of power and influence especially will be loath to give that up and go into hibernation for centuries. So this is the time when Orabis will decide.'

'Decide what?' Eddie wanted to know.

'Whether they should continue as before – maintain the status quo, carry on living in secret and feeding clandestinely off human society, some sleeping and others waking . . . or whether they should emerge and take over.'

'And which will they choose?' George asked.

'I wish I knew. For some vampires, this is the culmination of their life's work, the moment they have been waiting for. But others fear the changes that Orabis may bring.'

'And just who is this Orrible-iss?' Eddie asked.

'*Orabis* is the Lord of Death. Oldfield speculates he will have no qualms about declaring vampires lords of the Earth. His followers set up the Damnation Club – a so-called Parliament of Blood – many years ago to serve as a vampire government in waiting, ready to take over and rule the Empire.'

'They want to rule?' George exclaimed.

Sir William nodded. 'Already many of its members are in positions of power – in government, in the real parliament, in the police and the military and the scientific professions. Oldfield's actions and discoveries frightened them, delayed the process. But with the arising of Orabis, the time of the vampires will come at last and nothing short of a miracle can stop it . . .'

'So what do we do?' George asked. 'What *can* we do?'

There was a printed piece of card still in the metal box, beside the two bats. 'What's this?' Eddie asked, picking it up.

'Irrelevant,' Sir William said without looking. 'Got into the box by mistake, I fancy.'

'Really, Eddie, this is important.' George took the card from Eddie and glanced at it before handing it back. 'If you must know, it's a theatre bill. For some play in Norwich in 1866.'

'Just something that Liz's father kept as a souvenir of a play he went to,' Sir William agreed.

Eddie stared at it. 'That's not right,' he said slowly. 'That can't be right, can it?' He wasn't sure what the playbill was doing with the other papers, but he did know one thing. 'Liz's father hated the theatre. Thought it was the work of the devil, didn't he? So, he'd never go to see a play.'

As soon as Marie hurled herself forward, Liz stepped backwards, and fell through the trap door that the lever at the side of the stage had opened. Ironically, it was a so-called 'vampire trap' named after the play in which it was first used in 1820 – *The Vampire or The Bride of the Isles*. In the play it was the vampire who vanished apparently into thin air. Now it was Liz.

There was a long drop, and Liz just hoped it had been left set up. If not, she would land with a bone-shattering crash. Luckily, the trap was prepared, a thick blanket stretched out and suspended under the stage. Liz rolled off it, ready to run from the under stage area. Marie would soon realise where she had gone.

Under the stage it was almost completely dark. Liz hurried in what she hoped was the right direction, and almost immediately knocked into something. It fell with a clatter and Liz stifled a gasp of surprise. But it was just a broom that had been leaned against one of the supporting struts holding up the stage.

Liz hesitated. What if Marie was about to drop through the trap after her? Could she see in the dark? Liz picked up the fallen broom and jammed the wooden handle in the gap between the double upright supports. With strength born of desperation and fear, she heaved on the wooden handle, snapping it in two.

Then, shaking with fear, she crawled under the blanket, and propped up the two broken staves. The weight of the material pressing down on them held them in place, the brush slipping before holding against the edge of a floorboard.

Liz hurried as fast as she dared through the darkness and emerged, blinking in the dim light, at the top of a narrow wooden staircase. She was in the wings off to the side of the stage.

A hand came down heavily on her shoulder.

Liz leaped back with a cry, turning quickly.

'I'm sorry. I must have startled you.' It was Henry Malvern. 'I realised you wouldn't have got the message about the rehearsal. I came back to tell you.'

Liz's heart was pounding and she could scarcely speak. 'Marie . . .' she gasped.

'I know. I'm so sorry. It was very sudden.' Malvern turned away. 'Let me escort you home.'

'No, you don't understand. She's here. Marie is here.'

He turned back quickly, his surprise evident. 'What? What do you mean?'

'She's trying to kill me.' Liz grabbed hold of Malvern's arm, suddenly afraid he wouldn't believe her. That he might leave. 'She's a vampire,' Liz gasped.

Malvern was shaking his head. 'You're in shock. You've had a fright. Marie's death . . .'

'No – truly. She's here and trying to kill me. She'll kill us both.'

Malvern looked deep into Liz's eyes, as if assessing how distressed she really was. 'All right,' he said. 'I didn't see anyone else, but I'll take a look round.' He held his hand up to stop her protest. 'I'll be careful. You can wait in my dressing room. Lock the door. Let no one else in. No one at all. Once I'm sure it's safe, I'll come back for you. I have a carriage outside, we can be away from here in no time.'

Liz hugged him tight, grateful for the reassuring pat on her shoulder in return. 'Thank you. But please – be careful. She's dangerous.'

'Oh don't worry. If I see a vampire, I'll let you know.'

He led her the short way to his dressing room, and Liz closed and locked the door. The gas lamps were lit, but turned down low. She leaned against the door for a while, listening for any sound from outside. But all she could hear was the pounding of her blood in her ears and her ragged breath.

As she began to feel calmer. Liz sat on the chair in front of the table where Malvern kept his make-up. There were pots of different colour face paints. Beside them, she saw with a tinge of amusement, was the jar of jam she had given him. It was unopened.

Liz looked into the dusty mirror above the table and saw that her face was stained with tears. She wiped them away as best she could with her handkerchief. Behind her, reflected in the mirror she could see a rack of clothes.

With nothing else to do, she went to look through the costumes hanging on the rail, trying to guess what parts they might be for. But before she had even begun, her foot connected with something in the shadows under the rail.

But it was just a shoe. There were several pairs of shoes arranged under the rail of clothes. Liz lifted the shoe she had knocked to bring it back in line with the others. It felt surprisingly heavy. She tilted it slightly in her hand, and felt the weight shift.

Her heart once again pounding, and her mouth suddenly dry, Liz brought it out into the light, angling it so she could look inside.

So she could see the layer of dry earth lining the bottom of the shoe.

'Let me see that,' Sir William said, taking the playbill from Eddie.

'Someone must have given it to him,' George said. 'Or it belongs to Liz.'

'There's writing on it,' Eddie said. 'What's it say?'

Sir William opened the playbill on the table so they could all see. There were line drawings of the principal cast. One of them – a man – was circled in a scratch of blue ink. Beneath it was written:

'The one that got away,' Sir William read aloud.

George was staring at the picture, frowning. 'But this is from 1866?'

'I can read you know,' Eddie told him. 'Well, a bit.'

'But, that's twenty years ago,' George said. 'And that – surely that's Henry Malvern?'

'Harry Worcester, according to the text,' Sir William said. 'But if it is indeed the same man, unchanged after twenty years, and singled out by Oldfield . . .'

'The vampire that escaped from him,' Eddie realised. 'The worst of the lot. He was an actor.'

'He still is an actor,' George said.

'That's why Oldfield was desperate to keep Liz from the theatre,' Sir William realised. 'He was desperate to make sure she never came into contact with this creature if he ever reappeared. But because he would have nothing to do with the theatre himself, he didn't realise the man had already reappeared. If he had he would have exposed him – trapped him in some way.'

'And we've sent her straight there,' George said.

'At least she won't be alone. It's a rehearsal.'

'As if that'll stop him,' Eddie said. 'What we going to do?'

'There is only one thing we can do,' Sir William decided. 'Pray we are not too late.'

'And?' George prompted. 'I mean, that can't be all.'

'George, you must get to the theatre. Don't let Malvern know we suspect the truth unless you have to. But get Liz away from there safely.'

'I'll go with him,' Eddie said.

'No, Eddie. I need you to come with me.'

'Where to?'

'To see the one man who I hope has the power to act, before it's too late. The one man who can overrule the Commissioner of the Metropolitan Police and the other powerful members of the Damnation Club. Just so long as he is not himself a member already.'

'Who's that, then?' Eddie asked.

'The First Lord of the Treasury. Sometimes referred to as the Prime Minister.'

There was no sign of Malvern in the corridor, so Liz quietly closed the dressing room door behind her. There was no clue as to where Malvern had gone. The quickest way out of the theatre was to cut across the stage to get through to the backstage door. She went as quickly as she could without making too much noise. The stage was still in semi-darkness, and Liz was careful to give the almost-invisible open vampire trap a wide berth.

She was almost across the stage when Malvern called out to her: 'I sent Marie away. There's nothing to worry about.'

Liz froze, then slowly turned. Malvern was standing at the back of the stage. Perhaps he had been waiting for her there – watching her creep across in front of him. She turned away, ready to run.

'Come here.' His voice was commanding and confident. More than that – there was something compelling about it too. She struggled to resist, but felt herself turning, walking slowly back across the stage despite her intentions and efforts.

Malvern came slowly down to meet her. His voice

was dark, silky and persuasive. 'I need you, Liz. You know that. Soon you will assume the greatest role of your career. Of your *life*. I had intended to offer up Marie. She seemed perfect. But then I met you. And how could I resist? That's why I brought you here. That's why poor little Beryl had to die – so you could take her role as the maid and I could keep you close.'

He held up his hand, and Liz stopped. Malvern was three paces away, his head tilted as he regarded her with interest.

'What do you want?' Liz demanded, her voice stronger than she felt. Inside she was trembling and felt faint.

'Only one mortal ever got the better of me, you know. Only one man. He destroyed everything I had planned. Set back the time of the awakening simply by knowing too much. With the Coachman's own sister trapped in her sleep, he became cautious and the others became wary and slow to act. That man was weak and stupid but he defeated me. And I swore that one day I would be revenged on him.'

'My father,' Liz realised.

Malvern nodded. 'They wouldn't let me take him. Not then. In case it drew attention to us. Though the Coachman made him pay a high price for the loss of his sister. But how could I resist the chance to meet his daughter? To destroy *her*? More than that – to make her one of us. One of the greatest of us.' He drew a deep rasping breath. 'Oh, you will be so honoured.'

'What do you mean?' She couldn't keep the tremor from her voice this time.

'Clarissa is waiting for you in my carriage outside. Together, you have a visit to pay. An important person to see. And after that, at the whole assembly, in front of the risen dead and our Lord . . .'

He took a step towards Liz, and she found she was unable to move. His lips drew back in a smile, revealing his sharp gleaming teeth.

Then he told her what was going to happen, who she would become, and Liz felt sick and more afraid than ever in her life. As Malvern drew her to him, and pressed his icy lips to her warm neck.

CHAPTER 25

The secretary was flustered but adamant. 'You cannot see the Prime Minister this evening. It is, I'm afraid, quite impossible.'

Eddie had listened to Sir William insisting his way through several offices and past various officials to get to this point. Now here they were in a small room adjoining the Prime Minister's own office at Number 10 Downing Street.

'I cannot stress enough how vital this is,' Sir William said. He was almost shaking with anger now. 'And if you knew the sort of incompetence and obfuscation we have had to sweep aside to get this far . . .'

'Believe me, I can sympathise.' The secretary did not look sympathetic. He was a portly man in his thirties with receding black hair. 'But I can assure you I am being neither incompetent nor misleading. You cannot see the Prime Minister because the Prime Minister is not here.'

'We'll wait,' Sir William said. 'When do you expect him?'

'Tomorrow.'

'But that will be too late!'

'It is the best that I can offer, Sir William. But the Prime Minister is at this moment making his way to a special session of Parliament. It is, for me as well as for you, most inconvenient, in addition to being rather unexpected and at short notice.'

Eddie had spent the time they were talking walking round the room. It was similar to the other offices where he had listened to Sir William asking, begging, and cajoling his way up through the political hierarchy. There was a framed photograph on the panelled wall showing a group of people. One of them he recognised as the Prime Minister – which was a relief. He didn't know who any of the others were, but he guessed they were important.

The photograph was on the wall close to the door to the Prime Minister's office, and as he examined it, Eddie could hear movement from behind the door.

'Here – if the Prime Minister's gone to Parliament, who's in his office, then?'

'Who indeed?' Sir William demanded. He glared at the secretary and strode across to the door.

'You can't go in there!' the secretary insisted. 'I told you . . .'

But Sir William had already opened the door.

There was a man standing on the other side of the large desk that dominated the room. But it was not the Prime Minister.

It was a small, dapper man wearing a smart suit. His neat, dark beard gave him an authority that belied his size. He looked up in surprise at the interruption.

'That is Anthony Barford,' the secretary hissed. 'He is the Prime Minister Mr Gladstone's personal adviser. Now will you kindly leave!'

Barford was watching with interest. 'Wait a moment, Haskins,' he said. 'It's Sir William Protheroe, isn't it?'

'At your service,' Sir William said quietly.

'I confess I was actually waiting for someone else. Then I have to leave for the House of Commons in a few minutes, but if there is anything I can do to help?' Barford gestured for Sir William to come in. 'I am well aware of your department, Sir William, and of the work you do.'

'I have to get a message to the Prime Minister,' Sir William told him. 'Forgive my bluntness.'

'Oh, be as blunt as you feel necessary. I think you'd better tell me what's going on. I shall be seeing the Prime Minister before the emergency debate in a few minutes. I shall be more than happy to pass on your message, assuming you can convince me of the urgency.'

'About time,' Eddie blurted out. 'Someone who'll listen to us.'

'To *me*,' Sir William stressed. 'You'd better wait out there, Eddie, I think. And let me explain matters to Mr Barford.'

The door closed, leaving Eddie and the secretary Haskins alone in the office.

'It must be an important matter for Barford to bother himself with it,' Haskins admitted.

'Yeah, well. Could be the end of the Empire, I s'pose,' Eddie admitted. 'Important bloke is he? This Barford?'

'Between you and me, one of the most influential people in the country. There's little that the government does that Anthony Barford does not have a hand in.'

Eddie pointed at the picture on the wall between them. 'So who's this lot?'

'The Cabinet. The Prime Minister's most important ministers. That photograph was taken just last month, out in the garden. It was only delivered this week. Here,' he went on, pointing to the picture, 'you can see . . .' He broke off. 'That's odd.'

'What's odd?' Eddie had a sudden feeling of unease. 'What is it?'

Haskins gave a short, nervous laugh. 'You know, I was sure that Mr Barford was there as well. Perhaps he was called away. But he was standing just here, between these two . . .'

'But – there's no one there,' Eddie realised. He might already be too late. He wrenched open the door and rushed into the room beyond.

'How good of you to join us,' Barford said. He was still standing on the other side of the desk. But his expression had hardened, and he was holding a gun.

Eddie skidded to a halt beside Sir William. 'Oh,' he said. 'I expect you know, then.'

'I gathered,' Sir William said.

'You may go now, Haskins,' Barford called. 'I have matters under control. These two are, I am afraid, wanted by the police.'

Haskins looked shocked and pale. 'Shall I summon assistance?'

'There's no need,' said another voice. It came from behind Haskins in the outer office. A tall, thin man marched across to the door. 'As Mr Barford said, the matter is under control. You may leave us.' Sir Harrison Judd stepped into the Prime Minister's office and pulled the door closed behind him.

'It was you he was waiting for,' Eddie realised.

'And the Prime Minister?' Sir William asked.

'Oh, he really is at the House of Commons,' Barford said. 'Where we will shortly join him. In time to witness the Palace of Westminster become the Parliament of Blood.'

The back door of the theatre was blowing in the breeze. There was a faint light from inside, but the whole place seemed deserted.

George had the metal box with Oldfield's journals tucked under his arm. He had shuddered at pushing them back underneath the bats. Now the weight of the box was somehow reassuring as he made his way cautiously into the darkened building.

'Liz?' he called. 'Liz – are you there?'

The only reply was the distant sound of laughter. A woman's laughter.

'Is that you?' he called again, but more cautious now.

The corridor led past dressing rooms and store cupboards. Eventually he found himself at the side of the stage, looking out from the wings. He could see the darkened auditorium. A single light shone across the stage from the other side. It illuminated the figure standing there. A stark silhouette outlined in the pale green of the limelight. He could smell the bitter, acrid fumes of the burning lime. But his attention was on the woman.

She laughed again as George stepped out on to the stage. He still could not see her properly, and shielded his eyes from the bright light with his free hand.

'Liz?'

'She's not here.'

As she moved towards George, she blocked out the glare of the light and he saw that it was Marie Cuttler.

'You're feeling better? Do you know where she went?'

Marie took another step towards George. 'She had an appointment. She had to go.'

'Go? Go where?' George could feel his heart beating in the side of his chest. The thumping became more pronounced, irregular.

Marie was right in front of him now. There was something in her voice that froze George to the spot.

'How kind of you to come. I'm glad you are here. I'm so very, very hungry.'

There was a small looking glass on the back wall of the Prime Minister's office. It was in an ornate plaster frame, and when Anthony Barford stood in front of it, Eddie saw that he had no reflection.

'I am sorry that you will not live to see the culmination of so many centuries of work,' Barford told Sir William and Eddie as he turned from the mirror to face them again.

'Me too,' Eddie retorted.

'But you don't have the fifth canopic jar,' Sir William pointed out. 'Surely you need the Lord of the Undead's heart?'

'What do you know about that?' Sir Harrison Judd demanded.

'Only what I have read.'

'It isn't important,' Barford decided. 'The Coachman will find it. He can feel it, you know,' he told Sir William. 'The Coachman is so attuned to the Lord's desires and wishes and needs that he can feel his heart beating within the casket. With every beat, he gets closer to finding it. Tonight's ceremony will go ahead. We have everything we need for that now.' He turned to Judd and raised an eyebrow. 'I am assuming . . .?'

'Waiting in the office outside,' Sir Harrison Judd assured him.

'What about the Prime Minister?' Eddie blurted. 'Is Mr Gladstone a vampire and all?'

Barford laughed. 'Oh no. Not yet. But soon all that will change. The Lord of the Undead will have his heart,' Barford went on, 'be assured of that. The only other thing he craves is waiting outside. His heart's desire, you might say.'

'And what, pray, might that be?' Sir William asked.

'Please, show her in.' Barford told Judd. 'I think she can have the honour, the privilege of feeding on our guests. She must be hungry.'

'Who must?' Eddie said. He was feeling nervous enough already without the threats. He looked round desperately for a way of escape, but there was no other way out of the room.

Only the door that was opening to allow another figure to step inside.

'Allow me to present the Lord of the Undead's latest subject,' Barford said. 'His bride.'

The woman standing just inside the door was pale as death, except for her blood-red lips. She turned slowly to face Eddie and Sir William, eyes wide and unfocused. It was Liz.

Chapter 26

The thumping at George's chest was an insistent shaking now. Except – it wasn't in his chest. It was the metal box he was clutching. It juddered and shook so hard he struggled to hold on to it.

Marie was reaching out. Her eyes were deep and black. Her lips drew back and her eyes closed.

'So hungry.' She leaned forwards, enfolding George in her cold arms.

He felt her icy lips at his neck. He dropped the box.

It clattered to the floor, the lid springing open. Two dark shapes erupted from inside, wings battering against each other as they hurtled into the air. They climbed, turned, swooped down. One crashed into Marie's cheek with such force it knocked her head sideways. The other was clamped to her chest as she let go of George and staggered back.

She clutched desperately at the dark shape on her

face. Black wings battered against her, faster and faster.

'Help me!' Marie screamed, sinking to her knees and falling back.

George looked on in horror as Marie's face disappeared beneath the frenzy of black. A spray of scarlet misted the air, spattered across the stage. A hand beat and clutched at the bare boards. A leg kicked out, spasmed.

One of the dark shapes was flapping lazily at her throat. The other circled up and flew out of sight.

Leaving Marie's lifeless body stretched out across the stage.

'Oh my dear Elizabeth,' Sir William said, 'what have they done to you?'

'She has joined us,' Barford said. 'Just as it is time, sadly, for you both to leave. I am afraid, even though we will soon control this miserable country and its vast empire, you must take our secrets to the grave with you.'

Sir William frowned. 'To the grave,' he murmured, barely loud enough for Eddie to hear him. 'Of course . . .'

Barford sat down behind the Prime Minister's desk. He glanced at the gun he was still holding, then set it down on the blotter. 'Such a remote way to kill. How much better to experience it first hand. Close, and warm.' He waved his hand in the air – an invitation. 'You must be hungry, my dear. They are all yours.'

Sir Harrison Judd had also stepped away to allow Liz to approach Eddie and Sir William. She had her hands raised, like talons ready to rip out their throats. There was no way they could both get past her and out of the door. Even if they could fight off the creature that Liz had become, Eddie realised, Barford would grab the gun and shoot them down.

But while there was no hope that both of them might escape . . . Eddie didn't hesitate. He hurled himself at Liz, shouting at Sir William: 'Get out, while you can. I'll keep her busy.'

Liz grabbed him, pulling his head back. Eddie struggled to break free. He could feel her warm breath on his throat as she leaned over him. He could see Barford snatching up the gun again. Sir Harrison Judd catching hold of Sir William as the old man tried to escape – pushing him back towards Liz.

She turned, pulling Eddie with her. Then Liz pushed him away from her and grabbed for Sir William. Eddie collapsed to the floor.

As he fell, he managed to roll into Sir Harrison Judd, sending the man staggering backwards. At once, Eddie was back on his feet. He grabbed Sir William's arm and dragged him clear of Liz. She gave a hiss of anger and disappointment as Sir William staggered after Eddie.

A gunshot tore through the frame of the door close to Eddie's head. He pushed Sir William ahead of him and dragged the door closed.

'There's no key,' he gasped.

'Then we had better run.'

The house seemed deserted. The officials they had seen earlier had all gone home or left for the Houses of Parliament. Eddie and Sir William raced along half-remembered corridors and through hallways, emerging finally into the foggy night of Downing Street.

They stood gasping for breath on the pavement.

'Is it true?' Eddie asked. 'Is Liz one of them now?'

Sir William nodded gravely. 'I fear it is so.' He shook his head and sighed. 'Now that we have lost Miss Oldfield, we must find out what has happened to George.'

George was sitting on the edge of the stage, looking out into the darkened auditorium. Behind him, in a puddle of limelight, was the body of Marie Cuttler.

'What's happened?' Eddie said. 'Did the vampires get her?'

'In a manner of speaking,' George agreed. He stood

up, and Eddie was surprised how pale he looked. 'She tried to kill me. Wanted to drink my blood.'

'How did you stop her?' Sir William asked. He knelt by the body. 'This is fascinating. She has been entirely drained of blood. Already the body is dry and brittle.'

Eddie crouched down beside Sir William, and immediately saw the dark distinctive shape at the woman's neck. ''Ere – look out, it's one of them bats!'

'Indeed it is,' Sir William agreed. 'But it seems quite docile, doesn't it?' The bat's wings fluttered as Sir William cautiously prodded it with his finger. 'You know, if I didn't know better I might think that . . .'

'It was the bat that killed her,' George said, joining them.

'Indeed. That is exactly what I might think.'

'No, I wasn't speculating,' George told them. 'It really *was* the bat that killed her. The two of them that were in the metal box. As soon as she got close to me. It was like they could sense her and woke up. I dropped the box, they flew out and . . .' He gestured at the prone body. 'Well, you can see.'

'You mean *they* drank *her* blood?' Eddie said. 'That's a bit of a turnaround.'

'The other one flew off somewhere.'

'Sated, I should think,' Sir William said. 'Such a capacity for blood. But perhaps the vampires don't have much to offer. That would explain why the heart is so important, why they don't like thin air and a lack of oxygen. They need to keep what little blood they do have as rich as possible, and replenish it frequently.'

'So, what are you saying?' Eddie wanted to know. 'Bats eat vampires?'

'Not all bats. But this bat. Where is the box?' Sir William asked George.

George fetched it, and Sir William carefully lifted the bat from Marie's throat. It flapped its wings in a weak protest before Sir William dropped it into the box and snapped the lid shut.

'The Great Lie,' Sir William said. 'We have heard it mentioned several times. Now I think we have discovered what it is.'

'The bats?' Eddie asked.

'Vampires would have us believe that they have some affinity with these bats. Perhaps they even change into them. We believed it – at the house, we thought the bats were attacking us, helping the vampires buried there. In fact, the bats were the trap that Oldfield left.'

'They sensed the vampires,' George said. 'Maybe smelled their blood as they woke.'

'And like this one and its fellow,' Sir William patted the lid of the metal box, 'they were dormant, waking to feed. It is fortunate they like only the rich, thick blood of the vampire or they really would have attacked us too.'

Eddie wasn't convinced this was so useful a discovery. 'One bat isn't going to help much,' he pointed out. 'No matter how hungry it is.'

'It's the knowledge that is important, Eddie,' Sir William told him. 'Put it all together, and we may be getting somewhere.'

'Not a moment too soon then. Tonight's the night whatever they're planning happens, remember? And what about Liz?.'

'Liz!' George leaped to his feet. 'I should have asked you. I was too surprised and preoccupied by what happened here.' He walked slowly and carefully across the stage. 'I do hope she is all right. But as well as Marie . . .' He paused and pointed down at the floor. 'I found this.'

Eddie and Sir William walked over to where George was standing.

'Careful,' he warned them. 'You don't want to fall in as well.'

'As well?' Eddie could see as he approached that there was a hole in the stage where a trap door had opened. 'As well as what?'

'As well as him.'

Eddie peered into the blackness. His eyes slowly got used to it and he could make out a shape. The shape of a man. He was stretched out on his back, his eyes wide open in frozen surprise and fear. A broken spike of wood thrust up from his chest, and the dark form of a bat was flapping gently as it fed on the blood that had welled up round the wound.

'Henry Malvern,' George said. 'Or whoever he really was.' As he spoke, the body slipped further down the wooden spike. The face was ancient – cracked and crumbling away.

Sir William nodded grimly. 'It becomes clear.'

'Not to me it don't,' Eddie told him.

'I think you had better prepare yourself for a shock, George,' Sir William said. 'While I think we can deduce that Liz was confronted here by Malvern and got the better of him in no uncertain terms, it appears she was bitten. And that Malvern was not alone. It may already be too late. She is well on the way to becoming a vampire.'

George sank to his knees. 'Oh good God,' he murmured. 'Please tell me it isn't true.'

'Maybe it ain't too late,' Eddie said. 'Maybe we can sort it out and make her better. She didn't actually bite us, after all.'

'We know,' Sir William went on, apparently oblivious to their anxiety, 'that they are planning some ceremony tonight, and that a part of it at least will take place in the Palace of Westminster – at the Houses of Parliament.

We also know that they do not yet have the fifth casket containing the heart of the Lord of the Undead.'

'But how can that help Liz?' George asked, distraught.

'We don't know that anything *can* help her,' Sir William admitted. He put his hand on George's shoulder and squeezed gently. 'I am so very sorry. But you must be strong. And we all have to think about the wider situation now. About how these creatures can be stopped once and for all. And the fifth casket might give us something to bargain with.'

'I don't see how,' Eddie said. 'It's hidden, or lost, or destroyed. *We* don't have it either.'

'Ah.' Sir William jabbed a triumphant finger at Eddie. 'But I know where it is.'

'How?' Eddie demanded.

'Where?' George asked at the same moment. He sounded weary, but he was making an effort to pull himself together.

'That scoundrel Anthony Barford told us, don't you remember?' Sir William said to Eddie. 'Now, I wonder if there's anywhere in a theatre this size that they keep spades and shovels.'

'What would they want those for?' Eddie wondered.

'Not what we want them for, I'll be bound.'

'And what is that?' George asked.

Sir William's spectacles flashed as they caught the limelight. 'Grave robbing,' he said.

The cemetery was shrouded in fog. George could feel it cloying at the back of his throat, and it muffled their voices. He held the spade tight, aware that he might have to use it as a weapon. His body was tense with dread and anger. He couldn't get the image of Liz out of his mind. Perhaps, despite Sir William's fears, it was not too late to save her.

'Anthony Barford said we would take their secrets to our graves, you recall, Eddie?'

'I do, yeah.' Eddie was carrying Oldfield's metal box, clutching it tight to his chest like a talisman.

'Sounds like what Hemming had written in his journal,' George remembered.

'That's exactly what I thought,' Sir William said. He was a vague shape somewhere in front of George, leading the way along the narrow curving path. 'And it occurred to me that perhaps Hemming meant it literally.'

Eddie's voice floated out of the thickening air: 'And he's buried somewhere here, is he?'

'I never actually met Hemming. But I had already taken up my position at the Museum when he passed away after his illness. I went to the funeral.'

Sir William stopped so abruptly that George knocked into him. But he seemed not to notice.

'This way,' he decided, setting off again. 'I think.'

'Christopher Kingsley's grave is just along here some-where,' George realised as he recognised a statue of an angel standing close to the path. It was barely more than a silhouette in the foggy gloom.

'Don't I know it,' Eddie grumbled. 'Still got dirt from it down my back, I reckon. It's itchy.'

'Which means that right underneath us, at this moment . . .' George's voice tailed off as he realised Sir William had disappeared.

'Over here,' came the old man's voice. George and Eddie found him kneeling beside a grave. The grass was long and neglected, the headstone had tilted to a drunken angle.

'Forgive me, Xavier,' Sir William murmured. Then he straightened up. 'Right,' he told George, 'you've got the spade, so you'd better get digging.'

The earth was cold and damp, but George managed to make swift progress. He was spurred on by Sir William's comment that the ceremony must be due to start soon so they hadn't much time. He was less encouraged by Eddie's mention of how the Coachman could somehow detect the very casket they were looking for.

'Perhaps we're too late,' he said, handing the spade at last to Eddie and sinking down on the damp turf.

'Let us hope not.'

Eddie jumped down into the shallow pit that George had excavated and set to with more enthusiasm than expertise. Earth went flying, scattering across the ground and spraying George and Sir William who quickly moved out of range.

Sir William took his turn, and by the time that George took over again the hole was so deep they needed to help each other in and out.

'Can't be far now,' Eddie said.

'I wonder what's happening to Liz,' George said out loud. Neither of his friends had an answer. Before George could dwell on the possibilities, he felt the spade hit something solid. From the sound and feel, it was rotting wood.

He scraped the last of the earth from the top of the remains of the coffin. There was a smell coming from it that George tried to keep out by clamping a handkerchief over his nose and mouth. But it did little to help. As quickly as he could, he prised off what was left of the wooden lid and without giving himself time to think too much about it, reached into the darkness beneath.

'I can feel something,' he said, excitedly through the

hanky. It was a regular shape – smooth and cold. He dropped the spade and lifted what he had found out up for Sir William to take.

'I'll check there's nothing else.' Gingerly, George reached back inside the broken wooden coffin, trying not to think about what else he might find. His fingers brushed against something, and he gasped in horror as he realised it was a skeletal hand.

And the hand clutched at his wrist.

'Help me out, quick. There's someone else down here.' The hand grabbed George's leg as he tried to climb up and out of the grave.

'How can there be?' Eddie said, reaching down to help George. His expression changed as he realised. 'They're coming from below?'

'They've found us,' George agreed. With all his remaining strength, he heaved himself out of the pit.

'Well done, George,' Sir William said. He held up the casket for them to see. It was like the other canopic jars that had been in the crate in the Museum basement, but the lid was in the shape of a scorpion with its vicious tail curled up over its body.

'Just in time,' George gasped.

'Or just too late,' Eddie said.

There was a scraping from behind George. Something was pushing up through the bottom of the grave. The remains of the coffin tilted and fell as a figure forced its way into the pit. A skull-like face turned to look up at them.

The Coachman.

George turned to run. But like Eddie and Sir William he froze in terror.

The moonlight filtered through the fog just enough for them to be able to make out the vague shapes of the gravestones. And thrusting up between them were hands, arms erupting from the dead earth.

Pale, emaciated figures pushed through the graveyard soil and staggered to their feet as the graves opened and the undead awoke.

CHAPTER 27

'Run!' Eddie yelled. He wrapped the metal box inside his jacket, put his head down and charged into the figures appearing out of the fog and the ground. He hoped Sir William and George were following.

Bony fingers clutched and tore at him. There were so many of them – the undead waking from the long sleep in their graves. Eddie felt his foot disappear down a hole in the ground, and wrenched it free, almost dropping Oldfield's box. It was agony when he put his weight on it, but he ignored the pain and ran on.

A strong arm grabbed him, and he cried out. But it was George, helping him as he limped on.

George's face was the colour of the fog. 'Where's Sir William?'

'Right behind you. Keep running. Head for the river.'

The ground sloped upwards. Eddie hoped and expected at any moment to break through the last group of vampires. They were slow and seemed still tired as they continued to struggle free of the cold, damp earth. But Eddie could see no end to them.

They reached the top of the rise, and Eddie found himself lurching towards a high iron fence. On the other side, he could hear the lapping of water and just make out the murky dark expanse of the Thames.

'We'll never climb that,' George said.

Sir William was holding the canopic jar. He sank down to his knees and fumbled with the top. All around them the vampires were turning, moving slowly towards them. Hissing in anticipation.

'It's sealed,' Sir William said.

'Here, let me see.' George crouched down beside the casket. 'Might be wax, or . . . No – look, there's a lock. Strange shape, but I think I can force open the catch.'

'Never mind that,' Eddie said. 'The catch is they're going to catch us.'

They were surrounded by a semicircle of the pale creatures. Taloned hands reached out at them. The fence was cold and unyielding as Eddie pressed against it. Inside his jacket he could feel the metal box thumping and juddering as the bat inside sensed vampire blood close by. But just one bat wouldn't save them now.

'Stop right there!' Sir William's voice was loud and confident.

The vampires hesitated, but then started to press forwards again.

'We have something you are looking for,' Sir William
went on, and now Eddie could hear the tremor in his
voice. 'Come any closer and we shall destroy it.'

There was a sound like the rustling of leaves. It took
Eddie a moment to work out what it was. The vampires
were laughing. The sound grew, and then suddenly
stopped. The figures closest to Eddie and the others
moved aside, and the tall cadaverous Coachman stepped
into the moonlight.

'Your only chance is to give me the casket,' he rasped.
'Then we might allow you a quick death. A *lasting*
death.'

'No!' Eddie yelled. He leaped forward, ignoring the
shooting pain in his ankle, and grabbed the scorpion-
lidded jar. It was heavier than he expected. He struggled
to lift it, the lid moved as his fingers pulled nervously at
the catch George had loosened. Eddie had a lot of experience of opening locks . . . He staggered back, away
from the circling vampires. Then, pressing the catch
shut again, he held the jar up high so they could all see.

'You back off or I destroy it,' he said.

'It is what's inside that matters,' the Coachman said.
'Break the jar, and we shall still have what we need.'

'Not if it's in the river, you won't.' Eddie had moved

close to the fence. His hands were shaking, the jar trembling in his grip. 'Now back away, or I chuck it over and it'll sink for ever.'

The Coachman stretched out his arms, as if to keep his fellows back. 'Give me the jar,' he said. His voice was calm and reasonable-sounding. 'Just give me the jar.'

Eddie blinked. He could feel the voice eating into his will. He *wanted* to just hand it over. This must be how the Coachman persuaded Remick to go with him. Eddie felt himself stepping away from the fence, holding the jar out towards the Coachman's waiting hands. With a massive effort, Eddie turned.

And hurled the jar as far away as he could.

It was too heavy to get over the fence, so Eddie instead threw it into the fog. He heard the canopic jar rolling across the ground.

'Quick!' George yelled, pushing Eddie ahead of him into the fog. Eddie felt Oldfield's metal box slip from his grasp and tumble to the ground. But he had no time to stop and pick it up.

Sir William was running too. He and Eddie raced down the bank as the vampires scurried after the Coachman, searching for the fallen jar.

'Find it!' the Coachman was shouting. 'I must have it!'

'Well done, young man,' Sir William said.

They drew up breathless on the path through the

cemetery. Either side of them, Eddie could see the ground was churned up and broken open.

'There must be hundreds of them,' Eddie said. 'Their tunnels are all under here. This must be another vampire resting ground, like the house, and now they're waking up.' He looked round, peering into the swirling fog and trying to gauge the enormity of it all. Then he realised: 'What's happened to George?'

The fog closed in around George, smothering him. He did not dare to shout for Eddie and Sir William – the chances were that it would be someone else who heard. He resolved instead to find his way out of the cemetery as quickly as possible.

The moon had disappeared again and the world was a wash of grey. He picked his way carefully round the dark, gaping holes in the ground hoping to find the path. A figure loomed up in front of him, and George stepped quickly back.

But the figure did not move. He crept towards it, careful to make no sound. And almost laughed out loud as he saw it was a stone angel, weeping into its hands.

'I know how you feel,' he muttered.

Behind the angel was another dark shape – broad and high. George thought it might be a sepulchre or a large tomb. But it seemed to be a stone-built hut. It was windowless, with a single heavy wooden door. George walked slowly all round the little building. On the back wall, water dripped from a gargoyle's mouth in the eaves, splashing into a large trough below on the ground. In the foggy night, the liquid was dark as blood.

He barely glanced at the angel as he arrived back at the front of the building. Until it moved. And George realised that it was not the statue he had seen earlier at all, but a woman standing watching him.

'The sexton keeps his tools in there.' Her scarlet cloak was a stain of red in the grey night. Clarissa stepped smiling out of the fog.

'There is mention in Oldfield's journal of the Vrolak, or Wolf Bat,' Sir William said thoughtfully. 'Not many details, obviously, but I think that must be the pertinent species. He notes that it spends much of its life dormant, waking when it senses food.'

As they made their way through the deserted, foggy streets, Eddie's thoughts were elsewhere. 'But where's George? Is he all right? Shouldn't we be looking for him? And what about Liz? We'll never get her back to normal if we hang around nattering all the time.'

'Oh, George is old enough to look after himself. Liz is

another matter, I fear, and I do appreciate the need to act rapidly. George is a clever fellow. He should work out what we're up to.'

'And what are we up to?'

'It would have been useful to examine the creature again,' Sir William said. 'I don't suppose you still have Oldfield's box?'

'Dropped it,' Eddie confessed.

'Pity.'

'There's, er, something else I ought to tell you,' Eddie said sheepishly.

'Oh?' Sir William stopped beneath a street lamp. 'Well out with it, whatever it is.'

So Eddie told him what he had done.

Sir William's mouth dropped open in surprise. 'You did *what*?'

Eddie shrugged. 'Sorry.'

Sir William was silent for several moments. He tapped his forefinger against his chin. Then he drew a deep breath. 'Well . . .'

'I said sorry,' Eddie murmured.

'My boy, this changes everything,' Sir William went on. 'What an inspired strategy.' His spectacles gleamed in the lamplight.

'So, it's good, is it?'

'Good? Capital. Excellent. Top notch. Come on.' Sir

William strode off into the fog, a renewed vigour in his step.

'Where are we going?'

'We're going to a haunted house. It's a pity we have mislaid George, as we have a long and difficult task to perform in a very short space of time.'

'Let's go this way then,' Eddie suggested, pointing down a side street.

'Short cut?'

'No. But I know where we can get some help,' Eddie said. 'The Kenton Workhouse is just down here.'

George backed away, down the side of the small building.

'There really is nowhere for you to go,' Clarissa said, following him. Her icy smile bit through the fog. 'Why not give yourself up to us. I'll make it quick. It won't hurt. Join us.'

'Not likely,' George said.

'Then join *me*. Now I have lost my brother, you and I could be together for ever.'

'Your brother?' George didn't know what she meant, and he didn't care. He had reached the end of the wall, and was preparing to run for it.

But Clarissa sensed his intention. 'You wouldn't get

far. And anyway, after tonight there will be nowhere to hide.'

'Why? What's your precious Lord of the Undead planning to do?'

Clarissa laughed. 'What all lords do. Rule.'

George backed away as Clarissa moved towards him. There was something hypnotic about her – about her voice, about her smile. Would it really be so bad to live for ever? Then George thought of the terrible cost, of the lives that would have to be spent just to extend his own.

'What do you say?' Clarissa asked. 'Our Lord shall have his heart soon, but we still need your help. Come to me.'

George could feel the pull of her words, could sense his mind clouding over as if the fog had got inside his head. 'No!' he gasped. He struggled to remember Marie – her feral attack on him at the theatre. And he thought of Liz. George turned and ran.

Straight into stone. His knee connected painfully with the water trough, and he stumbled and fell.

She was there at once. Clarissa's cloak billowed out behind her like wings as she fell on him – mouth open, ready to bite.

CHAPTER 28

George rolled aside, desperate to throw her off. But she was incredibly strong. He managed to crawl backwards and struggle to his feet. But Clarissa still held him tight.

With all the strength he could muster, George hurled himself towards her. She had expected him to try to break away, and staggered back in surprise. But her teeth were still closing on his neck. Her legs met the stone water trough and she fell backwards with a cry. George was falling too, his weight forcing her over and into the trough. Together, they plunged into the freezing water.

George's head broke the surface and he gasped in foggy air, before she pulled him back. But she was no longer trying to attack George. She was struggling to get out from under him.

Clarissa's dress and cloak were heavy with water. George's weight pressed her down. Her grip on him slackened and he broke free at last and tumbled out of the stone trough to lie gasping on the ground.

His lungs felt ready to burst, but George forced himself to stand up. He hadn't been in the water that long, and neither had Clarissa. She would be back at him in a moment – up and out of the water. Flying at him in a rage.

But it didn't happen.

Cold, wet and shivering, George stepped warily towards the trough. Clarissa's eyes were closed. Her black hair was spread out in a dark halo. A drip from the gargoyle high above broke the surface over Clarissa's face, sending out ripples. The cloak stirred and moved then settled round her like a shroud. Staining the water red.

Nervously, George leaned closer. There was still no movement. No sign of life. Then suddenly Clarissa's eyes snapped open. A hand erupted from the water and closed on his neck. He tore it away, surprised at how weak the woman's grasp was. Her arms were flailing wildly, desperately, grabbing at George as he staggered back. He fell, breaking free, but pulling Clarissa with him so her head was now out of the water.

She was retching and choking. Her hand slapped back into the water and she slumped over the side of the trough, motionless. Her long, wet, black hair trailed in the mud.

Not daring to look closely, George hauled himself to his feet and staggered off into the mist.

The dormitory was alive with snores and the creak of the old iron beds. Eddie and Sir William stood in the semi-darkness, looking along the length of the room.

'I imagine boys and men have to share,' Sir William whispered.

'Guess so,' Eddie said. 'I'll see if I can find my mates. They'll help. They'll do it for Charlie.' Now that Sir William had explained what needed to be done, Eddie was sure that the workhouse kids would be up for it. He made his way quietly between the beds. All the shapes huddled under their single blankets looked too big. The children must be at the other end.

A shape moved in the darkness as someone sat up. 'Oh, it's you. Up to more mischief, are you?' a rough, scraping voice mumbled at Eddie.

Eddie peered into the gloom and saw it was the old man who had been chopping wood, the man who had helped him hide from Pearce. 'Yeah, it's me,' he whispered, tiptoeing to the man's side. 'I'm looking for my friends – for Jack and Mikey.'

'Midnight escape is it? Good for you, son. Good for you.' The old man sniffed and settled back into his thin blanket. 'You'll find 'em down the end.'

Eddie managed to find and wake Jack – who was so

excited to see him that Eddie had trouble keeping the boy quiet. Together they roused Mikey. An older boy in the next bed sat up, interested to know what was going on.

'I'll come with you,' he offered. 'I'm awake now.'

'Did you know Charlie?' Eddie asked him quietly.

'He was all right, was Charlie.'

'Then you can come.'

Eddie led them back along the dormitory to where Sir William waited patiently. Then together they trooped down the stairs.

They were almost at the bottom when a large shape loomed out of the near-darkness. 'And where do you think you lot are off to?' a gruff voice demanded.

'Strewth!' Eddie said. 'It's Mr Pearce.'

'Leg it!' Jack said.

'No, no,' Sir William said quietly. 'There's no call for that. I'm sure Mr Pearce is a reasonable man.'

'Then you don't know him,' Eddie said.

'And who the hell are you?'

'I am Sir William Protheroe, and I have need of the assistance of these young men.'

'Oh do you?' Pearce was blocking the narrow corridor at the bottom of the stairs that led to the outside door. He was holding a cudgel and smacked it threateningly into the palm of his hand. 'No one takes my boys.'

'Really?' Sir William took a step towards the man, and Eddie was tempted to grab his coat and yank him back. 'But that's not true is it, Mr Pearce? The Coachman,' Sir William went on, 'he takes your boys. Boys, girls, I don't suppose he cares. I don't suppose *you* care. Just so long as no one misses them. Just so long as you get your cut.'

'Are you from the Coachman?' Pearce asked, nervous now.

'No. But the Coachman won't be coming again. I shall see to that. And you, Mr Pearce . . .' Eddie was surprised to see that Sir William was shaking with anger. 'You had better pack whatever bags you have.'

Pearce raised the cudgel. 'Be careful what you say, old man.' He took a step towards Sir William.

'You like hitting old men, don't you?' The voice came from further up the stairs.

Eddie looked back, and saw that the stairs were now crowded with figures from the dormitory above.

'Well, we've had enough of it.' It was the old man who had befriended Eddie. 'You let them be about their business.'

'Or else what?'

A younger, stronger voice shouted down the stairs. 'We're not all old men and kids, you know, Pearce. We might be out of work and homeless, but we're not going to be bullied by you. This Sir William bloke – he's got something to do. Something important by the look of him and the sound of what he says. So you let him be about his business.'

There were cheers and shouts of agreement.

Pearce backed slowly away, scowling. But beneath the scowl he looked pale and anxious.

'Oh, and Mr Pearce, *sir*,' the old man on the stairs called above the noise. 'Reckon you'd better pack your bags like the gentleman says. Before the peelers come asking about Charlie and the others.'

'I'll get you for this,' Pearce said in a low voice as Sir William and Eddie pushed past him.

'Oh I very much doubt that,' Sir William said.

Eddie grinned. 'In your dreams, mate.'

They were halfway across the courtyard when Eddie heard the sound of running feet behind them. Afraid it might be Pearce, he whirled round. But it was Eve, pulling a threadbare cloak over a grubby nightgown.

'You ain't going without me,' she said. 'Whatever you're up to, I'm coming too.'

Eddie grinned. 'Good,' he said. 'Cos we need all the help we can get.'

'Indeed we do,' Sir William agreed. 'Now gather round and let me explain what needs to be done.'

The children stared at him as he quickly told them about the vampires, about the gathering at Parliament, and about what he and Eddie had decided to do.

'Some of the women make baskets,' Eve said. 'Sort of square, wicker baskets with lids. I help them, so I know where they are.'

'And I know where to take them,' Eddie said. 'George told me just the place.'

'Excellent.' Sir William clapped his hands together. 'You know, this might just work. Now, I must leave you in Eddie's capable hands.'

'Aren't you coming with us? Where are you going?' Eddie asked in surprise.

'I have an appointment with Mr Gladstone.'

'The Prime Minister?' Eve said.

'The very same. I'm going to see if I can stop or at least delay the ceremony.'

'The Coachman will kill you,' Eddie said.

Sir William put his hand on Eddie's shoulder. 'If we don't stop him, the Coachman and his kind will kill us all.'

The graveyard was like a battlefield. Fog drifted like smoke over the churned and broken ground. George picked his way round the holes and crevices back to the path. Gravestones had tilted and fallen as the ground opened. The place seemed deserted, but George listened carefully for any sound, staring into the grey night for any sign that he was not alone.

He was still half expecting Clarissa to appear fully recovered out of the mist in front of him. He didn't know if she was dead or merely unconscious, but George remembered what Sir William had said about the mountains being a place of sanctuary, and the vampires' fear of running water. It was all to do with oxygen, with breathing, with the strength of the heart pumping richer than usual blood round the body.

The grave he was looking for was a short distance from the path. It had no headstone of its own. It never would. George looked down into the gaping hole, remembering with a shudder how he and Eddie had forced their way out of it. It would be a brave man who went back down there. Or a foolish one.

He wasn't sure which of those he was; but George had a plan. He sat by the edge of Christopher Kingsley's grave and swung his feet into it, then lowered himself carefully into the catacombs below.

There were several MPs in the Central Lobby, talking quietly.

'You any idea what this is all about?' one of them asked Sir William as he hurried in.

'I'm afraid I have,' he said grimly. 'And I would advise

you to go home immediately.'

The man stared at Sir William. 'I beg your pardon?'

'Sir William will have his little joke,' a voice said from behind him.

Sir William turned to find Anthony Barford standing there. 'How kind of you to join us, Sir William. Please, if you will come this way? We are nearly ready to begin.'

It would have been easy to walk away, but Sir William needed to know what was happening. He needed to buy time for Eddie. And in any event, he could see the pale emaciated figures standing beside the exits. It was not difficult to guess what they were, or what would happen to him – and the genuine Members of Parliament – if he caused any trouble now.

'I've been looking forward to it.' He turned to go.

But Barford's hand caught his arm. 'Not that way. Not to the House of Commons. Mr Gladstone and his colleagues are taking their seats there, but I am afraid it will be necessary to bring them along to the other chamber.'

'To the House of Lords?'

Barford's bloodless lips drew back in a smile. 'Where else would the Lord of the Undead watch over his parliament?'

'Right,' Eddie declared. 'Time to get going.'

They hurried along Mortill Street, each with a basket clutched tightly. The wicker was rough and grazed Eddie's hands.

'You do this sort of thing a lot?' the new boy asked. He'd told them his name was Alex.

'Seems like it,' Eddie admitted. 'I used to be a pickpocket. But things have got a bit hectic since I gave that up. Come on, let's find a cab.'

'We'll never see a cab in this,' Alex said.

'And how do we pay?' Jack wondered.

Eddie jammed his basket under his arm and with his free hand pulled a bulging wallet from his pocket. The leather was scuffed and worn. 'I think I can afford it,' he said proudly.

'Where did you get that?' Alex said.

'Just sort of fell into my possession,' Eddie admitted. 'When I pushed past Mr Pearce. And a policeman gave me tuppence.'

They all stopped as they heard the sound of carriage wheels. A cab rattled out of the fog, and Eddie shouted and waved with his free hand. But it did not stop.

Mikey had to leap out of the way as the cab sped past. He glared after it, as usual saying nothing.

'He could have killed Mikey,' Eve said angrily.

The next cab was going so fast it almost knocked Jack

down. Eddie hauled the small boy out of the way as the cab clipped the kerb.

'What's got into them?' Eddie said. 'No call to be driving like that, especially in the fog.'

The next cab stopped. But only for long enough for the driver to yell at them from his seat above and behind the horses.

'Don't go that way. Get off out of it while you can.'

'Why?' Eddie shouted back. 'What's going on, what's wrong?'

'They're coming. Out of the graveyards, out of the derelict houses. Out of everywhere. You got to keep out of their way. Get in, I'll take you. Don't worry about the fare.'

'We need to get to the Houses of Parliament,' Eddie said, grateful but confused.

The driver immediately cracked his whip down at the horses. 'I ain't taking you there,' he yelled back. 'Looks like Westminster's where they're heading.' The cab lurched off into the fog, gathering speed and leaving Eddie and his friends staring after it.

'What's he mean?' Jack asked anxiously.

'I think we'd better get a move on,' Eddie said.

The next cab they found was abandoned. The horse stamped its feet and puffed in the cold of the night. The driver and several passengers were lying on the pavement a few yards away. Their broken bodies were pale and bloodless. Eddie spared them a brief look, then climbed up on to the driver's box and settled his wicker basket beside him.

'Get in then,' he called down. 'Next stop, the Houses of Parliament.'

Eve climbed up beside him while the others clambered into the body of the cab. 'You know how to drive, do you?' she asked.

'Can't be that hard. Cabbies do it.'

'Thought not.' Eve took the reins from Eddie. 'So leave it to someone who does.'

'Take your hands off me, sir!' the Prime Minister demanded.

Sir William was seated in the front row of the ornate red cross-benches, facing forward. Barford had promised him a good view, and he certainly had that. The House of Lords was almost full. Pale, drawn figures sat and stood so closely together that only the central aisle was empty. He could see several figures he knew – the small grey-haired Mrs Brinson, and the Curator of one of the other departments of the British Museum, as well as several peers of the realm and other notable people . . .

The whole place was more like a chapel than a

debating chamber. The end of the high-vaulted chamber was dominated by the ornate gold-leafed throne and the canopy behind it. There were two less ornamental chairs in front of the canopy, either side of the throne. On one of them sat Liz, looking every bit as pale as the other vampires. On the second seat was the Coachman, still wearing his cloak and his hat. On the floor beside him stood the canopic jar with its scorpion-shaped lid containing the heart of the Lord of the Undead. The Coachman's skull-face stared out over the assembly, and Gladstone's voice rang out again.

'I have never known such a thing!'

'Be silent!' the Coachman roared as Gladstone and several other people were dragged to the front of the chamber.

Sir William recognised many of them – prominent government ministers. All were doing their best to look dignified and confident. All were obviously terrified as Anthony Barford, Harrison Judd and several others dragged them before the empty throne.

'Henry Malvern should be here,' Barford said quietly.

'I'm sure he will make an appearance,' Sir Harrison Judd said. 'He had to cancel his dinner with Stoker from the Lyceum Theatre. You know how touchy the man can get.'

Alone of the half-dozen men now arranged before the throne William Gladstone looked angry rather than fearful. He was in his seventies, stooped but assured. Wisps of white hair clung to his balding scalp and his heavily lined forehead and face made him look even more severe.

'I demand to know what is going on,' Gladstone said. 'What is the meaning of this, Barford?' he demanded, turning to face the man who held him tightly by the arm.

'All will be explained,' Barford said.

As he turned back, Gladstone caught sight of Sir William watching him. He frowned, looking round at the other pallid faces staring back at him. Then he looked again at Sir William's more ruddy complexion. His eyebrows arched in a silent question.

Sir William could not answer, but he nodded slightly, hoping to give whatever reassurance the Prime Minister needed to get through the long night ahead.

The cab thundered over Westminster Bridge, sending the fog skidding away. There was little other traffic. But ahead, through the heavy air, Eddie could see the indistinct shapes of figures – people walking towards Parliament.

Eve drove the cab between them. People turned to look. Pale, bloodless faces peered out of the fog. Someone jumped aside just in time as the cab hurtled past.

'You done this a lot?' Eddie shouted above the sound

of the hoofs and the wheels.

Eve grinned at him. 'First time. I just wanted to have a go.'

'Terrific,' Eddie muttered. 'Scared by mummies, attacked by vampires, killed by a runaway cab.'

The crush of people got tighter as they approached the end of the bridge. The horse was forced to slow down to a fast walk.

'Where are they all coming from?' Eve wondered.

'Out of the ground,' Eddie said. 'Or the walls of other haunted houses. They must have resting places all over London. Let's just get through them.'

A hand clutched at Eddie's arm and he thumped at it, wrenching himself away from its grip. More hands reached up. The cab was slowing. Eve gave a cry and lurched to the side as someone tried to pull her off the driver's seat. Eddie held tight to her and struggled to pull the girl back.

'Go on!' he yelled at the horse. There was a whip in a holder beside the seat and Eddie grabbed it. He hated himself for doing it, but he cracked the whip as hard as he could above the horse's back. The cab lurched forwards. A pale figure was thrown aside as the horse forced its way through the crowd. Eve lurched back towards Eddie as the vampire that had hold of her fell.

Eddie looked down at the mass of clutching hands as

the cab kept going. A woman – pale, drawn, with angular features – leaped up on to the running board and reached in through the cab window. There was a shout from inside:

'Look out, Jack!'

Eddie realised with surprise that it was Mikey's voice.

The woman was fumbling with the door, trying to open it and climb inside.

'Do it now!' Jack yelled.

'No,' Eddie shouted back. 'It's too soon.' He turned to Eve. 'Keep going – fast as you can.' He handed her the whip, then he jumped down on to the running board, beside the woman. And within reach of the vampires racing alongside the cab.

The Coachman lifted the canopic jar and held it high above his head as he strode to the front of the dais on which the throne stood. Then he slowly lowered it and placed it in front of the throne.

'Now it begins,' he announced. 'We are gathered here to witness the birth of a new empire. An empire not of steel and sweat, but of fear and blood. From here we will govern the whole world. Our Lord has returned and our brethren have risen. Now begins the Parliament of Blood.' He turned to face the empty throne, and bowed.

'And here is our new sovereign: Orabis, Lord of the Undead.'

All around the chamber echoed to the chant: 'Orabis, Orabis, Orabis.'

Sir William watched in horror, saw Liz's eyes widen in astonishment, felt suddenly empty and sick. The ornate golden throne disappeared. With a crack like thunder, a hole had opened in the floor and it fell away beneath the dais.

For the first time, Sir William saw that there were ropes hanging from the ceiling of the chamber. They were hard to make out against the ornate canopy and screen behind where the throne had been, until they moved. Somewhere deep below a powerful engine sputtered into life. There was a grinding and clanking of gears.

A new throne was rising slowly, majestically out of the floor. It was oily and industrial, wrought from iron and wood. The figure seated on it was held in place by pipes and tubes that fed directly into its shrunken, emaciated form. Strips of ragged bandage hung from the body. A golden ankh hung on a chain round the neck. Long-dead eyes stared out from wizened features as Orabis surveyed the assembled mass of vampires. From the catacombs deep below the earth, the Lord of the Undead was rising to take his place at the heart of the Parliament of Blood.

CHAPTER 29

George hurried along a tunnel, keeping to the shadows and trying to avoid the groups of vampires making their way from the Damnation Club to the main chamber.

The roof of the cavern where he had arrived was pitted and scarred and broken open. Earth was scattered across the floor. It seemed that just as many vampires had burrowed down into the cavern as had forced their way up through the ground into the graveyard above.

Now the tunnels themselves were alive with the undead. The walls shimmered and heaved as pale bodies forced themselves out of the rock. The ground was slick with congealing blood that seemed to seep out of the floor and the walls. Bricks fell into the tunnels as more and more of the grotesque figures erupted from the very architecture. It was as if the place had been built round them, George thought. Perhaps it had. Who knew how long they had slept there, waiting for the return of Orabis.

George evaded the clutching hands and the people that staggered back and forth as they regained their balance, remembered how to walk, woke into an older world . . .

At last he found himself at a junction he recognised. He was not far from the main chamber. And behind that was the pumping machinery.

As he approached the chamber he could hear the chanting: 'Orabis, Orabis, Orabis . . .' But it wasn't the chamber he needed to get to, it was the cavern behind it. With luck that would be deserted.

Just round the next corner, George realised. If he could sneak past the entrance to the main chamber without being seen, he would be there. There was a patter of dust on George's shoulder. He brushed it off without thinking, then hesitated and glanced up.

The roof was coming down. Chunks of stone and masonry tumbled out of the darkness towards him. George leaped back and the stones exploded as they shattered on impact. Shards whipped past George's cheek. Then a dark shape dropped to the ground in front of George. A figure straightened up, teeth gleaming in the light from the flickering wall lamps.

❖

Eddie barged into the vampire woman on the cab's running board, and she fell. Her hand was still on the handle of the door and she clung on, feet dragging along the roadway. Slowly, she started to haul herself back up.

Claw-like hands clutched at Eddie, trying to prise him off the side of the cab. He kicked out at them, at the same time struggling to keep his balance. But the sheer mass of them would drag him down if he stayed here. He kicked out again, this time at the woman as she pulled herself back up on to the running board.

She gave a cry and lost her footing. One of her feet dangled in space. The other caught in the wheel of the cab and she screamed as she was dragged down and under. The cab rose in the air, then thumped down hard on the street again. The force of it broke Eddie free of the clutching hands, and he leaped back up to the driver's box to rejoin Eve.

But now he could see there was a man on the roof of the cab, crawling towards Eddie and Eve. His teeth were bared in a hungry grin of triumph.

'Just drive,' Eddie shouted at Eve. 'Drive like the devil!'

The cab surged forward as Eve cracked the whip again. Bodies tumbled away from the sides. The man on the top of the cab slid rapidly backwards as it accelerated and was thrown off with a cry.

Then suddenly the road ahead was clear. Eddie and Eve were laughing with relief. Eddie banged on the roof and shouted: 'You all right inside? Nearly there now. Don't fret. Have your fares ready.'

George stared at the figure in front of him. It was a man, so thin that his ribs were poking through the pallid skin beneath his tattered shirt. His head tilted back as if he was sniffing the air – hunting.

'They're all in there,' George said quickly, pointing to the entrance to the huge underground chamber.

Dark eyes stared back at George. The head tilted slightly as the creature that had once been a man listened to the chanting of his fellows. Then it turned and shuffled towards the chamber.

With a long, deep breath George continued down the tunnel to the next opening – the entrance to the Hall of Machines. He could hear them above the sound of the chant as he approached. Rhythmic hissing and clanking as they kept the river water out of the tunnels and fed blood into the pipes running to the throne where Orabis sat.

Except, George realised, the throne was no longer in the next chamber. The pipe work had been changed. Flexible rubber tubes now led upwards. The ropes he had noticed before led to a vast pulley system suspended near the roof of the room. There was an opening in the roof to allow the ropes and tubes through and George could see light. He could hear echoes of the chanting coming from high above.

And he could see the dark silhouette of the throne of Orabis held by the ropes in its new location above the catacombs.

The whole House of Lords seemed to throb. Dark liquid ran and dripped from the tubes feeding into the body enthroned before Sir William and the others. From deep below came the sound of the engines and pumps that sustained the grotesque figure.

Orabis, Lord of the Undead, opened his mouth and a thin trickle of blood escaped and ran down his chin, dripping on to the stained linen wrapped across his chest. When he spoke, his voice was soft and rich – a contrast to the ancient wizened figure.

'I have slept,' Orabis said. 'I have slept for so long. But now I have confounded my enemies. I have awakened and I shall have my heart restored.' He turned his head slowly to look at Liz. 'With my new bride, I shall rule over you all. And together, my friends, we will take our rightful place as the supreme power over humanity.'

He leaned forward, tubes rippling with the movement. His whole body pulsed in time to the heartbeat throb of the pumps. He seemed stronger and less frail by the moment. 'Today the British Empire. And soon – the world.'

They abandoned the cab two streets away. The vampires converging on the Palace of Westminster were heading for the entrance that opened on to the street. The crowds were thinning out now as the last of them arrived at Parliament.

'Must be packing them in,' Jack said.

'The more the better,' Eddie said.

Each clutching a wicker basket, the five of them hurried to a small grassed area at the end of the palace away from the Big Ben clock tower.

'We must be able to get in down by the river somewhere,' Eve said.

'Where we heading for?' Jack asked. 'It's a big place.'

'See the three towers, one at each end and another in the middle,' Eddie told them. They had to peer into the fog to make out the vague shapes. 'That's how they get ventilation. The bad, hot, smelly air is pushed out, and good air is pulled in through the tops of the towers.'

'How?' Alex wanted to know.

'There's a smaller tower, down towards Big Ben, and

that's a chimney. I dunno how it works exactly,' he confessed, wishing he'd paid more attention to George when
he explained it. 'But the hot air from the fire in there goes
up the chimney and pulls more air through behind it.'

'So?' Alex said.

'So, there's like vents and shafts all through the place
for the air to go round. We need to get to them.'

'You mean find where they start and end?' Eve asked.

'I mean, get right inside them,' Eddie said.

But first they had to get into the building. Mikey and
Jack found a door that opened on to a terrace above the
river, and they carefully eased it open.

Eddie could see the dark silhouette of a man standing
just inside the door. He gestured urgently to the others
to be quiet. They needed to distract him somehow, and
quickly. He gently pulled the door shut.

A few moments later, the door opened once more
and a boy with a blank, staring expression stepped confi-
dently into the Palace of Westminster. The man turned
towards Eddie, his own face pale and drawn.

Before he could speak, Eddie said: 'Sir Harrison Judd
wants you. Out there.' He pointed back at the door he
had come through.

The man's dark eyes narrowed in suspicion. 'Why
would he want me?'

'Perhaps so you can explain why this door isn't locked.'

The man stared at Eddie for several seconds. Then he strode angrily past him and out into the night.

No sooner had he set off along the river terrace than four more children slipped ghost-like into the building behind him. Eddie pushed the door shut.

'He'll be back in a minute, so we've got to hurry. Let's find those ventilation openings that George told me about.'

They soon found vents – close to the floor and under the ceiling. They were far too small for what Eddie wanted. Their search was hampered by the need to keep as quiet as possible. The place seemed almost deserted, but they could all hear the rhythmic thump of machinery and Eddie shuddered as he remembered the sound from his encounter with Orabis.

'This big enough?' Eve asked at last. She and Eddie had found their way down a narrow winding staircase to a basement area. A metal grille covered a rectangular hole in the wall.

'Could be.' Eddie prised away the grille with his fingers, wincing as he felt his nails tear. 'Take a look, see if you can get inside.'

'Why me?' Eve demanded.

'You're the biggest.'

'Am not!' she protested.

'You are,' Eddie insisted. 'If you can get inside then

all of us can.'

'And what if I get stuck?'

'Don't get stuck,' Eddie said. 'That wouldn't be good.'

Eve glared at him. Then she nodded and climbed into the opening. It was tight, but she could crawl along inside. 'Seems all right,' her muffled voice came back. 'Now what?'

'Now you can come out. For the moment. I'll fetch the others,' Eddie said. 'You have a look for any more of these vents down here.'

Sir William was pulled to his feet and led to stand with Gladstone and the other ministers. He stood defiantly before the Lord of the Undead.

'Soon you will join us,' Orabis said. 'The key to our power is continuity. Mr Gladstone, you will still be a figurehead, but answering to me.'

'Never!' Gladstone told him.

'What about Her Majesty?' one of the other ministers asked in a trembling voice.

Orabis laughed. Beside him, the Coachman also laughed. Soon the whole chamber and then the entire building was echoing with laughter.

'Her Majesty?' Orabis said with scorn as the sound died away. 'She could not even bring herself down from

Balmoral to witness the birth of our new empire. But the empire she has ruled will continue. Only the way it is governed need change.'

The Coachman stepped forward. 'Let us welcome new blood,' he said.

The vampire holding each of the ministers turned to his captive. Teeth flashed white as they lowered their heads. More vampires stepped forward to hold the victims, pulling their heads to one side to expose the necks. Sir William felt the cold breath on his neck . . .

'Wait!'

The ceremony froze in tableau as a figure stepped to the edge of the dais. 'I too shall feed.'

The vampire poised to bite into Sir William's neck hissed with disappointment, but stepped back. Allowing Liz to walk forward and take his place.

Clarissa had been telling only part of the truth when she said that the pumps were there to keep the tunnels dry. Most of the engines were pumping something other than water. George remembered how the walls had seemed to seep blood, and tracing the pipes he now knew why.

They were feeding blood from huge storage tanks into the walls, sustaining and feeding the vampires that had slept there perhaps for centuries. Now, as the vampires awakened, the pumps had stopped.

George was pleased to find that the engine nearest the back wall was also the biggest. The furnace that heated the water to drive the system was still alight, and George shovelled on more coal. Then he checked the pressure, closed the valves, and smiled with satisfaction.

Although most of the fires were still lit, there were only two other engines operating. One of them George saw fed blood into the pipes and tubes that now ran up to the world above. Close to it another, smaller pump was linked to the drainage ducts. It would take years – maybe even decades – for the tunnels to flood. But these vampires measured time by a different scale. The engine was barely ticking over, just working enough to pump the water seeping from the Thames out into the nearby sewers and drains.

George traced the pipes of the two pumping systems as far as he could follow them, working out which was input and which outlet. He inspected the junctions and the stop taps, adjusting some and ignoring others. He took a length of tubing from one of the other pumps to make the connections he needed between the two systems. His hand hesitated for a moment on the final flow valve.

And in that moment a figure stepped into the Hall of Machines. The light from the tunnel outside threw the man into silhouette. But it didn't cast a shadow.

George's hand tightened on the small wheel that would open the valve. Now or never. He twisted – and nothing happened. The wheel was slippery with oil and too stiff to turn.

'What are you doing?' Kingsley demanded as he advanced on George.

'My job.' George's heart was thumping in his chest, imitating the rhythmic pulse of the pumps. He moved so that he was standing in front of the pipes and tubes he had rerouted. His hand was behind his back, still trying desperately to turn the valve. Still without success.

'It was to be your job to maintain these pumping systems,' Kingsley said suspiciously.

'I can see I was wrong to try to shirk it, to escape.'

'Really?' Kingsley was walking slowly along the length of the hall, between the pumps and boilers, glancing at each in turn.

'I want to join you,' George called after him. He had to stop Kingsley seeing what he had done at the back of the hall. 'Now!'

Kingsley turned abruptly. He walked slowly up to George, dark eyes deep with suspicion. 'I know you, George. You can't lie to me. What have you been doing here?'

Puzzled, Kingsley ran his hand along one of the tubes

that fed blood up to the Lord of the Undead. 'No,' he murmured. 'That's all fine.' He stared suspiciously at George. 'Perhaps I found you just in time. What were you *going* to do?'

George had managed to take out his handkerchief and wrap it over the stubborn valve wheel. The extra grip was enough, and he could feel it just starting to turn.

'Nothing,' he said. 'Nothing at all.'

From the far end of the hall came a whistle of steam and a loud, insistent knocking was added to the rhythmic pump of the blood.

Kingsley turned immediately towards the noise. He hurried down the hall to see what was happening.

George turned the valve wheel as far as it would go, then hurled himself after Kingsley. His arms wrapped round Kingsley's legs, bringing him crashing down. With a cry of anger Kingsley broke free of George's grip. His foot lashed out, catching George across the cheek.

From high above, and from the nearby chamber, George could hear the rising chant of the assembled vampires. From the far end of the hall he could hear the protesting steam engine as the pressure built.

Kingsley stared down at him, smiling with anticipation. 'You're bleeding, George,' he said. 'That's good.'

The shaft was hot and cramped. Even without his jacket on, Eddie's shoulders touched both sides as he eased himself slowly along. He was pushing the wicker basket in front of him.

It was dark and humid and he was tired. But he forced himself to keep going. He couldn't let the others down. They must be every bit as weary and scared as they each crawled along their own shaft.

He just hoped he would find a suitable place before the signal they had agreed. Wherever they were when they heard it, that was the time: when Big Ben struck the hour. Midnight.

Sir William stood his ground as Liz approached. Her lips seemed redder than ever, her features incredibly pale. She leaned forward, mouth open. And winked.

Sir William took a short step backwards, his own mouth open in surprise. Up close, he could see that Liz's face was powdered with pale make-up.

As her lips closed on his throat, Sir William could feel the stickiness at his neck. He reached up, suddenly afraid, but Liz caught his hand.

'Father's raspberry jam. What do we do?' she whispered in Sir William's ear as she pretended to bite into his neck.

'Just wait,' Sir William murmured. 'Eddie has it all in hand. I hope.'

'He may be too late,' Liz replied.

Beside them, Gladstone's body was held up by one of the vampires while another bit deep. Blood was running down the Prime Minister's neck and dripping on to his jacket. His head lolled sideways.

The Coachman was standing triumphant at the front of the dais. 'Our time has come!' he thundered over the chanting and the sound of the pumps below. 'When we have fed, our Lord will be restored.' He picked up the canopic jar and raised it again. 'He shall have his heart. It will beat once more in his chest. He will be complete and will walk among us. And where he walks, he will leave only death.'

The Coachman turned back towards Orabis on the throne behind him. The chanting faded away to a hush of anticipation.

'My touch is death and my breath is destruction,' Orabis said. He paused, his ancient withered brow creasing. 'My . . . my . . .' He coughed, spluttered, then continued: 'My heart will be restored and my reign of terror will begin.'

Liz had stepped away from Sir William. No one was

watching them now. All eyes were on Orabis as he struggled to speak. His whole body suddenly convulsed in
another fit of coughing.

'My heart!' he gasped. 'Give me my heart!'

'Now this,' Sir William said quietly, 'is where it gets
interesting.'

Orabis was shaking, his hands clutching the arms of
the throne tight as his whole body shuddered. It pulsed
and shook in time with the rhythm of the pumps. As Liz
and Sir William watched his wasted body seemed to
swell, bloating and expanding. Strips of rotting linen fell
away as he shook. The trickle of blood from his mouth
was becoming a steady stream as he coughed and spluttered and choked.

Not blood now. But water.

Chapter 30

The words of Orabis, Lord of the Undead echoed round the Hall of Machines. Kingsley paused to listen, feet either side of George's prone body, hand clamped on George's neck.

As Orabis spluttered and choked to a halt, Kingsley's expression changed from rapt awe to anger. 'What have you done?' He hauled George to his feet and slammed him back against the massive boiler of one of the larger pumps.

'Nothing,' George gasped. 'Well, nothing much. I just rerouted some of the pipes, changed the direction of flow.' He did his best to shrug while being held tight against the hot boiler.

There was a clamour from overhead. A dark shape appeared high above George – someone climbing rapidly down the ropes from the opening in the roof. The coughing and choking was getting more emphatic and desperate, but it was barely audible now over the noise of the steam engine at the end of the hall as it shuddered and hissed frantically.

Kingsley's grip slackened slightly as he too looked up. George braced himself, ready for any opportunity.

'I swapped over the tubes,' he told Kingsley.

Kingsley looked round confused, checking the state of the various systems. 'But the pump is working. The flow is open and the pipes are full.'

'Yes,' George admitted. 'But it isn't blood that's being pumped round your precious Lord's body any more. It's water from the drains.'

As soon as he said it, as soon as Kingsley registered with horror what had been done, George tore himself from the vampire's grip. He turned to run.

Only to find Sir Harrison Judd was standing at the bottom of the ropes that looped up over the pulleys into the chamber above. Blocking George's escape.

His body heaved and bucked as the Lord of the Undead coughed and spat. He was dripping with oily water. It seeped from the points where the pipes and tubes attached to his body, glistening like perspiration as his body continued to pulse and swell. With a frantic effort, Orabis pulled at the gold ankh hanging round his neck.

The chain broke and he reached out, the ankh dangling from his trembling hand.

'The heart!' the Coachman roared, having ordered Sir Harrison Judd into the catacombs below to discover what was wrong. 'He must have his heart.' He waved back the vampires that were pressing forward to help. 'No – the heart must be given in accordance with the ceremony.' His skull face turned towards Sir William and Liz. 'By his bride!'

'Your cue,' Sir William murmured.

Desperately trying to remain in character as a vampire, Liz stepped solemnly back up on to the dais. The Coachman took the gold ankh on its broken chain from the trembling hand of Orabis and gave it to Liz. 'They thought they could taunt our Lord by burying him with the key of life. Believing he could never use it.' A shuddering laugh escaped from his bloodless lips. Then he lifted the canopic jar and held it out like an offering.

'Unlock the jar. Remove the lid. Take the heart. Place it in his chest and it will take root. It will strengthen and heal him. All will be well.'

The ankh was a key, Liz realised. The way the Coachman had handed it to her made that obvious. The empty eyes of his skull-like face were deep and dark, boring into Liz, eating into her as she slotted the end of the ankh into the lock and turned.

The retaining catch sprang open, and Liz lifted the carved scorpion from the top of the jar. She could hear Big Ben starting to chime midnight as she peered into the dark interior of the jar. Deep inside, something was moving, beating . . . alive.

The Coachman lowered the jar slightly so that Liz could reach inside. As he did so, the light spilled in, illuminating the inside of the jar. Liz gasped in astonishment.

'I cannot give him his heart,' she said in a trembling voice.

'Why not?'

'Because it isn't there.'

The ceramic interior was stained red. Lumps of grey meat spattered the inside. And the bat that Eddie had slipped into the jar beat its leathery wings in time to the chimes of midnight and sucked the last drops of blood from the remains of the heart of Orabis.

Some light filtered into the ventilation shafts from vents and grilles and narrow openings. In five of the many shafts that drew the hot air from the Palace of Westminster to allow cooler fresher air to be sucked in, a child paused as Big Ben struck midnight.

The warm air was drawn past Eddie in a breeze that ruffled his hair. The basket in front of him was trembling and juddering.

Eve fumbled with the catch on her basket. She had to hold the lid down to undo it, feeling it shaking and rattling under her palm.

Finally Mikey got his undone. He took a deep breath of humid air and closed his eyes.

Whoever this Eddie was, Alex thought, he was certainly more than a pickpocket. He let go of the lid of his basket.

The lid whipped open, and Jack clasped his hands over the back of his head as a black cloud enveloped him. The black shapes were drawn along the shaft by the breeze.

Through half-closed eyes, Eddie watched in fascination as the bats thundered through the near-darkness. The transformation was incredible. In the house on Mortill Street they had been dormant and still, hanging immobile from the rafters. Collecting them and putting them into the wicker baskets had been easy. Now they were swarming aggressively through the shafts – awake, and scenting blood.

Without the constant chanting Kingsley could hear the protesting hiss and clank of the huge engine at the back of the hall and hurried to investigate, leaving Sir Harrison Judd to deal with George.

George backed slowly away, trying to circle round and get past the furious vampire. But other figures were appearing from the tunnel outside now, watching George hungrily from the doorway.

'You will die for this,' Harrison Judd hissed. 'We shall drain the blood from you slowly, drop by drop.'

The vampires in the doorway were pressing inwards, advancing on George. Something struck his shoulder as he backed away, and he whirled round, ready to fight for his life.

But it was the swinging end of the rope that Harrison Judd had climbed down. George was directly under the hole in the roof. He could see the throne of the Lord of the Undead. Water was splashing down like rain, and George wanted to laugh. It had worked. His legs knocked into a huge, heavy, hessian bag of earth – the counterweight at the end of another rope that had hoisted Orabis up into the chamber above. He stumbled and almost fell, grabbing at the rope.

The vampires closed in.

The sound of the tortured engine at the other end of the hall reached a crescendo. George had stoked the fire, and closed off all the valves, even the safety valve. The water would be boiling furiously inside the metal drum, the steam unable to escape, the pressure building and building, until –

The boiler exploded. Huge chunks of twisted metal were hurled across the Hall of Machines. A plate torn from the side of the boiler sliced through Christopher Kingsley as he was caught in the blast. At once the whole place was full of steam, rolling like fog between the engines and pumps and swallowing the light.

But that wasn't why George had sabotaged the engine. The far side of the boiler was almost touching the back wall. As it exploded it ripped into the ancient brickwork and tore apart the wall, gouging a hole deep into the area beyond.

A trickle of murky water splashed through. Becoming a small stream that washed the hole ever bigger as the pressure of the water behind bore down on it.

Then the river Thames erupted through the broken wall into the catacombs.

A massive wave crashed down on the engines, smashing them from their fixings and hurling them across the hall. The vampires advancing on George turned in shock and fear. One went flying as the water swept him off his feet. Then another.

Sir Harrison Judd's clawed hands grabbed George and slammed him back against the wall. 'You'll die for this!'

'Very probably,' George admitted. 'But you'll drown before I do.'

They struggled to stay on their feet as the water

reached their waists. Harrison Judd's face was a mask of terror. 'But I can't *die!*' he protested.

The water surged onwards. The lifeless body of a vampire woman floated past and was carried out into the tunnels beyond. The grip on George was slackening. He could hear the crash of the water from the other side of the wall as well now. Shrieks and screams.

'You'll drown,' George told Harrison Judd. 'You'll *all* drown!' The water was up to his neck.

Harrison Judd was spluttering and coughing, struggling to keep his head above the water. 'You'll drown with us,' he roared. Then the water rolled over his head.

George ducked down. The world was in darkness. Sound was muted and distant. He fumbled round in the black water until he found what he was searching for. A bag of earth attached to a rope. His cold, numb fingers struggled with the knot.

He managed at last to get it undone. He couldn't hold his breath any longer. Bubbles rose in front of his face. A hand grabbed his neck.

The Lord of the Undead was trying to stand up. He ripped out tubes and pipes. Water spurted from the holes they left. He was retching, great gasps of murky river water spattering the dais.

But the assembled vampires hardly noticed. A dark cloud was rising from the narrow vents close to the floor. Another was falling from the vents under the ceiling. The air was thick with the leathery shapes of the wolf bats. The beating of their wings was like applause as they rose and descended on their prey.

Shouts, cries, screams. A sudden crush of panic as they all tried to get out of the chamber of the House of Lords. But it was the same throughout the Palace of Westminster. In the Commons too, vampires fought towards the exits, disappearing under the black cloud.

In the Central Lobby, a woman in a faded dress tore at the creatures lodged in her hair until the last blood was drained from her undead body and she slumped to the floor, beside so many others.

Sir William stood unflinching before the dais. He saw Mrs Brinson tearing at the dark shapes that clawed and tore at her. A single bat lodged on the unconscious Gladstone's neck, drawing out the infected blood. Anthony Barford lunged at Sir William, his face contorted with rage. But before he got close, his whole body was covered with bats. Several slammed into his face, their wings tangling with his hair and his beard. Flailing and shouting, he collapsed to the floor, smothered by a black wave.

Just Sir William and Liz stood unscathed.

And the near-bloodless Coachman. He swatted away the few bats that came at him. He clawed at the bats now descending on the swollen form of Orabis, ripping them off his Lord and hurling them away. But as quickly as he pulled them away more appeared. Until the whole of the Lord of the Undead disappeared under a pulsating blanket of darkness.

With a muffled scream of agony, fear, and defiance, Orabis, Lord of the Undead exploded. His whole swollen body burst open from the pressure of the water still pumping into it. Wolf bats went flying off in all directions. Thames water sloshed across the dais, murky dark and mixed with blood. The throne disappeared through the floor of the House of Lords as it fell back into the Hall of Machines below.

Standing beside the hole in the floor, the Coachman lashed out and grabbed Liz's arm. He dragged her towards him.

Sir William tried to get to them, but the way was blocked by the writhing, dying bodies of the vampires and the air was thick with the bats as they sought fresh blood. He forced his way through, eyes fixed on Liz as the Coachman drew her to him.

'You may have defeated us,' the Coachman rasped as he held the struggling woman tight. 'You may have made fools of my colleagues and destroyed my Lord, but now – before I die – in my sister's memory and to avenge her, I shall feed again at last.'

Sir William was still ten feet away as the Coachman's teeth descended on Liz's neck.

With the rope untied and free of the heavy bag of earth, the weight distribution changed. George had been hoping he was lighter than the large bag. But the hand on his neck was holding him down. He kicked at the floor, pushing himself upwards.

George broke the surface of the water. It was over ten feet deep now. Sir Harrison Judd's face was close to his, coughing and gulping air.

'We drown together,' Judd gasped.

'I don't think so,' George managed to say. The vampire had been weakened by his time in the water. George looped his arm round the rope, gripping it tight, as he prised Judd's fingers from his neck.

As he loosened the last finger, he felt the rope pulling. The weight holding George back – the weight of Sir Harrison Judd – fell back into the water with a cry. The counterbalanced weight of the throne high above was now far heavier than the weight of George on the rope. The throne fell.

And George was hauled up and out of the surging

water towards the square of light far above.

As he neared the top, speed increasing, the throne crashed into the rising water below, smashing apart. Wooden struts from the arms and back bobbed and floated on the surface.

George caught a brief confused view of the adjacent chamber as he neared the roof and saw over the high dividing wall. The water in there was rising too, seething and churning. A hand clutched at the air before sinking. Pale bodies floated face down. The sound of the Thames rushing through the catacombs was an almighty roar as George raced upwards.

Liz felt the cold prick of the teeth on her skin. She had managed to pull one arm free and thumped and slapped at the Coachman. But with no effect.

Then someone grabbed her arm.

With a gasp of astonishment she saw George rising rapidly from the centre of the dais where the throne had been. He caught hold of her, and she was pulled suddenly, painfully up and out of the Coachman's grip as George continued to rise towards the roof of the House of Lords.

'George! Oh thank God.'

George was staring at her nervously as they rose rapidly into the air. 'Liz – are you . . .?'

She shook her head. 'Just an act. Make-up and jam.'

'Jam?'

Bats flew out of their way. Liz clung on tight, grateful for George's strong arm round her as they stared down at the carnage so far below. Dark bats and pale bodies and red blood. The Coachman was looking up at them. He reached for the rope.

'He's coming up after us,' Liz realised in horror.

Before his skeletal hand caught the rope, it was knocked aside. Sir William had hurled himself across the dais, catching the Coachman in the chest. Sir William sank exhausted to the wet floor.

The Coachman staggered back, right to the edge of the hole in the floor. He teetered for a moment on the brink, arms flailing as he tried to regain his balance. Then he fell backwards into the churning waters below.

Even from high above, Liz could hear the sickening crunch as he landed on a strut of wood from the shattered throne. The Coachman stared down at the wooden stave emerging from his chest. Then the waters closed over him and he disappeared for ever.

Gasping for air and feeling exhausted, Eddie hauled himself out of the vent. He flopped down on the floor, breathing heavily, and wiped his face on his sleeve. After giving himself a few moments to recover, he went to find the others.

Pretty soon, all five of them were hurrying up to the floor above.

'It's very quiet,' Mikey said.

'You can talk,' Eddie told him. Then he laughed. 'You *can* talk.'

'He's right though,' Eve said.

'I wonder where all those bats went.' Jack was hurrying to keep up on the stairs.

'What is it with the bats anyway?' Alex wanted to know.

They found the first body at the top of the stairs – a man lying crumpled, his legs bent under him. His face was a withered dry husk that had collapsed in on itself. Beyond him, Eddie could see many, many more.

'Did we do this?' Jack asked, awestruck.

There was a breeze through the Palace of Westminster. Maybe the children had been blocking the ventilation as they crawled through, or perhaps it was something more elemental, but the breeze whipped at the clothes of the desiccated husks lying along the corridors and in the debating chambers of the Commons and the Lords.

'Look at that,' Eddie breathed as the dry features of

the fallen man fell away, crumbling to dust.

The wind stirred the dust, drew it up into the air and out through the vents and grilles. Until all that was left were empty funeral suits and mourning dresses, the clothing of the dead.

Sir William looked round the House of Lords. The breeze was gone as quickly and inexplicably as it had arrived. Its last gasps rippled the empty clothes.

Gladstone was sitting ashen-faced on one of the cross-benches, his ministers silent and confused close by.

'You had a lucky escape,' Sir William told the Prime Minister. 'We all did. The wolf bats drew out the infected blood. You still had enough of your own to survive. You'll probably feel a little weak for a while. Shocked too.'

'I shall remain shocked, sir, for the rest of my life.' Gladstone looked round warily. 'And the bats? What happened to them?'

'Flew up into the rafters. They'll sleep now until they scent more food.' He smiled sadly. 'I would suggest you leave them there. Don't disturb their sleep.'

He peered up at the high, vaulted roof of the chamber, trying to make out the dark shapes of the bats. But the sound of a voice drew his attention.

'I say!' George called down from where he and Liz were suspended high above the chamber. 'The other end must still be attached to something heavy. Can you possibly give us a hand to get down from here?'

Eddie and the workhouse children lined up with Liz, George and Sir William. The Prime Minister had despatched his key ministers to get the police and assess the damage done by the events of the night. Then he insisted on hearing the whole story.

'We must keep these events to ourselves,' the Prime Minister said. 'I'm sure there will be some form of recognition, although I must thank the Good Lord that Her Majesty was not here tonight. And I do mean the *Good* Lord.'

'I'm sure she would have been a figure of calm and fortitude in our time of need,' Sir William said.

Liz laughed. 'Though I doubt she would have taken too kindly to hanging off a rope above the House of Lords.'

'Or being half drowned in a tunnel full of vampires,' George said. His arm was tight round Liz's shoulder, as if he was still afraid to let go. 'Though I suppose that was my own fault.'

'Gawd help us,' Eddie said, grinning at his friends. 'I'd

fancy a medal if there's one going, but you'd better not tell Queen Vic what really happened here.'

'You think not, young man?' the Prime Minister said. 'Why is that?'

Eddie looked him square in the eye. 'Cos she'll think we're all bats, that's why.'

A pale gas lamp glowed through the foggy night on the other side of the Thames. Beneath it, a figure stood looking out across the river, watching the dark shapes of the last few bats circling over the Palace of Westminster.

She still stood there, unmoving, as the first streaks of sunlight painted the sky. Then at last she turned, her long black hair spilling over the scarlet cloak she was wearing, and walked away. Until she was swallowed up by the morning fog.